Laurie Gilmore is
Globe and Mail b
romance. Her firs
TikTok Shop Book of the Year award in 2024. Her Dream
Harbor series is filled with quirky townsfolk, cozy settings,
and swoon-worthy romance. She loves finding books with
the perfect balance of sweetness and spice and strives for
that in her own writing.

www.thelauriegilmore.com

instagram.com/lauriegilmore_author
facebook.com/lauriegilmoreofficial

THE GINGERBREAD BAKERY

Dream Harbor Series
Book 5

LAURIE GILMORE

HarperCollins*Publishers*

HarperCollins*Publishers* Ltd
1 London Bridge Street
London SE1 9GF
www.harpercollins.co.uk
HarperCollins*Publishers*
Macken House, 39/40 Mayor Street Upper,
Dublin 1, D01 C9W8, Ireland

This paperback edition 2025
25 26 27 28 29 LBC 6 5 4 3 2
First published in ebook by HarperCollins*Publishers* 2025
Copyright © Laurie Gilmore 2025
Map illustration © Laura Hall
Laurie Gilmore asserts the moral right to
be identified as the author of this work

A catalogue record of this book is available from the British Library
ISBN: 978-0-00-872809-0

Printed and bound in the United States

For all the readers that demanded Annie and Mac's story from the beginning…

Here we go!

LOGAN'S FARM

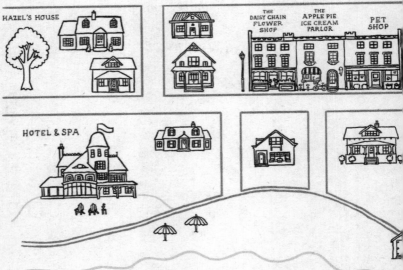

HAZEL'S HOUSE

THE DAISY CHAIN FLOWER SHOP

THE APPLE PIE ICE CREAM PARLOR

PET SHOP

HOTEL & SPA

DREAM HARBOR

KIRA'S
CHRISTMAS
TREE FARM

SULLIVAN'S
PUB

THE
PUMPKIN
SPICE CAFÉ

THE
GINGERBREAD
BAKERY

THE
CINNAMON BUN
BOOK STORE

CENTRAL AVE

THE
STRAWBERRY PATCH
PANCAKE HOUSE

MAC'S PUB

THE
PUMPKIN
SPICE CAFÉ

THE
GINGER
BREAD
BAKERY

THE
CINNAMON
BUN BOOK
STORE

THE MARINA

TOWN SQUARE

NOAH'S BOAT

Playlist

Landslide - Haley Klinkhammer ♥
is it new years yet? - Sabrina Carpenter ♥
So It Goes... - Taylor Swift ♥
Astronomy - Conan Gray ♥
good 4 u - Olivia Rodrigo ♥
Stick Season - Noah Kahan ♥
Fine Line - Harry Styles ♥
True Love - Ariana Grande ♥
MAYBE - Gabriela Bee ♥
IDGAF - Dua Lipa ♥
Merry Xmas, Please Don't Call - Bleachers ♥
Christmas Song - Phoebe Bridgers ♥
Dress - Taylor Swift ♥
Coffee - Chappell Roan ♥
us. - Gracie Abrams, Taylor Swift ♥
Wildest Dreams - The Native ♥
Overkill - Holly Humberstone ♥
Please Please Please - Sabrina Carpenter ♥
Sweater Weather - The Neighbourhood ♥
Here With Me - d4vd ♥
Juna - Clairo ♥
Mystical Magical - Benson Boone ♥
18 - One Direction ♥
Iris - The Goo Goo Dolls ♥
So High School - Taylor Swift ♥

Chapter One

Now

Annie Andrews liked most people. She was friendly and outgoing, very involved in Dream Harbor affairs, never missed a town meeting, supported local business with a fierce loyalty, and ran the Dream Harbor High alumni committee. In high school she was voted most school-spirited and most likely to become president. Her bakery was a beloved, town institution and had won 'best window display' three Christmases in a row. She babysat for her nieces and nephews, she dutifully petted every dog she passed on her morning walks, and she'd had the same best friend since kindergarten, which she felt spoke highly of her character. Frankly, she was a freaking delight.

There was one person, however, that her delightfulness simply could not extend to. One human on this planet that she *could not* be nice to. Mostly because she didn't want to. Mostly because she hated him.

And for the next three days, she was stuck with him.

'Annie,' Hazel hissed, nudging her shoulder. 'You're glaring again.'

She *was* glaring again. Right at the stupid face of Macaulay Sullivan. And she would have kept glaring until his head went up in flames if it weren't for the fact that they were at Jeanie and Logan's *rehearsal before the rehearsal* brunch, which was not even a thing but Jeanie wanted a mini-celebration with just the wedding party before the craziness of the wedding weekend really kicked off this evening with the actual rehearsal dinner. And who would deny the bride her wish? Not Annie. Because Annie was a nice person. Unlike some people.

Mac winked at her like he was reading her thoughts.

'I object,' she blurted out, interrupting Logan's very brief, very gruff thank-you speech to his groomsmen. The group was currently crowded around a table at The Strawberry Patch Pancake House. Unfortunately, it was rather dead at 11 a.m. on this particular Friday in December, so the whole table heard the words she hadn't actually been meaning to say out loud.

Logan, Jeanie, Hazel, Noah, Kira and Bennett all turned to look at her. Mac smirked. Annie barely restrained herself from reaching across the table and strangling him.

'I don't think this is the part you get to object to,' Noah pointed out with a grin. Hazel elbowed him in the side, and he yelped.

'You don't think we should get married?' Logan asked, brow scrunched like he was working through a puzzle, because why the hell wouldn't she want her best friend and his lovely fiancée to promise to love each other in front of the whole town?

'No! Of course, I don't think that! That's not … I didn't … that's not what I was talking about.'

'Then what were you talking about, *Annabelle*?' Mac asked, his stupid smirk smirking even harder.

'You! I was talking about you!' She was nearly shouting now and several patrons from other tables were turning in her direction. 'I object to you being part of the wedding party,' she said, lowering her voice and leaning across the table toward him, narrowly avoiding her syrupy plate. 'I don't know how you weaseled your way in here. You were never friends with Logan. You *bullied* him.'

Mac put up his hands in defense. 'First of all,' he said. 'I didn't bully him. Some good-natured teasing, maybe.'

'You called him Old MacDonald all through second grade! You 'e-i, e-i, oed' at him every time you walked by!'

Mac shook his head. 'How do you even remember all this shit, Annie? Do you have a little notebook where you write down every offense I ever committed?'

Annie scoffed. 'Wouldn't you love it if I cared about what you did that much?'

'Well, you seem to.'

'Ha! I couldn't care less about you, *Macaulay*. I just don't understand why you're even here… Oww! Haze, why are you jabbing me with your pointy elbows… Oh.' Annie looked up to find Jeanie looking at her with tears in her eyes. Shit. She'd made the bride cry.

'Is it going to be like this all weekend? I just wanted us all to have a good time.' Jeanie sniffled and Logan looked like he may actually strangle Annie, if she didn't fix this immediately.

'No, no, no. We'll behave. Right, Mac?'

'Yep. Best behavior. Promise.' He crossed his heart, and Annie had to bite back every word she wanted to say about how Mac's promises were worthless. But her friends still had no idea why she hated Mac so much, and she sure as hell wasn't about to tell them. And besides, she'd just made a promise to Jeanie to behave like the grown adult she was. And *her* promises did mean something.

She could suck it up for a few days. She could resist her urge to throttle the man across from her for a mere seventy-two hours. For her best friends, she could do it. Logan had been like a brother to her since they were five. With Hazel, they were inseparable. And now Annie loved Jeanie just as much. She would not screw up their wedding weekend.

'Really, Jeanie. I'm sorry. I will keep all Mac-related commentary in my head from now on.'

The entire table, including Mac, looked skeptical.

'I'm serious! I will put all my personal feelings aside for the weekend.'

Bennett leaned toward Kira and whispered, 'Do we know why she has such strong personal feelings?'

Kira shrugged. 'Complicated history?' she whispered back.

'Not complicated,' Annie cut in. 'We don't have any history at all.'

Mac flinched at that, something like sadness or regret flickering in his eyes. But Annie didn't dwell on it. She couldn't. Not if she wanted to keep her sanity. She pushed a smile onto her face and turned back to Jeanie.

'Nothing is complicated. In fact, it's all quite simple. Two of the people we all love most in the world are getting married. And we,' Annie gestured to the table of friends in front of her. 'Are going to make sure it's the best wedding weekend ever.'

'Good,' said Logan. 'Because Mac is here as one of *my* groomsmen. Some of us have put second grade behind us.'

Annie was getting nauseous from all the words she was swallowing, but she did it. For her friends. For the sake of this wedding, she would not say that it went far beyond second grade for her. 'Of course,' she said instead. 'Mac's your friend. I get it.' She raised her glass of orange juice and everyone joined in.

'To Logan and Jeanie.'

'Cheers!'

Everyone clinked their plastic, juice glasses together, and Annie was relieved to see the smile back on Jeanie's face and a slightly less murderous expression on Logan's. Phew. Wedding-crisis number one averted. Sure, she was the one who started it, but at least she'd fixed it.

No thanks to Mac.

Her gaze flicked back across the table to where he sat, laughing with Bennett and Kira. It didn't help matters that he was still as infuriatingly handsome as he had been in high school. Not that she would have admitted it at the time.

She'd never been friends with Mac. They'd never made sense together.

It was exactly what she'd told him eleven years ago.

But Mac had never been good at listening.

Chapter Two

Then

Mac wandered aimlessly through the stalls at the Dream Harbor Christmas market. There was just under a month until Christmas and he needed a gift for his mom. A *good* gift. And this seemed like as good a place to shop as any. They set up the market every year after the tree-lighting festival, but Mac hadn't been since he was a kid.

He was determined to get his mom a real present this year. At nineteen, he figured he could no longer get away with crappy, homemade gifts. Even though his mom still insisted on hanging that wonky reindeer-ornament he made her in kindergarten and would probably do the same if he made her an equally deformed ornament right now. It was time he leveled up his gift-giving game.

Unfortunately, aimless wandering seemed to be all he was doing lately. Six months out of high school and he was still stuck in this stupid town, still living in his childhood bedroom, still without any plan for his future. Or a plan for next week, even. Mac was adrift.

He stopped at The Pumpkin Spice Café stand and was greeted with a big smile from Dot, the owner.

'Hello there, Macaulay. Merry Christmas.'

There were very few people who could get away with using his full, objectively terrible, name. And Dot was one of them. Dot had always been kind to him even when he didn't deserve it.

'Hey, Dot.'

'What can I get you?' she asked, her enormous jingle-bell earrings tinkling merrily with the movement of her head.

'How about a hot chocolate?'

'Extra marshmallows?'

'Please.'

As soon as she handed him the red to-go cup overflowing with marshmallows and a candy cane hooked on the side, he felt completely absurd. This was a child's drink. And Mac was trying desperately to figure out how to be a grown-ass man.

Unfortunately, it was very hard to feel grown up when your mother was still the one doing your laundry.

He needed to move out. To move away. He was feeling increasingly suffocated by this town and their preconceived notions about him.

'Thanks, Dot,' he muttered, taking his ridiculous drink with him, suddenly grateful that all his friends were away at school and wouldn't see him carrying this sugary confection around.

He took a sip. It was delicious, though. Hard to feel bad about anything with a mug full of cocoa in your hands.

Mac continued his stroll through the market, pausing every now and then at a crafter's table in an attempt to find the perfect gift. It wasn't an entirely selfless act. He was hoping a thoughtful gift would help soften the blow when he told his parents his new plan. Well, it wasn't so much a plan as a general notion. An idea to wander somewhere other than Dream Harbor. His half-baked thought that he could drive cross-country to help him figure out what the hell to do with his life. He figured several months in a car by himself would help with that.

A familiar face snagged his attention.

Annabelle Andrews sat in front of him in fifth-period Economics. Or she did last year, anyway, before they'd both graduated. He'd spent a lot of the year resisting the urge to tug on her sleek ponytail and he only occasionally poked her in the back with the eraser end of his pencil to ask her what assignment they had due that day. She'd always answered with an exasperated sigh, like he was disappointing her in every way.

He'd gone to school with Annie since they were five and she had never liked him, so in fairness, he had never liked her, either. She was a classic over-achiever, the type who practically begged the teacher for extra credit, whereas he preferred to achieve just enough to pass. Unless it was on the lacrosse field. That was where he was more than happy to give it all he had. Not that Annabelle Andrews gave a shit about sports. Or the people that played them.

Not that he cared what she cared about.

And here she was, still in town, just like him. Interesting.

She was set up at a table with a sign on the front reading *Annie's Baked Goods*. An assortment of Christmas cookies wrapped in holiday cellophane were displayed on the table. Mac waited while an older couple picked out some cookies and paid a smiling Annie. The smile dropped when she saw him standing there.

'Annabelle,' he said, dipping his head in acknowledgment.

'It's Annie, and you know it. What are you even doing here?'

He shrugged, wishing he'd tossed his stupid marshmallow-topped drink before this encounter. 'Shopping. What are you doing here? I figured you'd be off at Harvard or something like that.'

Annie scowled. 'This isn't some teen movie where everyone goes to an Ivy League school at the end. My family has six kids. Do you really think they can afford for me to go to Harvard?' She rolled her eyes like he was an idiot—one of the many habits that unsurprisingly made him not like her very much.

'My mistake,' he ground out. 'I just wasn't expecting to see you running a *bake sale* after all that extra homework you did in Econ.'

Annie slapped her hands onto the table and leaned forward. A slight flush had worked its way up her pale cheeks in a way Mac chose not to find appealing.

'This bake sale is the start of my new business venture. I'm taking business classes at the community college and selling cookies from an online shop for now. But give it a few years and you'll see. I'll be a very successful small-business owner.'

He didn't doubt that for a second, but he wasn't about to admit it.

'Wow, I guess you have it all figured out.'

'I do, actually,' she said with a smug smile. 'And what about you? Just hanging around Dream Harbor letting your mom cook and clean for you?'

He scoffed as if that was absurd, even though it was one hundred percent true.

'Actually, I'm outta here after the holidays.'

'Really?'

'Yep. Heading cross-country.' The half-assed plan he'd been brewing in his head was cemented as soon as he spoke the words out loud.

'Heading to what?'

'It's about the journey not the destination,' he said, and instantly regretted how douchey that sounded.

Annie raised her eyebrows, but surprisingly didn't call him out on that bullshit answer.

'So, are you going to buy some cookies, or what?'

'Uh … yeah. I'll take some of the gingerbread ones.'

Annie gave him a genuine smile and, for a second, he felt like he couldn't breathe.

'Those are my specialty,' she said, handing him the small bag. 'Try one.'

She waited while he opened the package and took out a small gingerbread man with icing features and buttons. Mac bit his head off.

It was quite possibly the best cookie he'd ever had. Spicy and sweet with just the right amount of crunch.

'Damn, Annie. This is delicious.'

She beamed and he nearly choked on his cookie. For

thirteen years, she'd looked at him like he was at best an inconvenience and at worst an enemy, and now she was *smiling* at him. It was disorienting, to say the least. Which was probably why he said what he said next.

'We should hang out later.'

Annie's smile dropped and her brow furrowed in confusion. 'We've never hung out.'

He shrugged, trying to feign casualness, even though now his heart was thumping at an alarming rate as though he *cared* if Annie wanted to hang out with him.

'I know, but no one's home for the holiday break yet. We might as well keep each other company, right?' God, he hoped that didn't sound as desperate as he suddenly felt.

Annie's lips twisted to the side as she considered his offer. 'Well, Logan *is* on that cruise with his grandparents and Hazel's not back from her semester studying abroad yet … so I guess we could … do something…' She seemed as confused by his suggestion as he was, but he couldn't turn back now.

'Great, let's meet at the diner at eight.'

A small frown played on Annie's lips even as she agreed. 'Okay, yeah. The diner at eight.'

'Perfect. See you then, Annabelle.'

'Don't call me that!' she yelled after him as he walked away. He waved over his shoulder and strode off before she could take back her agreement to see him later.

Because, suddenly, he was very eager to hang out with the girl he'd always thought he didn't really like.

Chapter Three

Now

The rehearsal was a bigger deal than Mac was expecting. He'd left the pub in Amber's capable hands for the night and had shown up to The Christmas Tree Farm right on time to find a nervous-looking Logan getting ready to walk down the aisle they'd set up through the center of the newly renovated barn.

'Hey, here he is,' Noah said, giving Mac a hearty pat on the back when he joined the group of groomsmen.

'Sorry, I'm late.' Mac tossed his coat over the closest chair.

'You're fine,' Logan said. 'They're still figuring things out over there.' He gestured to where Jeanie was surrounded by her bridesmaids, all animatedly talking about timing and music and procession order.

Annie caught him looking and narrowed her eyes.

Christ, that woman was never going to let it go.

How long did he have to repent for sins committed when he was nineteen?

He winked at her just to see her cheeks redden in anger before she tore her attention away from him and redirected it to Kira who was explaining how things would look on the big day. He had to hand it to Kira; it already looked amazing in the old barn. The fact that it had a roof was a big improvement, but she'd really transformed the whole space. It was large enough to have rows of white chairs leading up to the makeshift altar on one half, and then tables and chairs for the reception on the other.

There was still a lot to be done before Sunday, but it looked good. Of course, if Mac ever got married, he'd much rather just go to the courthouse. Judging by the slightly ill look on Logan's face, he felt the same way.

'Excited?' Mac asked him.

'To be married to Jeanie? Yes. To stand up in front of everyone? No.'

Mac laughed. 'Just don't say the wrong name and you'll be fine.'

Logan looked at him in horror. 'Why would you even say that?'

'I was joking! It's going to be fine!'

'You're going to do great,' Noah chimed in. 'It's just a few words to recite.'

'Says the man who eloped,' Logan grumbled.

Noah grinned. 'I couldn't wait to make Hazel my wife,' he said with a shrug. 'What can I say?'

It was at this point that Mac seriously regretted not finding a date to this wedding. Apparently, while he was slinging drinks every night, everyone in his life had paired up.

'Looks like the girls are ready to start,' Bennett said as Kira came to stand at the end of the aisle. Not only was she the owner of the barn, she was also the wedding planner. Word at the last town-hall meeting was that she was throwing herself fully into this new event-planning venture. And selling Christmas trees one month a year, of course.

'Okay, this is how it's going to go…'

Mac didn't pay too much attention to the directions. How hard could it be? Walk up the aisle, stand next to other groomsmen, don't stare at Annie, walk back down the aisle. It wasn't some elaborate dance sequence or something. Logan looked like he wanted to run away as it was; if they tried to get the man to do some fancy steps down the aisle they might lose him completely.

Mac made his way between the mostly empty chairs and stood in position between Noah and Bennett. A few family members were seated in the first two rows. Mac said a quiet hello to Logan's grandparents, Estelle and Henry.

'Good,' Kira said, still in half bridesmaid, half wedding-director mode. 'Now it will be me, Annie, and Hazel. And then, of course, the star of the day, the bride.' Jeanie beamed at Logan and suddenly the man looked like he would perform a one-man show if she asked him to.

'Remember not to walk too fast,' Kira instructed. 'And hold your flowers down here like this.'

The women all mimicked Kira's stance with their invisible bouquets, which Mac assumed would be real on Sunday during the actual ceremony.

'All those years attending her mother's benefits and fundraisers have really paid off,' Bennett whispered.

It was true. Kira clearly knew how to wrangle people, set up an event space, handle the logistics of a big occasion, and do it all with a smile.

'She's killing it,' Mac said with a quiet laugh. 'She did a great job in here.'

'Yeah, man. She's been working really hard.' The pride in Bennett's voice was obvious. It made Mac think of how he'd talk about Annie's bakery, if she would let him. How he sometimes did when she wasn't around. She'd come so far from the little table at the Christmas market eleven years ago.

'No chitchat during the ceremony,' Kira chided, flashing Bennett a flirty smile.

'Sorry, babe.'

'That's okay. Now, Jeanie's dad will be here for the actual ceremony, but for today you can walk down alone.'

Jeanie nodded and the women began their procession.

Kira, Annie, Hazel, and Jeanie, but all he really saw was Annie. Story of his life since he moved back here. Annie was all he ever saw.

Annie frowning at him. Annie scowling at him. Annie huffing and sighing and occasionally, if he was lucky, yelling at him. And because he was some kind of masochist, he still wanted to be around her.

He wasn't sure what the women would be wearing at the actual wedding, but today Annie was wearing a cream-colored sweater and dark jeans. Her blonde hair was pulled back in her usual ponytail. A light blush graced her cheeks, and her glistening eyes gave away that she was already emotional about her friends' wedding.

Mac didn't hear most of the run through of the ceremony. He was too busy thinking about a different Christmas season. The one, and only one, when Annie had let him hold her. When she'd smiled at him like he wasn't the bane of her existence. His favorite Christmas, if he was being honest. Which was so pathetic he could barely admit it to himself.

He'd tried to forget Annie so many times, tried to purge her from his system, to replace her with other women. But it never worked. No one ever lived up to her memory, to the memory of that one perfect Christmas. A memory that he had been hoping had been blown way out of proportion over the years. But then he'd moved back here and found she was just as perfect as he'd remembered.

And it sucked.

It sucked that life hadn't worn down some of her shine, that she was still just as enthusiastic and loving and hard-working as she always had been. She still threw her whole self into everything she did. She was still that beautiful, over-achiever he'd known all those years ago. And now he was stuck here, forced to admire her in all her Annie-ness, and just pretend like it wasn't slowly killing him.

Jeanie and Logan practiced their kiss to the delight of the small crowd, who cheered loud enough to bring Mac back to the present moment. As the couples paired off to walk back down the aisle, he was of course paired with Annie. He offered his arm, and she took it begrudgingly.

'You look beautiful,' he whispered in her ear as they marched down the aisle.

'Mac, don't.'

'Annie, I just…'

'I said, don't,' she snapped. 'I'm emotional enough about this wedding, and I really don't need you messing with my head like you did after Hazel's thirtieth.'

Mess with *her* head? Ha! It was his head that was a mess. He hadn't stopped thinking about that night in over a year.

'I wasn't trying to mess with your head.'

They got to the end of the chairs and everyone else was drifting off to where the food had been set up along the wall. Archer had done the catering, and it smelled fantastic.

Annie turned to face Mac, her familiar glare burning into him.

'Well, you did.'

The memory of that night was enough to kill him. They'd been so close. *She'd* been so close. Her face just a breath from his, her lips *right* there. She'd been warm and willing in his arms, and then she'd looked up at him and it had been as though every reason she hated him came crashing back into her. She'd run from the pub like Cinderella from the damn ball.

He'd obviously been deluding himself. They'd drunk too much that night and Annie had been emotional because her friends were settling down. Letting him get so close to her had been motivated by some kind of panicked desperation on her part. But still it had been nice while it lasted.

'I'm sorry. It won't happen again. But you do look beautiful. That's just an objective fact,' he said with a shrug.

Annie softened slightly, her scowl becoming less scowl-y, which was the best he could hope for these days.

'So, are you bringing a date to the wedding?' she asked, steering the conversation away from their messy past.

'Nah, not this time.'

Annie's eyebrows rose in surprise. 'Really?'

Mac shrugged. 'I guess I forgot to find one.'

Annie's gentle laugh was a reward. 'Yeah, me too.'

It was Mac's turn to be surprised. Annie seemed to love parading new guys in front of him, although he supposed he was guilty of bringing a random date or two to things, just so he didn't have to be alone in front of her.

They'd played a lot of stupid games over the years.

'Maybe you'll save me a dance,' he said.

Annie's laugh was bigger this time as she patted him on the shoulder. 'Not a chance, Sullivan.'

She was still laughing as she walked past him to the buffet. Mac shook his head at his own stupidity.

Not a chance was right. It was probably time he got that through his thick skull.

Chapter Four

Then

Hours after she'd sold out of cookies at the Christmas market, Annie was still trying to figure out how she'd ended up sitting across from the captain of the lacrosse team, sipping cocoa and eating French fries on a random Thursday night, four weeks before Christmas. It was not something she'd ever expected to add to her agenda.

But here she was.

With Mac.

A boy she hadn't spoken more than a few words to over the past year, most of which were just the page numbers he was supposed to have completed for class.

They'd been sitting in awkward silence since they ordered, probably because this whole thing was weird, and they had no business hanging out together. But Mac was right. There was no one else around and she was bored.

That was why she'd agreed to this bizarre meet-up. Boredom. Not because of some ill-placed crush she'd had on Macaulay Sullivan ever since ninth grade when he'd shot up about two feet and stopped being a dick to her friends. It definitely wasn't that, because Annie was smarter than that. Despite her steady diet of teen movies from the last thirty years, she knew that in real life the hot, popular guy did not in fact have a thing for the type A girl. It just didn't make sense.

As a rule, Annie didn't date jocks, especially ones that were mean to her friends. She had nothing to say to them. She didn't particularly care about how hard anyone could throw a little ball into a net, or hit a ball with a bat, or catch a ball and run, or really do anything at all with a ball. So, even though she found Mac pleasing to look at, she'd never considered him as dating material. And she was sure he felt the same about her. Because, again, this was not a teen movie.

It was weird that they were here.

Even though it *was* nice to look at him across the booth from her, all dark hair and bronzed skin. Annie happened to know, thanks to a sixth-grade ancestry project, that although Mac's name screamed Irish, he was also half Italian. So even here in the midst of a cold, dark New England winter, Mac's genes apparently still thought he was in the Mediterranean.

He lifted long dark lashes and caught her staring at him. His immediate smile was enough to make her stomach flutter.

Shut up, stomach.

'So, Annie,' he said, leaning back in the booth. 'Should we clear the air first?'

'Clear the air about what?'

'About why you hate me so much?'

Annie choked on her French fry. 'I don't hate you.'

Mac scoffed. 'Yeah, okay. You definitely do.'

'I do not! Just because we've never been friends doesn't mean I hate you.'

'Ha! Every time I look at you, you frown at me.'

Annie rolled her eyes. 'I'm sorry that I don't fall all over you like everyone else at our school used to.'

'They did not.'

'Please! Captain of the lacrosse team? Girls love that crap.'

'But not you.'

Annie shrugged. 'I'm not that interested in sports.'

'Or the people who play them.'

'So what? It's not like you were showing up at student council meetings.'

Mac shoved three more French fries into his mouth. 'Fair. But I still think you don't like me.'

'I don't like how you treated Logan when we were little.'

Mac's eyes widened. 'Logan?'

'Yeah, you used to tease him. And his mom had just *died*. I guess it did make me hate you.'

To his credit, he looked abashed about his behavior toward Logan. 'I'll apologize.'

Annie rolled her eyes. 'Yeah, I bet.'

'I'm serious. Give me your phone.'

'What? No!'

'Pull up Logan's number. I'll text him right now.'

'You're kidding.'

'I'm dead serious. I was a little shit. Let me apologize, and then me and you can have a fresh start where you don't hate me anymore.' Mac held out his hand expectantly. He was serious. Whatever she had been expecting from him, this was not it.

She took her phone out of her purse and pulled up her text chain with Logan. The last message was a picture of a grinning Nana Estelle in between a frowning Grandpa Henry and a squinting Logan. They all had sunburn across their noses and Estelle's giant sunhat nearly covered Logan's and his grandfather's faces. Annie hoped she was having the best time. She'd been waiting to go on this cruise her whole life.

Mac's eyebrows rose in amusement when he saw the picture, but he didn't comment. Just took the phone and typed out a message. He handed it back to Annie to approve before sending.

ANNIE

Hey, man. It's Mac. Sorry I was an asshole to you when we were kids. Hope you're having fun on your old-folks cruise.

'You know this is very weird, right?'

Mac nodded. 'Yep.'

Annie hit send.

They both stared at the phone on the table and waited for a response.

It didn't take long before a string of question marks came through.

LOGAN

????

ANNIE

I'm at the diner with Mac

Annie texted back to clarify.

LOGAN

Why?

ANNIE

Not sure, really

LOGAN

Okay...

ANNIE

He wanted to apologize, I guess

LOGAN

Weird. Apology accepted.

'He says he accepts your apology.'

Mac sighed. 'Phew. So do you forgive me, too?'

Annie's phone buzzed again, and she looked down.

LOGAN

Wait, are you on a date with Mac??

She tossed the phone back in her bag. She would deal with Logan later.

'Okay, fine. I forgive you.'

There was that damn smile again. So maybe it wasn't just the sportiness that had the girls lining up at Mac's locker.

'Great. I don't know about you, but I feel better.' His arms were stretched over the back of the seat, showing off the breadth of his chest. Annie swallowed a half-chewed fry and nearly choked again.

'Shouldn't you be playing lacrosse somewhere?'

Mac laughed. 'You know I was captain of a not very good team in a very small school. College scouts weren't exactly lining up to recruit me.'

'Oh.' She wasn't sure how he felt about that. He didn't seem overly bitter, but the slightly lost expression he'd had when he told her about his cross-country plan was back.

'So, what have you been doing since graduation?' she asked.

Mac shrugged. 'Mostly working at my dad's pub. What about you? You didn't want to go away to school somewhere?' he asked. 'Somewhere other than Harvard?'

'Why would I want to go away? I love it here.'

Mac laughed but cut himself off when he realized she was serious.

'You don't feel the same way, obviously,' she said, her earlier convictions that they had nothing in common and this whole thing was stupid returning.

He leaned forward again, arms on the table. Whatever position he was in, he seemed to take up so much space.

'I'm just bored. I guess. Or restless? I don't know. I feel like I need to figure things out.'

'And you have to leave to do that?'

He nodded, taking another fry and dragging it through the ketchup. 'I think so, yeah.'

'But you're still here.'

His cheeks flushed red at that observation and Annie

thought maybe this big, strong guy was just as freaked out about the future as she was.

'I can help you map a route, if you want,' she blurted. 'I mean, I'm a pretty good planner.'

His smile grew again. 'That'd be cool. Thanks, Annie.'

The pleasure that warmed her body at his praise was almost embarrassing. But lucky for Annie, no one was around to witness it.

They spent the rest of the night with heads bent over Mac's phone, periodically scribbling places and ideas in the notebook Annie always carried with her, plotting the route that would take him far away from her.

But, by the time Gladys was kicking them out, they were closer than ever.

Chapter Five

Now

Kira had set four of the wedding-reception tables for the rehearsal dinner. She'd kept it simple with only candles for the centerpiece and little sprigs of rosemary on each napkin. The tablecloths were white and the plates mismatched china. The whole thing felt homey and intimate. As it turned out, Kira was quite good at this. Annie was impressed.

She was seated between Iris and Bennett for dinner, and luckily Mac was at a different table because she really couldn't make any more promises about being on her best behavior if she had to sit next to him. After walking down the aisle, where she had been subjected to memories of the other times she'd let her body get too close to his, she'd been trying to avoid him as much as possible. Which was tricky to do since it wasn't exactly a big crowd. The guest list consisted of the bridal party, Logan's grandparents, a couple of Jeanie's cousins, Mayor Kelly who was officiating, and Archer and Iris. The rest of Jeanie's family didn't get into town until the next morning and everyone else had to wait for the big day on Sunday to be part of the fun.

Annie slid into her seat, setting her plate down on the table. She'd filled it with slices of beef tenderloin, mashed potatoes, and haricot verts, which she'd learned this evening were just green beans, but Archer had made them all fancy.

'This looks heavenly,' she said, and Archer smiled at her as he placed a full plate in front of Iris and sat down beside her.

'Enjoy,' he said.

'Does he feed you like this all the time?' Annie asked Iris. 'If so, it makes complete sense why you agreed to have his baby.'

Iris laughed and the water she'd been drinking nearly sprayed from her mouth. She coughed into her hand and Annie patted her back.

'Sorry, didn't mean to make a pregnant lady choke.'

Iris shook her head. 'I'm fine. I'm fine,' she said, waving away Annie's ineffective life-saving efforts. 'And yes, he does feed me like this all the time.'

Annie laughed. 'Damn, girl.'

'I know.'

'I would carry the man's baby for a meal like this every night,' Bennett said from Annie's other side, and Iris burst out laughing again.

Archer winked at Bennett and the girls laughed even harder.

'What's so funny over there?' Mayor Kelly asked from across the table.

'Oh, we're just discussing what we would do for Archer in exchange for this food every night,' Annie said with a smile, and the mayor's eyebrows rose above his glasses.

'So, Pete, do you have the ceremony ready for Sunday?' Estelle asked, changing the subject before the mayor could weigh in. Which was probably for the best.

'Mostly. I want to get a few more thoughts from the bride and groom, but I think I'm ready to go.'

'You're going to do great, Dad,' Hazel said, patting him on the back from her seat beside him.

'It's going to be lovely, I'm sure,' Estelle said, and then turned her attention to Jeanie who was seated at the next table. 'Jeanie!' she called. 'Have you given any thought to what you're wearing on the wedding night?'

Annie could see the furious blush on Logan's face from across the room. She and Iris descended into more giggles.

'Um, not really,' Jeanie said.

Estelle smiled. 'Okay, very good. I have just the thing.'

'Well, that's ominous,' Annie whispered and Iris agreed. 'I don't think I want to know.'

The evening went on with more drinks and food and laughter. Archer had outdone himself and Annie couldn't imagine how Sunday's meal would be any better, but she knew it would be.

'We should probably test out the dance floor,' Noah said, coming up beside Hazel and putting out a hand to her.

'We probably should.' Hazel smiled up at him and Annie couldn't help the small pang she felt anytime she was around her friends lately. She loved them all, and she was so happy that they had each found their person. But, when everyone had their person, it really emphasized the fact that she didn't.

She could feel Mac's eyes on her from the other table as more and more guests got up to dance. She didn't allow herself to look at him. Instead, she very gratefully accepted an offer from Jeanie's cousin when he asked her to dance.

The music was slow and romantic, and Annie had had enough wine to feel pleasantly warm. She couldn't help but think that, if she had been dancing with someone she cared about, the moment would have been quite lovely.

Hazel's head rested on Noah's shoulder as they danced, Iris and Archer couldn't take their eyes off each other, and Kira had taken a break from her hosting duties to dance with Bennett. Her laughter filled up the room when he dipped her. And never mind Jeanie and Logan. Annie wasn't sure their feet even touched the ground as they danced, whispering quietly to each other in their own little world. They were all so happy, so settled. And in a group of couples, Annie had quickly become the only single left.

Well, and Mac.

She really needed to get more friends.

'So that's why I don't feed my geckos crickets.'

Annie blinked.

'What was that?' she asked. She'd totally not been listening to whatever her dance partner had been going on about. In fact, she wasn't even sure she caught his name.

'Crickets,' he repeated. 'They give off a weird smell, so I prefer to feed my gecko pellets only.'

Annie stared at him in horror before she remembered to be polite. 'Of course, that makes sense,' she said, forcing a smile on her face. 'Well, thank you so much for the dance.' She pulled away, even though the song was not over. She'd had enough cricket talk for one evening.

As she made her way across the dance floor and away from gecko guy, she caught Mac following her with his gaze. He still sat at the table chatting with Henry and Mayor Kelly, but his eyes were on her.

She needed to get out of here. She needed a break from all of it, from Mac, from the happy couples, from the insanely romantic wedding Kira had planned. It was all too much.

She stepped out of the barn and into the cold night air and took a deep breath. She was fine. Everything was fine. She took another deep breath of the pine-scented breeze as she tried to convince herself that everything really was fine. She stared up at a sky filled with stars.

Annie didn't make a habit of being lovesick and she certainly wasn't going to start now. Once this wedding was over, everything would go back to normal. She could go back to avoiding Mac, and her single-ness wouldn't be quite so painfully obvious. She had her friends and her family and her bakery. She didn't need a dance partner.

Right. Two more days to go.

She could do this.

But by the time the already small crowd had dwindled even further to just Iris, who was waiting for Archer and his crew to finish clearing the food, and Mayor Kelly who was going over his notes for the ceremony with Logan, Annie was looking for any distraction to keep between her and Mac.

Hazel and Noah had left to drive a tipsy Jeanie home and Bennett had gone to escort the Ellis cousins to the inn.

'What else can I do?' she asked Kira, to avoid watching Mac spin Iris in a slow circle on the dance floor.

'I think we're done for the night.' Kira plopped down into the nearest chair. 'We should probably get some sleep. We have more work to do tomorrow.'

'Right.' Manicures and pedicures, followed by finishing up the secret, wedding dessert and helping Kira decorate the barn. She was hoping Mac wouldn't be a part of any of it. Maybe she wouldn't have to see him again until Sunday and then there would be enough other stuff going on, she'd barely have to interact with him. Except for the whole pesky walking down the aisle business.

'What happened between you two, anyway?' Kira asked, following Annie's gaze to where Mac was now talking with Archer and Iris, the dance over.

Annie sighed. 'It really doesn't matter.'

'It kinda seems like it does.'

Mac looked up and caught her in his gaze. Sometimes it felt like a million years ago that she had let herself fall for that cocky team captain, and sometimes it felt like she was still that girl letting herself trust that boy. Mac's lips tipped into a tentative smile and Annie was right back in that diner booth trying to convince herself that they didn't make sense together, that he couldn't possibly like her.

But he had convinced her that he did. And, for that one December, she'd let herself believe him.

And look where it had gotten her. Stuck on a guy who would never be right for her.

She turned away from Mac's smile.

'We were young and stupid.'

Kira's brows rose. This was the most Annie had ever confessed about what happened between her and Mac. For some reason, it felt a little easier to tell Kira, who hadn't been around Annie and Mac her whole life and had only showed up in town a year ago.

'You were young and stupid and…'

'And … it was over before it really started.'

Kira sighed in disappointment. 'I feel like you're holding out on me, but I'm exhausted so I'm going to let you get away with it for now.' She stood up and planted a kiss on Annie's cheek. 'I'll see you in the morning.'

'Okay, yeah. See you in the morning.' Annie went to find where she'd stashed her purse and coat and, by the time she turned around to leave, the barn was empty except for one person. Of course.

'Walk you out?' Mac asked, heading toward her across the dance floor. Annie's body went into fight-or-flight mode.

'I think I can make it down the driveway to my car without your assistance, thank you very much.' Okay, so fight it was.

Mac blew out a frustrated sigh. 'Can I walk out with you, Annie, or do I need to give you a five-minute head start so you don't have to endure being next to me for a second longer?'

She glared at him and was about to tell him he could walk right off a cliff when Kira popped her head back into the big barn doors.

'Forgot to turn out the lights!' She hit the switch and the lights in the barn went out save for the strings of twinkle lights crisscrossed over the rafters. And the traitor scurried away before Annie could accuse her of being just as bad as everyone else in this busybody town.

She turned back to Mac with a huff to find him staring at her in the warm glow of the Christmas lights. He wasn't smirking or winking or doing any of that bullshit that made it easy to hate him. He was just watching her with such fondness in his eyes that Annie thought she might choose flight now.

'Damn that Kira,' she whispered, and Mac let out a low laugh.

'It's a nice effect.' He glanced up at the ceiling where the strings of lights hung.

'Very Christmas-y,' Annie mumbled back, falling deeper into the trance of staring at Mac in the low lights. It reminded her too much of another time she'd seen Mac in the glow of Christmas lights. When she'd seen the way he looked flushed and happy and undone, the twinkle of lights on his bronze skin something she'd seared into her memory.

When he looked at her again, she knew he was remembering the same thing.

'Annie,' his voice was rough when he spoke and at some point, he'd moved closer. She could feel herself being pulled toward him. 'Do you remember that night...'

'Of course, I remember that night,' she snapped. The night of Christmas lights and Mac's bare skin against hers? How could she ever forget it?

Mac smirked a little at the mention of it. 'Not *that* night. The night we went on the Christmas-lights tour.'

Now Annie was smiling, too, lost in the memories. 'Yeah. That was fun.'

Mac was even closer now, his nose practically brushing her cheek, his words gentle and warm against her skin. 'That was my favorite night.'

Her breath caught. *That* was his favorite night? The night he held her hand and they laughed and talked until 2 a.m., and they didn't even kiss but the promise of it was there. Thinking about it was like pushing on a bruise. It still hurt. Even all these years later.

'I wish we could have that back,' he whispered, and Annie wanted to close her eyes and give in to that thought. She wanted to have that feeling back, too. But she remembered all too well what came after that feeling. All the months she had thought about him, she had *waited* for him. It wasn't only her heart that had been bruised, it was her ego, and somehow that was so much worse.

She swallowed hard. 'We were so young,' she said, instead of all the other thoughts racing through her head.

'I still feel like that when I look at you.'

When had his hands landed on her hips? When had he tugged her close? When had they started to sway to some imaginary song, having the slow dance she'd avoided earlier?

Annie let her head rest against his chest, and she felt the sigh shudder through him. She gave herself exactly three breaths to remember the good times and forget everything else. Three inhales of Mac's familiar spicy scent, three exhales to steel herself before she pulled away. Mac's fingers dug into her hips just for a second before letting her go.

'We should go,' she said, unable to meet his eye.

He still stood close to her, and she was afraid he would touch her again, afraid of what she would do if he did. But finally, he nodded.

'Right. We probably should.'

They walked out into the cold air and the dreamy moment in the barn was wiped away. It didn't matter if Mac knew how to sweet-talk her these days, it didn't matter if the memories were tempting, it didn't matter how damn good his arms felt around her. Annie had made a promise to the girl she was all those years ago. The girl who had let herself fall for a guy she knew she had no business falling for. To the girl who decided to trust and to love against her better judgement. To the girl who'd waited around for Macaulay Sullivan for a goddamn *year* only to be left in the dust.

She'd sworn she'd never let him back into her life.

And she wasn't about to break her promise now.

Chapter Six

Then

'How can you possibly be this excited? You know you can just drive past any of these houses on your own.' Mac breathed into his hands in an unsuccessful attempt to warm his frozen fingers.

'How could you *not* be excited?' Annie was standing next to him on the lawn in front of the town hall, bundled up in a puffy coat, knit hat and mittens that he was frankly jealous of. Her cheeks were rosy, and her eyes were lit up in anticipation, and it suddenly seemed like a real oversight that he'd never noticed how cute she was. Although, to be fair, she was much cuter when she wasn't scowling at him.

Apologizing to her friend had really gone a long way. He knew now that messing with anyone Annie loved was a dealbreaker. And he also knew the girl could hold a grudge.

'I don't think I've done this since I was ten.'

'You've been missing out. The Dream Harbor Christmas Lights Tour is one of my favorite holiday traditions.'

They were waiting for one of the school-bus-turned-tour-buses to return to pick up the next load of passengers. It would then drive them around the Dream Harbor neighborhoods to admire the light displays. The crowd was almost entirely old folks discussing who they thought would have the best set-up this year and small children running in circles while their parents tried in vain to get them to calm down. The consumption of candy canes and hot chocolate while they waited probably wasn't helping.

Mac blew into his hands again. Annie watched him with a small smile.

'You're cold?'

'Not too bad.'

'Why do guys do that?'

'Do what?'

'Pretend they're never cold. Do they revoke your man card if you admit to being chilly?'

Mac huffed a laugh, his breath clouding in front of him. 'I'm fine.' He stamped his feet a little to get feeling back into his toes. Probably shouldn't have worn sneakers.

Annie raised an amused eyebrow. 'You'd rather freeze to death than wear a hat?'

He looked terrible in hats, so yes, he'd rather die than wear one in front of a cute girl. But he was not about to admit that level of fragility. 'I didn't think it was this cold out. It hasn't even snowed yet.'

Annie rolled her eyes and made a point of tugging her hat down over her ears. It looked soft and cozy. Damn it, he was an idiot. He wished he had a hat. And mittens. And lined boots.

'Where's this bus, anyway?' he muttered, rubbing his hands together until Annie finally took pity on him.

'Stop.' She took his hands between her mittened ones, enclosing him in her warmth. 'Better?'

So much better, but it wasn't only because of his hands. Annie was close to him now and all the things he'd never noticed about her were right there. Her cute little upturned nose, the dip in her full upper lip, the slight flush on her cheeks. A few wisps of blonde hair had escaped her hat, and he had the bizarre urge to tuck them behind her ear.

Annie was pretty.

Like, really pretty.

What the hell was wrong with him? How do you look at someone for thirteen years and not realize they're actually *beautiful*?

This gorgeous girl had been in front of him his whole life and, somehow, he was only now noticing?!

As he stood there staring at Annie's lips—had they always been so pink?—another inconvenient truth revealed itself. Mac wanted to kiss her. Like, he *really* wanted to kiss her. He wanted to kiss that mouth that used to do nothing but frown at him, the mouth that now looked so appealing and sweet, tipped up slightly in the corner like she was amused by him.

'Mac? Do your hands feel better?'

Oh, shit. He'd been standing here staring at her like an idiot.

'Much.' He cleared his throat. 'Much better, thanks.'

Annie smiled, rubbing her hands over his. 'Good. Can't have you losing any fingers and ruining the tour.'

'So glad you were worried about my wellbeing.'

Annie laughed. 'Nope. Just the Christmas lights.'

He laughed, too, because suddenly he was having fun at this stupid town tradition that he'd written off as childish; because Annie liked it, because maybe Annie liked him.

Or she at least didn't hate him anymore.

But leaning down to kiss her right now was probably a bad idea. Right?

Right. They were only hanging out because no one else was in town and they'd agreed they were both bored. Nothing about that was grounds for suddenly kissing someone.

Except for the fact that, the way Annie was looking at him right now, he thought maybe she wouldn't mind. Maybe he could. Maybe she wanted him to.

While Mac wondered if Annie was the kind of girl that wanted to be asked first or if he should just go for it, the bus pulled up, the screech and hiss of the brakes fully ruining the moment anyway.

'Let's go!' Annie dropped his hands and quickly joined the line of people slowly making their way onto the bus. He followed her up the steps and was greeted by his kindergarten teacher in a Santa hat sitting in the driver seat.

'Merry Christmas,' Nancy greeted each passenger.

'Merry Christmas, Ms. DeMarco!'

'Well, if it isn't two of my favorite students.'

That was certainly a lie. Mac had spent a considerable amount of time in the 'cozy corner' taking a 'break' when he was in Ms. DeMarco's classroom. His 'listening ears' and 'gentle hands' never seemed to be working right, and he'd had to spend a lot of time thinking about that. He really had been a little shit back then.

Annie beamed at their former teacher.

'Have you been good this year, Macaulay?' Nancy peered at him from under her Santa hat.

'I … uh…'

'He's working on it,' Annie said before they were forced to move on to allow more people onto the bus. They dropped into a seat in the back of the bus. He breathed out a sigh of relief as he sat and found Annie grinning at him.

'Worried you were going to have to stay in for recess?' she asked between giggles.

'Don't mock my trauma,' he said, causing Annie to laugh harder.

'Are you saying you were unfairly targeted?'

'Oh no, I definitely deserved it,' he said with a grin. 'But I'm trying to turn over a new leaf. I don't need people reminding you of my dark past.'

'So dark,' she said with a giggle. 'It's amazing you've been able to put it all behind you.'

As long as she had put it behind her, that was all he really cared about.

Annie pulled off her hat, shaking her hair free. While it had been freezing outside, the bus was uncomfortably warm. The windows were already fogged over. She took off her mittens and wriggled out of her coat and then sat back in the seat with a dramatic gasp.

'Phew! That's better.'

It was better, because now he could see all that golden hair he used to stare at instead of focusing on word problems and he could see the snug sweater Annie had been wearing under her coat.

Annie was *hot*.

Again, he wondered what the hell he had been doing his whole life not paying attention to this beautiful girl; all because what, she didn't come to his lacrosse games? Stupid. But he was here now, crammed into a school-bus seat with her, and this time he was not going to hesitate.

He casually slung an arm around Annie's shoulder, snuggling in closer so he could look out the window with her.

'All right,' he said with a smile, his lips dangerously close to Annie's ear. 'Let's see some lights.'

Annie plucked Mac's arm from her shoulder and wriggled out of his grasp.

'You're kidding, right?'

He grinned. 'Worth a shot.'

Annie rolled her eyes and turned her attention back out the window even as her cheeks heated at the way Mac was looking at her. What the hell did this guy think he was doing, anyway? Putting his arm around her like they were dating or something, when she knew for a fact he was outta here after the New Year. She'd helped him plan the damn route.

Not to mention, she'd never live it down if Hazel and

Logan found out she was hooking up with Mac, of all people. After she'd done nothing but malign his character for the past thirteen years, there was no way her friends would let it go.

She shuddered at the thought.

'You can't possibly be cold,' Mac said, misinterpreting her shiver. 'It's like eight hundred degrees on this bus.' He leaned across her to wipe the condensation from the window, forcing her to be subjected to his arms again. Strong arms. Muscular arms. And his warm, spiced scent washed over her, making her close her eyes and breathe deep.

Okay, so Annie hadn't exactly made dating a priority in high school. In fact, she may have forgotten to do it at all. But who had the time, really? Between student council and her AP classes, Annie barely had time to see her friends.

But now, with Mac so close and oozing his unique brand of masculinity all over her, she thought that not dating may have been an oversight. She hadn't had the chance to become immune to things like strong arms and whatever it was that made Mac smell so good.

Unless you counted Logan, which she one hundred percent did not, Annie hadn't spent much time around teenage boys. Sure, she'd slow-danced with Aiden Smith at the ninth-grade winter formal, and there had been that underwhelming make-out session with Seth Bates after she kicked his butt at mock trial. But, in general, she had never seen the appeal of adolescent males until right now.

Annie nudged Mac back onto his half of the seat in a desperate attempt to get her head on straight. His proximity was doing weird things to her judgement. 'Not cold. Just excited to see the lights,' she lied. The bus was slowly trundling down Main Street, Christmas music playing over the speakers, and she tried to focus on that instead of Mac's newly uncovered charms.

Annie had a life-plan to manage, a cookie empire to build. She did not have time for distractions. She'd only agreed to this second meet-up—she would not call it a date —because she wanted to see the lights and her sisters were all refusing to come this year.

She dug into her oversized purse and pulled out a bag of freshly baked sugar cookies she'd made for the occasion. She held them out to Mac and the sound he made when he bit into one was so obscene that the older couple in the seat next to them turned in shock, as though they thought something untoward was happening over here. Annie felt her cheeks go up in flames.

'Damn, Annie. You really know what you're doing with these cookies,' he said, eyes closed, head leaning back on the seat.

'Of course I do.'

Mac's lips tipped into a smirk even as his eyes remained closed. 'I should have known.'

'Known what?'

He opened his eyes and rolled his head to face her. 'That you would be good at anything you tried.'

Annie swallowed hard. 'I'm definitely not.'

Mac shrugged. 'Well, you're good at cookie-baking.'

'Thanks.' Had it gotten even warmer in here? Why had Mac's words had such an effect on her? She knew she was good at baking. But she also knew that she'd tossed three imperfect batches of those same cookies into the trash today and these were the only ones that made the cut and that sometimes she wondered how she would put this crazy dream of hers into action. What if she worked hard and it still didn't happen? What if she tried and failed?

'What's the matter? You look like I just told you your dog died instead of complimenting you.'

'I don't have a dog,' she said weakly, trying to avoid the topic of her paralyzing fear of failure. She forced a smile. 'I'm fine. I'm glad you like the cookies.'

Mac looked at her like he wasn't totally buying that, but they'd turned down a side street and slowed down so that passengers could admire the first row of lit-up houses.

'If you look to your left,' Nancy's voice came over the speaker as the whole bus turned their attention to the lefthand side, 'we have Mr. and Mrs. Harris's home, which has the county's biggest display of nutcrackers.' The crowd dutifully oohed and ahhed at the army of nutcrackers displayed on the lawn.

'To your right, is the first of many nativity scenes on our route, this one with life-size figures.'

'Jesus,' Mac breathed.

'Exactly,' Annie quipped, and he laughed, his warm breath brushing her ear again since they'd both turned to look out the window. Another shiver ran through her.

'I'm surprised they don't have a live camel,' he said.

'Just wait until we get up to the Christmas Tree Farm. It's the last stop, but I hear the owner, Edmund, rented a real camel and several sheep this year.'

'Wow.'

'Yep.'

Mac was encroaching onto her side of the seat again and she should really push him away. She had no business with a guy like Mac, and he was obviously just passing the time until his friends came home. They both were.

But then she remembered the sound he made when he bit into the sugar cookie and the way he'd looked at her as she warmed his frozen hands, and she thought maybe she could take a small detour from her grand plans. Just for the next few weeks. Just until life returned to normal after the holidays.

They turned a sharp corner, and she nearly fell into Mac's lap and the universe settled things for her. When he wrapped his arm around her again, Annie didn't push him away.

'This okay?' he whispered in her ear. She nodded and snuggled in closer as the lit-up houses passed by the window.

'Yeah, it's okay.' It was perfectly okay that she was cuddled up with the one boy she'd claimed to hate while secretly harboring a crush on him that she never would have admitted even under threat of torture, but his arms felt so nice and it was her favorite time of year and the bus was so cozy with its twinkle lights and Christmas music...

It was perfectly okay.

She leaned back on Mac as through the window the light displays got more and more dramatic. She smiled as he gasped at the giant house on the end of Elm Street that had a full-size sleigh on the roof pulled by eight lit-up reindeer and, by the time he was enumerating his reasons for preferring multicolored lights over white ones, she knew she'd officially sold him on the Dream Harbor Lights Tour.

When they got off the bus and Mac was still holding her hand as they walked back to his car, she wasn't sure what else she'd sold him on. Or if she was buying into whatever was happening here. But when Mac said he didn't want the night to be over yet, she said she didn't either.

And when he invited her to his place, she said yes.

Chapter Seven

Now

Annie was getting dressed when her phone rang.

'Hey, Haze. I thought we were meeting at nine?' Annie glanced at her watch. She wasn't late. She couldn't be late. Too much to do today. First the spa with Jeanie and the girls, then finishing up her special gift for the bride and groom, and then helping Kira set up the tables and flowers. And if she could manage it, she had a few dozen cookie orders that needed filling before Monday. Worse-case scenario, she could just skip sleep, she'd done that plenty of times before.

'The appointment got moved to the afternoon.'

'Okay, great.'

'But that's not why I called.' Hazel sounded frazzled and, frankly, that was ominous on the day before the wedding.

'What's going on?' Annie put her phone on speaker while she brushed some mascara on her top lashes.

'Have you seen Estelle?'

Annie paused mid-mascara-swipe. 'Why would I have seen Logan's grandmother at eight-thirty in the morning, Haze?'

'I don't know, but no one else has seen her, either.'

'Wait. Hold on. Are you telling me that Logan's grandmother, his *beloved Nana*, is missing the day before his wedding?!'

'Uh. Yes.'

'Hazel! What the hell?! Have you tried calling her?'

'Of course I did! I was supposed to take her to get her hair done today and I called her to confirm, and she didn't answer her cell phone, so I called the house and Henry said she left early this morning.'

'Left to go where?!' Annie was shouting and pacing in her tiny bathroom, which was really only two steps in one direction and two steps in the other. She was getting dizzy.

'I don't know!' Hazel wailed, having moved far beyond frazzled into panicked territory.

Annie sat on her toilet lid and took a deep breath. 'Okay, let's calm down for a second. Didn't Henry know where she went?'

'Honestly, he seemed kind of confused about the whole thing. He said Estelle had to go out to pick something up. Or maybe someone? I don't know. He was talking in circles about some kind of surprise, but I'm worried, Annie.'

Okay, so a missing elderly person was not ideal but, as elderly folk went, Estelle was pretty with it. Annie was reasonably certain that Estelle wasn't lost and confused somewhere, but she also knew that, if Logan caught wind of this situation, he would be a mess on the day before his wedding and Annie couldn't have that.

'I'll go look for her,' Annie said, rising from her seat and hastily finishing her makeup routine. 'She's probably just around town somewhere getting a gift. I'll track her down and then we can all rest easy for tomorrow, okay?'

'But then you'll miss the mani-pedis.'

'I'm sure I will have found her by then.'

Hazel let out a worried little sigh.

'It'll be fine. Everything will be perfect. Don't worry.' Annie would make sure of it. 'And don't mention anything to Jeanie about Estelle, either.'

'Are you sure? Maybe I should come with you.'

'No, you promised Kira you would help with the favors.'

'Oh, right. I would send Noah, but he and Logan are taking some of the Ellis cousins ice-fishing today.'

'Dear God,' Annie muttered. 'I swear, if those two idiots fall through the ice, I will revive them and re-kill them myself.'

'I know. I suggested paint and sip, but they didn't go for it.'

Annie smoothed her hair back into her signature ponytail. 'It'll all be fine. And I'll keep you posted on my search for Estelle. My guess is I'll be sipping a PSL with her by ten.'

'I hope so. Bye, Annie.'

'Bye, Haze.'

Annie took a minute to tidy her apartment before setting out on her quest. It only took a minute because the space was so small, but she loved her little attic apartment. She lived on the third floor of an old Victorian house that had been converted into several apartments. She loved the slanted ceiling and the way the light came in through the front window every morning. She had everything she needed here. Her cozy bed, her kitchenette, good for heating up soup or tea and not much more, and a clawfoot tub, which was perfect for soaking after being on her feet for hours. It was her oasis after a long day.

And most importantly it was *hers*. She'd spent years living with her parents while she got her business up and running. She was barely making enough money to buy ingredients in those first few years; she certainly couldn't afford rent, too. And then she'd been saving for the lease on her shop, the new equipment she'd need, and the money to actually pay an employee.

Owning a bakery was her dream, but it was an expensive one.

After years of working for it, she wouldn't trade her baking empire for anything. Annie strongly believed that everyone should have a passion in life. It could be anything, bird-watching, writing fan fiction for your favorite small-town TV show—where you make every character a werewolf—photographing the squirrels that live in your backyard. Whatever gets you out of bed every day. It just so happened that her passion for baking translated into her career, which was a mixed blessing.

Now, her other passions were napping whenever possible and watching reality TV. Not that she would admit to either of those things. She had a reputation to maintain, after all.

She grabbed her coat from the hook by the door and slung her bag over her shoulder. When she opened the door and found a man standing on her doorstep, she yelped.

'Damn it, Mac. What the hell are you doing here?'

He looked as shocked as she was, apparently not expecting her to be charging out the door right as he was about to knock.

'Logan sent me.'

Annie frowned. She did not have time for this. 'He sent you for what?'

'His tie and cufflinks.'

'Why the hell would I have—' Oh, right. She did have those things. As a close friend of the bride and groom, Annie had been helping them both. She'd forgotten that Logan had ordered a tie and special cufflinks but had them sent here so Jeanie, a notorious snoop, wouldn't see them. She had already ruined the surprise proposal Logan had planned. He, at the very least, wanted a part of his outfit to be a surprise. Annie had thought it was cute at the time, but now she was annoyed. And extra annoyed that Logan had sent Mac of all people.

'Shouldn't you be ice fishing or something right now? How are you the only groomsman available for this task?'

Mac smirked. 'You really think I'd agree to sitting outside freezing my ass off trying to catch a tiny fish I have to throw back anyway? No, thanks. And Bennett's parents just got into town this morning. They're all out to breakfast at the Pancake House. So, I told Logan I would run some last-minute errands for him.'

Annie sighed. 'Fine. Wait here.'

'You're not going to invite me in?'

She rarely invited anyone in. Her place was too small, and her bed took up most of it. It was awkward to have people over and then expect them to perch on your bed. But she also couldn't remember where she'd stashed Logan's stuff, and it would be weird to leave Mac standing outside on the tiny landing by her door. Even though her instincts told her to slam the door in his face.

But she was still on her best behavior.

'Fine,' she huffed. 'Come in. But don't touch anything.'

He chuckled a little as he followed her inside. 'God, Annie. You act like I'm going to come in and start rifling through your underwear drawer.'

'I wouldn't put it past you.'

'I typically like it to be consensual when I see a woman's underwear.'

'Hmm.'

'Like the last time I saw yours.'

She flung a pillow at his head, and he chuckled as he caught it. 'The last and only time,' she reminded him.

'Oh, I'm well aware of that, darling.'

She flipped him off as she knelt down next to her bed. Having such a tiny apartment made her get creative with her storage. She started pulling out the bins she kept under there.

'I don't have time for your crap today, Mac,' she said as she rifled through the first bin.

'Busy day of manicures and secret bridesmaid stuff?' he asked, kneeling down beside her.

'Yes, lots of secret bridesmaid stuff.' She nudged him

aside with her shoulder. 'I don't need your help.' She didn't need him looking through her things. This particular bin was filled with summer clothes she didn't have space for in her only closet, a few books she'd meant to loan to her mom, a box of blank Christmas cards she'd had every intention of sending out two years ago but never got around to it, and multiple bottles of her favorite face cream.

'Stocking up?' Mac asked, lifting one of the bottles.

Annie snatched it back and laid it next to the others. 'They were discontinuing it. And that's my favorite one.'

Mac made a small sound like he was adding this piece of information to everything else he knew about her.

'I feel like I'm getting a sneak peek into your inner workings here, Annie,' he said, peering deeper under the bed to look at the other bins.

'I'd rather you see my underwear,' she muttered, closing this bin and pulling out another one. The last thing she needed was Mac peering into her inner workings. In fact, she needed Mac far away from her inner workings. She'd let him get way too close last night, let him hold her. Which was really stupid.

Was it too late to find a date to this wedding? Maybe on her way to track down Estelle, she'd find an eligible bachelor walking down the street. She needed a buffer between her and this man who kept pulling her back in, despite her best efforts to push him away.

Mac sat back on the rug and let Annie sort through the next bin.

'Afraid of what you'll see in this one?' she asked, glancing over her shoulder.

His lips tipped into a smile. 'A little. I don't really want to know that there's a hit list and I'm the first on it.'

'You're the only one on it.'

'That's sweet.'

She shook her head, trying and failing to not be amused by this conversation.

'Aha! Here it is!' She pulled out the small paper bag that contained Logan's tie and cufflinks. 'Found them.' She handed them to Mac, and she didn't miss the disappointed look on his face, like he was upset the search ended so quickly.

'Let me help you,' he said, getting up from his spot on the floor and offering a hand to Annie.

'Help me with what?' She stood without taking the offered hand. No more touching. It was safer that way.

Mac sighed, tucking the rejected hand into his pocket. 'With whatever you have to do today. You clearly have a lot on your list, and this was the only task Logan gave me. Put me to work.'

Annie contemplated telling Mac to go to hell, but she did have a lot on her list today. Not that he could help with most of it.

'Fine,' she said, begrudgingly. 'You can pick up Estelle.'

'Great. From where?'

'I don't know,' Annie said, moving toward the door. She flipped off the lights, including the twinkle lights she'd strung up for Christmas. Mac followed along, still looking around at her apartment like he was taking mental notes about the fact that she had unfolded laundry in a basket and dirty dishes in the sink. She couldn't be perfect *all the time*.

'What do you mean, you don't know?'

'She's missing.'

The shocked look on Mac's face as he stood frozen in her doorway was almost entertaining enough to distract Annie from the fact that a missing grandmother was not funny at all.

And that she'd just recruited Mac to help her search.

Chapter Eight

M ac had spent most of his teenage years confusing lust with love. When he'd made out with Lauren Pepprell at the movies in ninth grade, he had been pretty convinced he was in love with her. And when Sadie Bates let him feel her up that time her parents were out of town, he was positive he loved her. And surely, when he lost his virginity to Parker Moore last year, he was in love with her, right?

Sitting in his basement bedroom with Annie, he suddenly wasn't sure about any of it.

Which was crazy, because he wasn't *in love* with Annie. But he'd never stayed up half the night or even like half an afternoon with any of those girls. He'd liked them and they'd come to his games, and he'd taken them on a date or two, but nothing like this had ever happened before.

Annie was currently lying on his bed, snuggling the

stuffed polar bear he'd had since birth, and teasing him for admitting that his favorite movie was *The Muppet Christmas Carol*.

'I meant like a favorite movie in general, not a Christmas movie,' she said between giggles.

'That is my favorite movie!' he insisted, and Annie started laughing all over again.

He threw a pillow at her from his position draped across the foot of the bed. 'It's a good movie.'

'It's singing puppets.' She added the pillow to the stack behind her head. It was after 1 a.m. and he should really take her home, but he was having too much fun.

'The world's most beloved singing puppets.'

She shrugged a little like she'd give him that much. 'Fair.'

'Thank you.' He stretched his arms behind his head and stared up at the old drop ceiling above them. He'd moved into the basement a few years ago for more privacy and, as much as his mom tried to make it homey down here, it was still a basement. At least twice a year, the whole damn thing flooded. He really needed to move out.

'Okay, my turn,' he said.

'My favorite movie is *Pride and Prejudice*, the Colin Firth version, obviously. Although, technically, it was a TV series but I'm going to count it.'

'I don't know what any of that means. And that wasn't my question.'

Annie huffed and he could hear her snuggling down into his pillows. 'Okay, go ahead with your question.'

'So, you and Logan never hooked up?' He wasn't sure

why he wanted to know, but he didn't really think you could be that close a friend with someone of the opposite gender, assuming you were both straight, and not hook up eventually.

Annie returned the pillow from earlier and it landed on his face.

'Ew.'

'It's not that crazy of a question.' He slipped the pillow behind his head.

'He is a brother to me in every way except blood. So no, I didn't hook up with him nor would I, even if we were the last two people on the planet.'

'Wow, harsh. Poor Logan.'

'I assure you he feels the same about me.'

'If you say so.'

'What's that supposed to mean?'

'I'm just saying, if it was me and I had a hot girl hanging around me all the time, but she only wanted to be friends, that would be tough.'

Annie sat up so she was looking down at him.

'You think I'm hot?'

Oops. Had he let that slip out?

'I mean, yeah.' He tried to say it casually, like he often had girls over, confessed his most embarrassing secrets, showed them his childhood stuffed animals and then told them they were hot. Just a normal evening for ol' Mac.

Annie's brow furrowed in a way that said she was skeptical, and Mac wanted to elaborate on exactly why she was hot, starting with that plush bottom lip and ending with the perfect curve of her ass, but he didn't want to ruin the night.

She flopped back onto the pillows. 'Okay, moving on. Biggest fear?'

'Wow, you're going to go from favorite movie to biggest fear?'

'Yep, biggest fear, go.'

He could have said bats, because that was true. They were essentially flying mice with fangs which was objectively terrifying. But he had a feeling that wasn't what Annie was going for.

'Getting stuck here,' he said, directing his words to the ceiling. It was easier to confess that way, without Annie's eyes on him.

'Define here.'

Mac blew out a long sigh. Damn, this girl was intense. Maybe he should have just complimented her ass and called it a night.

'Here in town, here in my mom's basement, here doing nothing with my life.'

'What do you want to do with your life?'

'Hold on, it's my turn and I want you to answer the same question. Biggest fear?'

Annie didn't skip a beat. 'Failure.'

'Failure?'

'Yep. And don't try and tell me all that inspirational bullshit about needing to fail before you succeed.'

'Nah, failing sucks. Getting stuck here would be failing.'

'Right. And never getting my business off the ground would be failing. And I would hate that.'

Mac sat up so he could look at her. She looked cute, all sleepy with wispy blonde hair escaping her ponytail.

'Okay, so don't fail.'

She scoffed. 'Piece of cake. No pun intended. I just won't fail. Thank you for that wonderful advice.'

'No, I mean, it's only failure if you stop, right? If you keep going, even after a set-back, then you'll eventually get there.'

Annie considered him for a minute. 'Yeah, I guess so.'

'Great. It's settled. You'll be running a baking empire in no time.' He crashed into the pillows next to her, so they were side by side. She rolled over to face him.

'So, what do you want to do with your life?' she asked.

'I hate that question.'

'It's okay to say you don't know yet.'

'Is it?' Everyone else seemed to have at least a vague notion and all Mac had was a half-assed plan to drive around the country until he figured it out.

'Of course it is. We're only nineteen.'

'Says the woman with a master business plan.'

She giggled and he liked it. Probably too much. This whole night was messing with his head. But he liked this girl. It was the only feeling he'd had in a long time that he was sure about.

'It's too bad we didn't hang out sooner,' he said, wishing they hadn't wasted so many years.

'What did you really think of me in high school?' she asked.

'That you were a stuck-up over-achiever with super shiny hair and a great ass.'

Her eyes widened in surprise. 'I don't know if I should be mad or flattered.'

Mac laughed. 'Same question.'

'That you were a dumb jock and a sometimes bully with beautiful eyelashes.'

'Eyelashes?! That's what you noticed about me? My eyelashes?'

'Yep.' Annie grinned and he couldn't help but laugh.

'Wow, there I was spending all that time in the weight room, and I could have just batted my lashes.'

'Truly.'

'And what do you think of me now?' he asked, almost afraid to hear the answer. He didn't even know what he thought of himself lately, who he was or who he wanted to be.

Annie thought for a moment, her lips twisting to the side. 'Now, I think you're actually kinda sweet and you're definitely not dumb. And I'm still jealous of your lashes.'

Mac fluttered them dramatically to cover his absurd relief at her assessment of him, and Annie giggled.

'Same question,' she said.

'You're still an over-achiever, but I don't see it as a bad thing when it doesn't end up in extra economics homework. Hair and ass, still perfect.'

She smacked him on the arm in mock outrage. 'Stop talking about my ass.'

'Sorry, I'll try not to.'

Annie reached out and looped her finger under the gold chain around his neck. She pulled slightly until the cross that hung on the end of it dangled between them.

'I always wondered what was on this chain.'

Mac resisted the urge to squirm. First his biggest fears and now this. Annie was seeing more of him than anyone had. But he wanted her to. He wanted her to know him, as though that would somehow help him figure himself out. Like, through her eyes, he would start to make sense.

'Are you very religious?' she asked, and he liked that she didn't seem put off by the thought. Mac hadn't been into organized religion in a while now, but plenty of his favorite people were.

'Not particularly.'

'But you wear a gold cross.'

'It was my grandfather's. He gave it to me for my confirmation.'

'So, you're a little bit religious,' she said with a small smile.

'When it suits me.' Mac broke more Catholic rules than he followed, but when his grandpa got sick, he prayed like hell for him to get better. Not that it did much good in the end, except maybe comfort his mom.

Annie gave a little nod, taking in this piece of information about him. She still had his necklace hooked over her finger. One gentle tug and he'd be close enough to kiss her. She realized it at the same time he did, her eyes widening slightly.

'Your eyes are very blue.' *Brilliant, Mac. Sheer freaking poetry.*

'Thank you?'

Her smile was quickly becoming his new favorite thing.

'They're beautiful.'

The smile grew.

'Thank you.'

'You're welcome.'

'I should probably go home.'

'I'll drive you.'

Neither of them moved. Annie released his necklace and let her hand rest in the space between them on the bed. They were only one of Annie's hand's-width apart. Annie had small hands.

'It's probably cold out,' Annie whispered, her eyelids beginning to droop.

'It definitely is.'

'I already told my mom I was staying with a friend...' Her voice trailed off as her eyes closed.

'A friend?' Mac whispered.

Annie smiled in her almost-sleep, giving him a contented sigh. 'Yeah ... a friend.'

He stayed like that, taking in all the details of her face, all the things that made her Annie. The little scar on the bridge of her nose, the curve of her cheek, the shorter, fine blonde hairs that surrounded her face. He knew he shouldn't kiss her. Despite what fairy tales would have you believe, he knew a girl should be conscious for that, but God, was it tempting with her lips right there.

'Stop staring at me, Mac. It's creepy.'

Mac rolled onto his back with a laugh. 'You scared the crap out of me. I thought you were asleep.'

'No one falls asleep that quickly, and I could sense you looking at me.'

'Sorry,' he said, the laughter still in his voice. 'So, are you staying over?'

'As long as you promise not to gaze at me longingly all night.'

'Ha! Who says I was doing it longingly?'

'I could sense that, too.' She was smiling now, even though her eyes were still closed.

'No more staring,' he promised as he pulled a blanket over her.

'Goodnight, Annie.'

'Goodnight, Mac,' she murmured, snuggling down into the blanket. It was then that he realized she was still holding his stuffed polar bear.

Of course she was.

He pulled his own blanket over himself and turned away from Annie to avoid any more embarrassing staring incidents.

And that was how Mac had his first sleepover with a girl, and he honestly didn't know if it was love or lust taking root, but it was definitely one of the two.

Or maybe both.

Chapter Nine

Now

Mac had insisted on driving them to the Y to look for Nana in his big, dumb vehicle that was some kind of half truck, half SUV monstrosity and older than both of them. *Vintage* was what he called it when she'd commented on it. A vintage Ford Bronco, he'd informed her like she was supposed to be impressed.

She was not.

And the only reason Annie allowed it was because she was out of gas. Again. She hadn't had time in between everything else she was doing to stop and fill her tank, but she could have. She *would* have this morning, if Mac wasn't being so pushy and insisting that he be the one to drive.

'I still think it would have made more sense for us to split up,' Annie grumbled, jumping down from the truck.

'You asked for my help, so you're getting it,' Mac said

with a sweep of his hands, like he was some kind of prize in a game show.

Annie scowled. 'Whatever. Let's just go in and find Estelle. She's probably at one of her classes and forgot to let everybody know.'

Annie strode across the parking lot to the front doors of the Dream Harbor YMCA with Mac trailing along behind her. She really didn't know what had possessed her to include him in this little search. For the three years since he'd been back in town, she'd done everything in her power to avoid time alone with him. She'd been busy, she'd been uninterested, she'd been down-right mean. Anything to protect herself from him. And look at her now, spending the morning with Mac like it was fine, like they were *friends*.

But when she went out to her car and that damn gas light was on, she didn't have much of a choice. Right?

Right. She needed to find Logan's grandmother, and fast, because she had plenty of other things on her to-do list and no time to do them. She rubbed the spot on the back of her neck that tightened up when she was stressed. The last few weeks had put a giant baseball-sized knot there. She dug her fingers in, trying in vain to loosen it up.

'What's the matter with your neck?' Mac asked as they went through the automatic doors. The lobby of the Y smelled like sneakers and cleaning solution.

'Nothing's wrong with my neck and, if something *was* wrong with my neck, it would not be any of your business.'

'My mistake,' Mac said. 'I thought you told Logan we would be friends for the weekend. And friends check in with each other.'

Annie bit back a scoff. 'I told Logan I would be on my

best behavior. I said absolutely nothing about being your friend.'

She ignored the flicker of hurt on Mac's face and continued her power walk to the front desk. She didn't have time for Mac's feelings. Just like he had never had time for hers.

'Hello,' she said in her friendliest voice. 'We are here for the seniors' aerobics class.'

The woman behind the desk had a short-cropped haircut that Annie wished she could pull off and a look that said she was not in the mood to deal with anyone's antics.

'That class is for members sixty-five and older,' she said, glancing over Annie's shoulder at where Mac was standing, not even trying to look elderly. So much for being helpful.

'Oh, of course!' Annie said, scrambling for another idea. She wasn't expecting such high security at the Y. 'We are actually here to—'

'We're here for a membership,' Mac interjected. 'And maybe some information on classes that would be more age-appropriate for us.' He flashed the woman behind the desk his most dazzling smile. It made Annie want to punch him in the face, but surprisingly it worked on the no-nonsense Y employee.

'In that case,' she said, no longer speaking to Annie, 'let me get you some forms.'

She hustled into the back office to round up the paperwork and Annie turned to glare at Mac.

'Now what are we going to do?'

Mac shrugged. 'Apparently get a gym membership,' he said.

'That's the last thing I want,' Annie said, causing his mouth to tip into a smile.

'How about you sneak off to the pool area and I will keep our new friend busy with plenty of membership questions,' he whispered, giving Annie's shoulder a gentle nudge. She was about to argue but that was actually a good idea. She hurried off to the pool before the woman returned with clipboards and pens, glancing only once over her shoulder at where Mac was now explaining that Annie had to take off but that he was very interested in the Platinum package.

Annie was dismayed to find a goofy smile on her face. Why did he have to be so charming? She shook her head, getting rid of that thought and barreled her way into the pool area. It was warm and muggy inside and smelled strongly of chlorine. At the far end of the pool, a small group of older women were bouncing up and down in the water, an energetic playlist pumping through the speakers. No one paid Annie any mind, so she hurried across the puddled tiles to where Iris was perched on the edge of the pool.

'Annie's here!' Carol called as she jumped up and down in the water. 'Did you bring us after-class snacks?'

The women turned to Annie, looking up at her with hopeful eyes. 'Sorry, ladies, not today. I've come on bridesmaid business, not bakery business.'

While the women looked disappointed at her lack of baked goods, they perked up at the mention of bridesmaid duties.

'How is the wedding preparation going?' Janet asked. 'Have you seen the dress? What does the barn look like?

Is it *actually* ready? Are we going to be freezing our butts off tomorrow?'

Annie shook her head. 'You won't freeze. The barn looks amazing. The dress is beautiful but... Have any of you seen Estelle this morning?'

The women looked at each other with varying degrees of shock and dismay on their faces.

'Estelle! You're looking for Estelle?'

'I just ... we aren't sure exactly where she is...'

The women stared up at her from the pool with their eyes wide.

'I'm sure she's fine,' Iris assured them. 'It's Estelle we're talking about. She wouldn't have just wandered off.'

Annie redirected her attention to Iris, who sat on the edge of the pool, hand over her growing baby bump.

'Right. Iris is right. Estelle wouldn't have just wandered off for no reason. I'm sure she'll turn up. I wanted to check here and see if maybe she came to her class, but clearly, she didn't so I will continue looking.'

'What if you don't find her? She can't miss the wedding!'

'She won't miss the wedding. I will find her.' Annie put her hands on her hips in her most confident pose, but the women still looked somewhat horrified. Annie sighed. 'Can you all keep this to yourselves, please? I really don't want to worry the bride and groom.'

The group nodded in agreement as though they would never even think of spreading this news all over town.

'I'm serious, ladies. I'm counting on you now to keep this to yourselves, and if you see Estelle anywhere give me a call. Okay?'

'You got it, Annie. We want this wedding to be perfect,' Marissa said with a smile.

Annie ignored the tightening knot in her neck at the mention of the wedding being perfect. Of course it would be perfect. She'd make sure of it; stiff neck be damned.

'Okay, back to your workout,' she said as she nodded to Iris to turn the music back up.

'Come on, ladies! Let's see those jumps. You can go higher than that,' Iris called to them as Annie hurried out of the pool area.

By the time she'd made her way back to the desk, Mac was still talking to the stern employee, except now she had a giant smile on her face and was finding Mac to be quite hilarious.

'There you are,' Mac said, looking up as Annie approached the desk. The employee shot her a disapproving look. Apparently, she wasn't thrilled that Annie had taken her own private tour.

'We should really be going now,' Annie said with an apologetic smile.

The woman's glare deepened. 'Make sure you take your paperwork and bring it back when you're done,' she said to Mac, pushing a stack of forms that Annie was positive could be filled out online across the desk to him.

'Thanks, Tina. You've been super helpful,' he said, that damn smile aimed in her direction again.

Annie groaned and grabbed him by the bicep that certainly didn't need any more time at the gym, tugging him away before he could invite Tina from the Y to the wedding.

'Yeah, thanks, Tina!' Annie called, dragging Mac toward the door.

'Did you find out any info?' Mac asked when they were back in the parking lot.

Annie blew out a long breath, the air clouding in front of her. The sky was gray and cold. She was glad most of Jeanie's out-of-town relatives had arrived this morning, because they were predicting snow later and having half the guest list stuck in a snowstorm didn't make for a perfect wedding.

'No, nobody has heard from her today.'

Mac frowned as he climbed up into the truck. Annie met him inside.

'Where should we look next?' he asked.

Annie tipped her head back on the seat, eyes closed, trying to breathe out some of the tension that was creeping into her skull. The last thing she needed was a headache. She opened her eyes at a strange but familiar sound to find Mac shaking a small bottle of painkillers. He popped the top, raising his eyebrows in question. Annie was too tired to argue. She held out her hand and Mac tapped two small pills into her palm.

'Thank you,' she grumbled, reluctantly accepting the Advil as a peace offering.

'What was that? I didn't quite hear you,' Mac said with a teasing grin.

'I said. Thank. You.' Annie enunciated each word clearly and loudly until Mac laughed.

'You are welcome. Now where to next?'

'Well, if I were Estelle out on some top-secret wedding

errand, the first place I'd go would be the café. Because how does anyone run top-secret errands without caffeine?'

'Great,' Mac said, backing out of the parking space, his arm draped over the back of Annie's seat.

'Did she give you her number?' she asked incredulously, glancing at the membership papers he'd tossed on her lap when she climbed in.

'Maybe. Why, are you jealous, Annabelle?

Annie scoffed. 'Why would I be jealous?'

Mac shrugged and Annie did her best to ignore the way his broad shoulders tugged at his coat.

'I'm surprised you didn't ask her to the wedding,' she said half joking, half fishing for information.

'How do you know I didn't?'

'Did you?'

'Would it bother you if I did?'

'Nope, not a bit. You are free to date whomever you please, Macaulay.' She was glad she didn't have to look him in the face when she said it.

'That's very generous of you,' he said. 'But I didn't ask her.'

Annie was not proud of the immediate relief that flooded her body. It was one thing to deal with Mac bringing dates to Christmas and other get-togethers, but she really didn't think she could handle watching him with a date at something as romantic as a wedding. Watching him hold another woman in his arms while they danced together. She might have to topple her secret wedding dessert just to cause a distraction and get the hell out of there.

'Well, that's your business,' she said, slumping in her

seat. She caught Mac's lopsided grin from the corner of her eye.

'Why did you come back, anyway?' she asked, needing to change the subject from exactly how jealous she got when she saw Mac with other women.

After enough years had gone by, she'd given up on the idea that Mac was ever coming back. Of course, she knew he visited his parents every once in a while, and she very deliberately avoided him when he did. She'd even planned an impromptu girls' weekend with Hazel one year, just to make sure she was out of town on Mac's mother's birthday.

And then, when he had returned for good, she hadn't given him the chance to explain anything. It had been nearly three years now and they hadn't done much more than snipe at each other, and she was perfectly aware that was primarily her fault. But it didn't mean she wasn't curious.

Mac looked over at her like he was surprised by the question, because of course he was. Annie rarely asked him anything that wasn't, *why the hell are you here?* Which basically, she still was asking, but nicer.

'My dad was ready to retire, and I figured I'd been gone long enough.'

He'd been gone for eight years.

Not that she'd kept count.

'And is it torture?' she asked.

'Is what torture? Running the pub?'

'Being back here in Dream Harbor. I thought you never wanted that to happen.'

'You remember more about that December than you let on,' he said with a chuckle. And Annie was immediately transported back to that night so many years ago. Lying face to face with Mac in his bed and pouring out their fears to each other. She hadn't done anything like that since.

She ignored his comment, not wanting to discuss that time any more than she wanted to discuss Mac's dating life or her reaction to it.

'So, do you hate it?' she asked and for some reason that question felt like the most important one. When Mac left, he'd abandoned not only her but the town she loved. It pissed her off that he was able to simply walk back in and everyone embraced him like some sort of prodigal son. Annie wasn't that forgiving.

'No, I don't hate it. I'm not nineteen anymore, Annie. I want different things than I did then.' He had parked in front of The Pumpkin Spice Café and turned to look at her. She wanted to ask what he wanted now but she was afraid of the answer.

'Well, I'm glad you don't hate it here,' she said. Her gaze flicked to his, and he was looking at her with such tenderness she wished she had never gotten in this truck in the first place; because if Mac kept looking at her like that, she didn't know how much longer she could pretend to hate him.

'How's your head?' he asked.

'It's fine. Just a tension headache, that's all.'

He was still looking at her like he wanted to lean across the center console and make all sorts of bad decisions. Annie was left to be the reasonable one.

'Anyway, I'm feeling much better now. Let's go get some coffee and see if we can find Nana,' she said in a rush, opening her door and tumbling out into the cold air.

She breathed deep in a vain attempt to clear her head, but there wasn't enough cold air in the world to purge Mac from her system. Especially when he came up beside her and pressed his large warm hand into the small of her back, guiding her into the café. She didn't even have the strength to push him away. Or maybe it was the desire she lacked because that hand felt damn good. And she couldn't always be the reasonable one.

Chapter Ten

Now

It was a freezing December Saturday, and the café was packed. Every table was filled, and the line ran from the counter to the door.

'She must be in here,' Annie said.

'Everyone in the entire town is in here,' Mac said, guiding Annie into the line. Miraculously she hadn't swatted his hand away and he was fully taking advantage of the opportunity to touch her, even if it was through several winter layers.

Annie stood up on her tiptoes scanning the crowd but, from what Mac could see, Estelle wasn't here.

'Maybe we should ask if anyone has seen her,' he said, getting ready to raise his voice above the crowd. Annie sensed it and clapped a hand over his mouth. Her skin was so soft against his lips he nearly groaned.

'No,' she hissed. 'We can't announce to the entire town that Estelle is missing.'

She dropped her hand before Mac could do something insane like run his tongue from her palm to her fingertips.

'Then how are we ever going to find her?'

'We'll find her. But if these people know we're looking for her, it will inevitably get back to Jeanie and Logan. And a missing grandmother is not part of the plan.'

She had leaned in close to him during this little speech, whispering in his ear. Her breath was warm on his face, and she smelled like mint and vanilla. He wanted to tug her closer and keep her there, but that was a surefire way to get a knee in the groin.

Instead, he flexed his fingers on Annie's lower back, putting a little more pressure there until she was nearly flush against him. He didn't miss the light tremor that ran through her at the proximity.

'Okay,' he said. 'So, what do you propose we do next?'

Annie blinked up at him like she couldn't quite remember what they were doing here or why they were standing so close. She gave her head a slight shake and little tendrils of blonde hair escaped from her ponytail.

'We should probably get coffee,' Mac suggested.

Annie nodded slowly, coming back to herself. She took a small step away from him. Annie was always taking small steps away from him.

'Right, coffee. We should definitely do that. And we can finish our search after.'

'Why don't you go take a lap, just in case she's sitting in a back corner somewhere. I'll get the drinks.'

'Okay.' Annie nodded, setting off on a circuit of the café, while Mac waited. He needed a break from her nearness. It was doing things to his brain, making him unable to think straight.

'What can I get you?' Crystal asked when he got to the counter.

'Peppermint hot chocolate, large, extra whipped cream and a spiced chai latte.'

Crystal raised an eyebrow.

'What?' Mac asked. 'It's the holidays.'

The barista smiled as she typed in his order. 'It sure is.'

Christmas music played quietly over the speakers, and the counter was trimmed in pine boughs and holly berries. The display case was filled with cookies he was sure Annie had made, not that he could figure out when she could have possibly had the time. Outside, a light snow had started to fall, as if on cue.

'Excited about the wedding tomorrow?' Crystal asked as Joe made his drinks.

'Of course. Love weddings. Any chance you don't already have a date?' he asked, suddenly feeling desperate not to end up alone around Annie again.

'Sorry. Travis finally locked it down.' She waggled her ring finger at him, the huge diamond sparkling in mockery of his situation.

'Lucky guy.'

Crystal smiled. 'Don't worry, Mac. You'll get her one day.'

He chose to assume that Crystal was speaking of a generic 'her' and not the specific 'her' the entire town knew he'd been after since he moved back here.

'Thanks. Hey, you haven't seen Estelle this morning, have you?' He knew Crystal wouldn't get the town talking.

'No, but Dot was in earlier and mentioned that she was meeting up with Estelle today.'

'She did? Any chance she said where?'

'Something about the inn. I figured they were greeting family coming in for the wedding.'

'Yes, amazing. Thank you!'

Crystal seemed understandably surprised about his enthusiastic reaction to Estelle's plans for the day, but he didn't have time to explain. Plus, Annie had sworn him to secrecy. He took his drinks, looking around to find Annie, when he bumped into a group of local high-school kids he'd had to take fake IDs from last weekend. They were still trying to get them back 'to dispose of properly'. Luckily Mac wasn't that big of an idiot.

'Come on, Mac! Be cool.' Hayden, the boldest of the group, tried to step in front of him.

'I haven't been cool in years. And you know I can't give them back.'

'In Quebec they can drink at eighteen.'

'Then go to Quebec to drink.'

'Mac…'

'Next time, don't try to use a fake ID at a pub filled with people who've known you since you wet your pants during the annual Christmas pageant.'

Hayden's friends burst out laughing at that and Mac gave him a hard pat on the back.

'That was way harsh, bro.'

'Sorry, *bro*. At least I didn't call your mother.'

Hayden blanched at that threat and relented on his

mission to reclaim the ID, shoving his friends toward the counter.

Mac shook his head with a laugh. Some days he still couldn't believe that he wasn't the one begging for his fake ID back. At least he and his friends would go a few towns over to drink. This kid needed to learn some life lessons on how not to get caught. But that was probably not something he should say out loud.

He'd spent so long putting off becoming a real adult that, when he first came back to town to run his dad's pub, he felt like he was faking it. It took him a year after he bought it to stop calling it his dad's.

But he'd wanted to make it his own. He'd worked for years to ensure that he was the Sullivan people thought of now when they came in. He'd added trivia nights and karaoke. He'd updated the menu. He'd put a lot of love into that place. Had Annie noticed any of it?

While he'd been out on the road, he'd realized the places he liked best, the ones that were the most fun to work at, were places that had regulars. The pubs, restaurants, and cafés that had repeat customers, that created a sense of gathering, of community, those had been his favorites.

And now he got to do that here in his hometown.

Annie had asked him if he hated it, running the pub. He didn't hate it all. He loved it. He wished she could see that, that she could see he belonged here as much as she did.

'Friends of yours?' Annie asked, sliding up next to him and taking her drink.

'Ha. No. But I do have a lead.'

'A lead?' Annie's face lit up and Mac wished he could

make her look that happy by doing something other than simply asking the barista where an old lady had gone off to.

'Yep. Crystal says Estelle and Dot were in earlier and they were headed to the inn.'

'Oh my gosh, perfect! Let's go.'

They were making their way to the door when they were intercepted by the book club. Because of course they were.

'Mac!' Jacob called, waving at him from his seat. 'Did you read the book this week?'

Annie froze in her mission to beeline for the door. She turned to stare at him. 'Macaulay,' she said, her smile growing. 'Are you a member of the book club?'

Was he a member of the book club if he'd only come to one meeting? He still felt like he'd been tricked into it. Jacob had left a book behind at the pub once and it happened to be a slow night, so Mac had read it. It wasn't Mac's fault that it was so *good*. He needed to talk about it with someone. So, he may have gone to *one* meeting months ago. The book club hadn't given up on him since.

'Not really,' he said to Annie, even as Jacob was waving wildly for him to come over to the table, yelling about the latest book they were reading.

'I really think you'll like this one,' Jacob was saying, even as Mac was trying to inch his way to the door. 'It's a second-chance romance. Very angsty. I think it's really your type of story.'

'Yeah, maybe I'll get it from you another time,' Mac said, trying desperately to get out of the situation. 'I'm right in the middle of my yearly reread of *War and Peace*.' Jacob shook his head at that, not buying a word of it.

'Come over here, you two!' Nancy called in her no-nonsense teacher voice and Mac felt compelled to obey. 'We have wedding questions.'

Annie shuffled over to the book-club table, looking like she'd rather be headed to a root canal.

'What are you all doing here on a Saturday?' she asked, clearly trying to avoid the wedding questions.

'This was an impromptu meet-up,' Kaori said. 'Not an official meeting.'

'Have you seen the barn?' Isabel asked. 'Is it going to be ready in time?'

'Of course. It looks great. Kira has everything under control.' Annie nodded confidently but the book club still looked skeptical. The Christmas Tree Farm had been open all month selling trees, but Kira had kept the barn a top-secret project, barricading off the back fifty acres to keep out nosy townsfolk. And the townsfolk hated to be kept out of anything. Kira had caught plenty of people 'accidentally' wandering around the barn claiming to be looking for the perfect Christmas tree.

Nancy had been escorted off the property several times.

'And how's Logan?' Linda asked, stealing the last piece of muffin from Nancy's plate. 'We haven't seen him in days.' She said it as though there was some conspiracy to hide the groom. In fact, Logan avoided town as much as possible, so it wasn't that big of a surprise that no one had seen him.

'Logan is great! He is very excited to marry the love of his life and everything is fine.' Annie assured them. The book club did not look appeased. It was like they sensed something else was wrong. Mac found himself biting down on his tongue to avoid blurting out that Nana was missing and they had no idea where she was or when she would be back or how Logan would react when he found out. Apparently, some of Annie's anxiety about the situation had seeped into him.

'We should really get going,' he said, his hand finding its way to the small of Annie's back again. Jacob's gaze tracked its journey and he smirked at Mac, a perfectly groomed eyebrow raised in question. Mac dropped his hand. They needed to get out of here before the book club knew about more than just the missing-Nana problem.

'Okay, but I really think you should read next month's book with us, Mac. He's loved her for years!' Jacob was clearly prepared to relay the entire premise of the book. Mac took Annie by the elbow and guided her away from the table before Jacob could make any life-to-text comparisons.

'Bye, everyone!' he said. 'Important wedding duties to attend to.' He steered Annie out the door. The last thing he needed was to read about another poor bastard who had loved the same woman for years. And, while he was sure the book would end up happily, he was not at all confident the same would happen for him.

Chapter Eleven

Then

Annie's face was burrowed against something warm and firm and her arm was draped over something solid and … breathing? Her fingers trailed along bare skin. She froze. Whose bare skin was she touching? And where the hell was she?

Oh, dear God, she was still in Mac's bed. And so was he. And apparently, before she had woken up, her fingers had been tracing little lines across his abs where his T-shirt had risen up during the night. She carefully moved her hand off his stomach, hoping that if she moved slow enough, she wouldn't wake him. This was so embarrassing! She was completely curled around him like some kind of deranged monkey clinging to his back. How was she going to get out of this without him noticing? Because obviously the solution to this problem was to run as far away from Mac and his cozy bed as possible. Cookies and light displays and late-night chats were one thing, but snuggling in his bed was an entirely different story. Before Annie could fully develop her escape plan, the body she was still inconveniently pressed against started shaking with laughter.

'Good morning, Annie,' Mac said, the amusement clear in his voice.

Annie rolled away from him in horror.

'Did you sleep well?' Mac asked, still laughing.

'Oh God,' she groaned. 'I cannot believe I was spooning you.'

'I've never slept better. I like being the little spoon.'

Annie was still groaning when Mac rolled over to face her. He had a huge grin on his face and, between that and the messy, morning hair falling over his forehead, and the abs she'd just been fondling, Annie felt more confused than ever. Why did he have to be so damn cute?

'You hungry?' he asked, still studying her with amusement.

Annie was so relieved to not have to discuss the spooning incident further that she said yes, not considering the implications of her answer.

Mac's smile grew. 'Great. You can stay for breakfast.'

'Stay for breakfast? Isn't this your parents' house?' Annie assumed he'd want her out of there as quickly as possible.

Mac shrugged. 'Of course it is. Lucky for you, feeding people is my mother's favorite thing to do.'

'And that includes feeding random girls that stay overnight in your bedroom?'

'Well, I don't know. This is the first time it's ever happened.'

With that interesting tidbit of information, Mac winked, rolled out of bed and left Annie staring at the ceiling wondering what she had gotten herself into with this boy and what the hell she was going to do next. Besides apparently eating breakfast with his mom.

Mac popped his head out of the bathroom, toothbrush dangling from his mouth.

'I've got an extra,' he said, pointing to the toothbrush. 'If you want to freshen up before breakfast.'

Annie covered her face, the new horror of what her breath must smell like dawning on her.

Mac laughed, continuing with his brushing. 'That wasn't a hint or anything. I just thought you might want to brush your teeth.'

Annie continued with her groaning. She was sure her hair was a mess, she didn't have a change of clothes or makeup, and she certainly didn't feel prepared to go meet Mac's mother or spend any more time with him before she went home and regrouped. She needed a plan. She needed to completely reevaluate her thoughts and feelings about Mac and then determine what the hell to do about them. This whole thing had thrown Annie completely off-kilter. And she did not like to be off-kilter. Annie was an on-kilter kind of girl.

'Maybe I should go. I could slip out before your mom wakes up.'

Mac popped out of the bathroom again. 'Nah, it's past seven. She's already up.'

Annie let her hands slide away from her face. She took a deep inhale to calm herself down and the smell of bacon filled her nose. Mac was right; she had clearly missed her window to sneak out.

She sat up and attempted to rake her fingers through her hair and get it into some sort of order. She found her bag from last night still slung over the chair in the corner. She probably had at least a ChapStick and a tube of mascara in there. She would never leave home without those. Okay, maybe this was fine. Maybe she would eat some bacon, chat with Mac's mom and then get out of here and pretend this whole weird night never happened. That was doable, right? Right.

New plan in hand, Annie swung her legs out of bed and went to join Mac in the bathroom. She froze in the doorway watching him splash water on his face. The whole scene was far too intimate. What did she really know about Mac besides that he liked sports, had more muscles than she knew were humanly possible, was sometimes a jerk—and sometimes, she thought, remembering last night, very sweet? And now here she was watching his morning routine, getting a sneak peek at a popular boy in his natural habitat. It was surreal to say the least and the whole thing was freaking her out because, if she was being honest with herself, she liked seeing Mac this way and, if she was being *completely* honest with herself, she wanted to see more of him this way. Sleepy and rumpled with his hair a little bit wet. He looked harmless this way, like he couldn't hurt her. He looked *nice*. She didn't know what to do with that or if there was anything she *could* do with that, but she definitely needed more than four hours of sleep to sort it all out.

Mac straightened and caught her looking at him in the mirror. He did that ridiculous winking thing again and

Annie was once again relieved that no one was here to witness the flush in her cheeks; thankful she was the only one to feel her stomach flipflop every time he looked at her.

This was getting ridiculous.

He scrubbed his face dry with the towel and then handed her his extra toothbrush. Annie was horrified at the thought of him watching her brush her teeth. That was one intimacy too far. She could not allow Mac to watch her brush and *spit*! He clearly sensed her hesitation, flashed her one more smile and left the bathroom.

'I'll give you a minute,' he said from the bedroom.

Annie closed the door with a sigh of relief. Why was she being so weird about this? None of this had to be a big deal. Nothing physical had happened between them last night. They'd had a chat. That was it. It was something that had happened between her and Hazel and Logan a million times before. Although, to be fair, neither Logan nor Hazel made her feel all hot and confused and twisty inside.

She focused on brushing her teeth, splashing cold water on her face and attempting to look like some semblance of herself instead of on the panic slowly building in her belly. She really needed her friends back before she did something she would regret. Because whatever was happening here, Annie already knew she would regret it.

By the time she was following Mac up the stairs for breakfast, Annie had made up her mind that this morning would be the last part of their bizarre week of friendship. Annie had plenty of friends, she had plans, she had a future here in this town. Mac had, well she didn't know what Mac had, other than the ability to make her completely flustered, but he was leaving anyway so there was really no point in delving into these insane feelings she'd been having. She'd let herself, for a brief moment, indulge in the idea of living out the fantasy of her silly high-school crush paying attention to her. But that was all it was, a silly fantasy, and Annie didn't go for fantasy.

'Morning, Mom,' Mac greeted the petite woman pulling sizzling bacon out of a pan on the stove. She turned to face them, and Annie gave her a polite wave from her spot beside Mac in the doorway of the kitchen.

Annie had seen Mac's mom before around town, of course, and she'd chaperoned a few field trips over the years, but Annie had never been in his house, and she had the same surreal feeling she'd had watching him brush his teeth. Like she wasn't supposed to be here.

His mother's eyebrows rose as she took in the two of them standing side by side, clearly still wearing last night's clothes. Annie shifted on her feet. Why did she feel so guilty when nothing had happened? Not to mention they were fully grown adults. She was allowed to do things like sleep at a guy's house, wasn't she? Although this wasn't a guy's house. This was a guy's *mom's* house, which changed the math a bit.

'I didn't know you had a guest,' she said, directing her attention to Mac.

Mac cleared his throat, suddenly less confident in the face of his mother's scrutiny.

'You know Annie,' he said as if that made things less weird.

'Annabelle Andrews.' Her eyebrows rose even higher. 'I didn't know you two were friends.'

Annie bit back the words, *I didn't know we were friends*

either, and instead she said, 'Hello, Mrs. Sullivan, it's nice to see you again.'

'It's nice to see you, too, Annie, although somewhat unexpected.'

Her gaze shifted back to her son. 'I hope you were a gentleman,' she said with a pointed look. 'And that you remembered that it's only fun if *everyone's* having fun. And in the bathroom cabinet we have plenty of—'

'I know!' Mac cut her off with a wince. His face was bright red. 'I know, Mom, but it's really not like that. Annie is just a friend.'

Mac's mom looked skeptical at that assessment, but she gave a little shrug and let it drop. 'Well, who's hungry?' she said, turning back to the pan on the stove. 'I made bacon and eggs but I'm happy to throw on some pancakes if you'd prefer, Annie.'

'Oh no, eggs are fine, thank you.' Annie sat where Mac had gestured at the table.

He nudged her shoulder. 'Sorry about that,' he whispered.

Annie let out a small laugh. 'Did your mom actually just remind you about the location of condoms in your house?' she whispered back.

Mac's face turned even redder, but he laughed with her. 'Yeah, and to make sure both partners get off.'

More giggles spilled out of Annie even as her face heated with Mac's words. What would it be like to *get off* with Mac?

'Now you've had a glimpse,' he added, 'of how horrifying my parents' sex talk was for me.'

Annie snorted. Mac grinned at her from his seat next to her.

Mrs. Sullivan turned back to the table with two plates heaped with bacon, eggs, and toast. She looked like she was about to ask what was so funny but seemed to change her mind halfway to the table. Instead, she smiled at them like she knew exactly what was happening here. Annie wished she would fill her in.

They spent the rest of breakfast chatting about Annie's plans and the upcoming holidays and about how Annie's family was doing. Mac was mostly quiet, but after her initial nerves, Annie found it easy to talk to his mom. She was nice and funny, and Annie had always been good at talking to adults.

'Mac was so attached to me when he was little,' his mom was saying. 'I couldn't even put him down long enough to bring in the groceries without him screaming his little head off.'

'Aww...' Annie teased as Mac groaned.

'Okay, Mom, I think that's enough stories that make me look like a sad little mama's boy for one day.'

His mom lovingly patted his cheek. 'There's nothing wrong with loving your mother,' she said. 'And next time,' she said, turning back to Annie. 'I'll bring out the photo albums.' She winked conspiratorially.

'That would be great. I'd love to see them,' Annie said, even as she wondered if there would be a next time that she sat and chatted with Mac and his mother after spending the night. It didn't seem likely.

'We definitely don't need to do that,' said Mac as he got up to clear the plates.

'But you were so cute and chubby.' His mom tried to take the plates from his hands. 'I can get that. I'm sure you two have plans for the day.'

'Actually, I really should get home,' Annie said before Mac could jump in with his next great idea.

'Yep. I'm wide open to get these dishes done for you, Mom.'

'Okay, sweetie, thanks for that. I need to get to work anyway.' Mac leaned down so she could give him a kiss on the cheek before she hurried out of the kitchen to get ready for her shift.

'I like your mom,' Annie said.

'Yeah, I like her, too,' Mac said, leaving the dishes in the sink for later. 'She's kind of the best, which is why I need to find her the perfect Christmas present this year.'

'What do you usually get her?'

Mac shrugged, leaning against the counter. 'Usually something last-minute, or if my dad's feeling generous, he'll let me throw my name on something he bought. Or some bullshit like that. Seems like it's time I up my gift-giving game.'

Annie happened to be an amazing gift-giver. It was one of her special talents, something she really prided herself in. But she needed to get out of here and away from Mac and back to her regular life. She could *not* volunteer to help him, and yet it was taking all of her energy not to suggest it.

'Anyway,' Mac said, 'I'll probably go back to the Christmas market to look for something good.'

Don't say it, Annie. Don't say it.

She tried to hold it in, she really did. But that was a terrible idea! He couldn't just keep wandering the market waiting for a good idea to hit him. He needed to think about it before he went. The market was huge. He needed a plan. He needed her help.

'I could come with you.' Well, there goes that. She was not doing this because of the confused feelings last night had stirred up, or the possible sexual awakening Mac's abs had inspired this morning. She was doing this for Mac's mom, who deserved a good Christmas present this year. And maybe a little bit because of the abs.

Mac's face lit up at the suggestion and Annie's plan to spend time away from him went right out the window.

She could live in the fantasy for a little bit longer. What was the harm in that?

Chapter Twelve

Now

M ac had offered to drop Annie off at home so she could get other bridesmaid things done and he would go check the inn, but as expected, Annie's control-freak tendencies were still in full swing. She didn't trust him to go alone.

And even though he'd been asking Crystal out only a few minutes ago, he couldn't help the excitement he felt at spending time alone with Annie. This was the first time in over a decade that she'd even allowed it, other than the night of Hazel's birthday. And that had ended before it even started.

He'd tried to give her the space she clearly wanted, but in a town like this, avoidance was impossible. Especially since he and Logan had bonded over their secret love for creating little woodland scenes in decorative glass containers at Iris's terrarium-making class and became better friends than they ever had been in school. Annie had become unavoidable. She was everywhere. Town-hall meetings, holidays at Logan's house, farmers' markets, festivals, school fundraisers. The woman was omnipresent.

He didn't hate it, but unfortunately, she hated him.

Not that he could really blame her. He'd fucked up all those years ago. He was perfectly aware of that but, Christ, could that woman hold a grudge. How could Annie possibly still hold him accountable for his actions when he was a kid? He'd attempted to apologize, to explain multiple times since he'd been back, and she wouldn't even let him try.

Right on track, Mac had swung from pining over Annie to being pissed that she wouldn't even hear him out. That was typical, too.

By the time they arrived at the inn, he was equal parts frustrated with her and eager to hang out with her.

'You should get me drinks more often,' she said as she hopped out of the truck.

He ignored her pointed look. 'What, so you can pour it on me? No, thanks.' He strode toward the front entrance.

'That was one time,' Annie protested, hurrying to catch up.

'Twice,' he said, pausing at the big double doors to the Inn. 'If you count the beer I bought you as a peace offering on my first night working at the pub.'

She was at least embarrassed enough to look mildly apologetic about that one.

'Right. Sorry, I forgot about that time.'

The other had been a (thankfully) lukewarm cocoa he'd bought her at last year's Christmas-tree lighting, a shameless attempt to bring back memories of a happier Christmas between them. The cocoa landing in his lap had ended that dream pretty quickly.

'Yeah, well, fool me twice...' He yanked open the door, rattling the giant evergreen wreath hanging from it.

'What crawled up your butt since the café?' Annie asked, scurrying in behind him.

'Nothing crawled up my butt,' he said, far too loudly for the quiet lobby. Several guests warming themselves by the fireplace gave him the side eye as he walked by.

'Sometimes these little trips down memory lane make me wonder why I ever want to spend time around you,' he said, lowering his voice as they approached the front desk.

Annie shrugged but he could see the flicker of hurt in her eyes. 'You're free to go. I can take it from here.' She rang the silver bell on the counter, flipping her ponytail over her shoulder and hitting him in the face with it.

'Oh no, I'm invested now. Besides, I know you think you have dibs on Logan but he's my friend, too and, as his best man, I should be involved in the Nana search.'

Annie rolled her eyes. 'Whatever. And you're not his best man. Noah is.'

'Fine. As one of his lesser groomsmen, it is still within my duties to find his grandmother.'

'Keep your voice down,' Annie hissed. 'We don't need the whole town knowing she's missing.'

'And why is that exactly?' It seemed to Mac that the more people who knew, the quicker they would find her.

Annie sighed like it should be obvious. 'Because then it will get back to Jeanie and Logan, and instead of spending the day before their wedding relaxing, they'll spend it being stressed out. And that is not what we bridal-party people are shooting for. Got it?'

Mac shrugged. He still thought Annie was taking her bridesmaid duties a bit too seriously, but he did want his friend to have a good wedding weekend. He leaned in closer to Annie. For Logan's sake.

'Fine. We'll keep it a secret,' he whispered.

He couldn't help his smug smile when Annie shivered at his nearness. She could deny it all she wanted but her body always gave her away.

'Right. Good.' Annie's voice was breathy and low, and it hit Mac then, the reason why she never wanted to spend time alone with him. It was way too hard to pretend they hated each other this way. His smug smile grew.

They were still standing way too close when Jack emerged from the back room wearing a red bow tie, a Christmas vest covered in reindeer and with not a hair out of place. Mac was glad they hadn't gone to school together because he probably would have teased him and then he'd have to be apologizing right now.

But, as it was, Jack gave them both a big smile.

'Well, hello! What brings you two here?' His gaze flicked between the two of them and Annie hastily backed away from Mac.

'We're looking for Estelle, actually,' Mac said, and Annie shot him a look for blowing their cover, but how else were they ever going to find this woman if they didn't ask?

'We heard she was here earlier, and we had a quick question for her,' Annie added with a polite smile.

'Hmm.' Jack frowned. 'I only got in an hour ago, so I'm

not sure if she's still here, but I know she has some family staying with us for the wedding, so it's possible.'

'Can you tell us the room numbers? For her relatives?' Annie asked.

'Well … I probably shouldn't…' While Jack weighed the moral implications of giving out guests' room numbers, the doors opened with a gust of wind and a man carrying a large load of firewood stomped his feet on the welcome mats.

'Oh, there's Gabriel.' A furious blush worked its way up Jack's cheeks and Gabriel's name came out on a breathy exhale. 'Maybe he's seen Estelle.' Jack hustled over to the man with the firewood and Mac knew he looked the exact same way every time he hurried somewhere for a chance to be near Annie. Jack had it bad for this guy and Mac could totally relate.

While they stood waiting for Jack to return with some answers, another man emerged from the back room.

'Hello,' Annie said, obviously curious about this newcomer.

'Hello,' the man said with a shy smile. 'I'm just waiting for Jack.'

'Are you a new employee here?'

'Architect, actually.'

'Really? How interesting! Are they doing work on the inn?' Annie leaned closer, her elbows on the counter of the check-in desk.

'That's what we're discussing,' the man said. He was soft-spoken with dark-rimmed glasses, and frankly Mac didn't love the way Annie was looking at him.

'I'm Annie Andrews. I own the bakery in town,' she

said, sticking her hand out to shake. 'Welcome to Dream Harbor.'

'Elliot,' he said, shaking Annie's hand. 'It's nice to meet you.'

Annie held onto his hand for a beat too long. She glanced at Mac before she said, 'Are you free tomorrow night, Elliot?'

Mac bit so hard on his tongue to stop himself from protesting that he drew blood. Was Annie actually asking someone out in front of him? This was a new low, and one that he could *not* handle.

'I … uh…' The man blushed to the tips of his ears as he stammered, 'I'm attending a wedding.'

'Oh, wonderful! I will see you there, then,' she said with a smug smile at Mac before Elliot slipped away into the manager's office once again.

Mac didn't have time to dwell on that little interaction for too long before Annie had his hand and was tugging him down the hallway.

'What—'

'Shh…' She took a hard left down the first hallway with guest rooms. 'It'll be easier for us to take a little look around ourselves,' she whispered.

'You know you're insane, right?'

She stopped and turned to glare at him. 'I just want everything to go right and— What was that?'

'What was what?'

'Shh!'

'Annie, I swear to God if you shush me one more time—'

Before he could finish his threat, Annie had his hand

again and had pulled him into the closest utility closet. It was pitch-black inside and smelled like lemon Pledge.

'Annie—'

A single finger met his lips but, to her credit, she didn't shush him. And he was too distracted by the feel of her skin on his mouth to do anything but stand in shocked silence. He didn't give a shit what was out in that hallway. If it kept him stuck in this dark closet with Annie, it could stay out there forever.

Voices drifted in through the doorway.

'I'm just nervous about tomorrow.'

'But you are head over heels for that man.'

'I'm not worried about Logan or marriage. It's the *wedding* part. It's a big event. I want it to go well and everyone to have a good time.'

Mac knew he recognized that voice. Jeanie was in the hall with someone, and Annie didn't want her to know they were here looking for Estelle. Hence the closet hiding place.

'You're the bride. All you have to worry about is saying yes. Leave everything else to the rest of us.'

'Thanks, Mom. Have you seen Aunt Dot? She's supposed to have my something old…'

A door down the hall opened and the voices faded as they went into the room.

Annie was standing so close that he felt her sigh of relief on his cheek. She let her finger fall from his lips and he wanted to grab it and put it back.

'I *told* you,' she hissed, snapping him out of his standing-too-close-to-Annie stupor.

'You told me what?'

'Jeanie is stressed about tomorrow and it's our job to make sure that's not the case.'

'I don't think her mom meant that we're responsible for a missing-persons search. I think she was talking about wardrobe malfunctions and drunk-uncle situations.'

Annie huffed, and even though it was dark he could picture her rolling her eyes at him.

'We need to go.' She lifted a hand to find the doorknob but in the cramped space ended up fumbling against his arm and his stomach. He grabbed her wrist before she could grab anything more … personal.

'Don't you ever rest?' he asked instead of dwelling on where he'd like Annie's hands to wander.

'I'll rest when I'm dead.'

'Annie.'

'Mac.'

He tugged a little on her wrist and to his surprise she leaned into him, her cheek pressed right over his heart.

'Your heart is beating really fast,' she whispered.

'I know.'

Still, she didn't move. For one agonizingly perfect minute, she didn't move. She just pressed her face against him and let him twine his fingers with hers. Her breathing slowed and her body relaxed against his. He took a risk and planted a chaste kiss on the top of her head. The soft sigh she let out at the contact was everything he'd dreamed about in the past eleven years.

But like everything else with Annie, it didn't last.

'I'm sorry I hurt you,' he murmured.

Annie pulled away. 'You didn't hurt me.'

'Christ, Annie, will you just accept my apology? I fucked

up, okay? We had one perfect month together and then I ruined it. Can we move on, please?'

She was fumbling for the doorknob again.

'I don't need your apology, Mac. Because I'm fine. We hung out for one month like a million years ago and it really doesn't matter to me anymore. Where the hell is the doorknob?' She groaned in frustration.

'If it doesn't matter, then why are you pissed at me all the time?'

'Did it ever occur to you that I simply don't like you?'

'Ha! Okay, sure, darling. You and I and everyone else in this town know the way you look at me.'

'Get. Me. Out. Of. Here.' She punctuated each word with a kick to the door.

Mac sighed and turned the knob. Annie spilled out, almost landing face-down on the hallway floor. As he blinked in the suddenly bright light, she glared up at him from the carpet. He reached out a hand to help her up, but she ignored it.

'I will find Estelle myself,' she said, getting upright and storming down the hallway.

'Annie, wait.' He followed her long strides.

'You know what, Mac?' She spun to face him. 'It wasn't *that* perfect of a month.'

'Oh, really? That isn't what you said at the time.'

'Well, I faked a lot of things at the time.'

Mac froze. She could not mean what he thought she meant.

'What are you talking about?'

Annie raised her eyebrows. 'I think you know exactly what I'm talking about.'

'But we … but you … I thought…'

She gave him a smug smile. 'You thought wrong. Bye, Mac.' She spun on her heel and left him there gaping after her, reassessing everything he thought he knew about Annie. About that December. About women in general.

Mac hadn't felt this punched in the face since he was actually punched in the face during a bar fight in Tulsa that he'd got in the middle of by accident.

But that blow hurt much less than this one.

'What the hell, Annie?'

Mac had followed her out to the parking lot and got to her just as she was realizing they had driven here together. There was no way he was letting her get away with saying something like that and then running off. She should have kept her mouth shut. But this was what happened to her when she spent too much time around Mac. Her sense left her completely and she reverted to childish behavior.

But she didn't hate the way Mac looked chasing her across the parking lot. She found it quite satisfying actually, which of course was part of the problem.

'We have to go,' she said. 'We don't have time to talk about this right now.'

'Like hell we don't.' Mac had caught up to her and had her crowded against his truck. His voice was nearly a growl. With anyone else she would have felt threatened and perfectly within her rights to use her favorite self-defense maneuver of a knee to the crotch, but with Mac, she found herself wanting to piss him off more, just to make him get closer.

'You can't drop a piece of information like that and then walk away,' he said. She hadn't seen him this mad since she spilled the cocoa in his lap last year. His chest rose with each angry breath and pressed against hers. Damn this winter weather. Why was she wearing so many layers?

Annie sighed like this was all very taxing for her and not at all like she wanted to throw Mac into the backseat of his big stupid vehicle and have her way with him. 'I don't know what you want me to say.'

'Say it's not true,' he ground out. 'Say you said it to make me mad.'

'You're being awfully dramatic about this.'

'Dramatic? *Dramatic*. After all these years you're trying to tell me you didn't *enjoy* yourself when we were together and I'm supposed to be okay with that?' His voice dropped on the word enjoy and Annie felt it down to her toes.

But she'd be damned if she'd let Mac know the effect he was having on her. She rolled her eyes, and she was sure, if it was physically possible, steam would have come out of Mac's ears at the sight of it. 'The sex was *fine*. I wasn't expecting much more than that. We were young and inexperienced. It's really not a big deal.'

Mac was pacing in front of her now, leaving scuff marks in the fine layer of snow that had accumulated in the parking lot. His brow was furrowed, his mouth set in a firm line. He looked like a man whose entire world had been turned upside down. With that one admission it was like Annie had completely rewritten their past. And she almost felt bad about it. She almost felt bad for *him*. She nearly relented and told him the rest of the truth. That, while she may not have had an orgasm, that night with Mac was still one of the best of her life. But he didn't deserve that truth.

'I thought … I thought you … I mean, I thought we…' Mac kept up his pacing, talking to the pavement instead of Annie. When he finally looked up, there was so much hurt on his face it took Annie's breath away. 'I thought that night meant something.' He stopped moving and the weight of his stare had Annie pinned to the side of the truck harder than his body had.

She could lie. But instead found herself telling the truth. 'It did mean something,' she whispered.

With that admission Mac stepped in closer until Annie could feel the heat of him, but he didn't touch her. She really freaking wished he would.

'Yeah?' he said.

'Yeah. It meant something.' She felt him nearly sag in relief.

'Let me try again,' he said, his voice tight.

'Try again?'

He was so close now that his words brushed against her ear. 'Let me try again.' His voice dropped, sending shivers through Annie's body that had nothing to do with the falling snow.

For a brief second, she actually considered it, letting Mac try again. Her body was very interested in what that might look like. She was hot from her head to her feet and was about thirty seconds away from tearing off both of their coats so she could press herself against him. They had only been nineteen the last time she'd had the chance, and she was sure Mac had acquired many new skills since then.

Maybe she should let him try. Maybe she was *owed* the effort. Hate-sex was a thing, wasn't it? Maybe they could do that.

But if Annie had one character flaw, it was her pride. And hers had been irreparably injured.

'I thought it meant something, too,' she said, meeting his gaze. They were so close their noses nearly touched. 'I thought it meant something until you ditched me like the whole thing meant nothing.'

Mac flinched. 'That's not how it happened,' he growled.

Annie laughed in his face, causing him to take a step back. 'Not how it happened? As I remember it, we had an agreement, and you never showed.'

'Annie, I *wanted* to.'

'Save it, Mac. I don't have time. I have a mani-pedi to get to and a grandmother to track down.' Annie opened the door and got into the car, slamming the door shut before Mac could get another word out. She'd heard enough from him for one day. If he had wanted to show up all those years ago, he would have done it. She wasn't going to let him rewrite the story now. Just because her body was fooled, didn't mean the rest of her would fall so easily.

All this reminiscing wasn't doing anyone any good.

Chapter Thirteen

Then

They'd been walking around the Christmas market for over an hour, and honestly, Mac was surprised Annie had showed up. Almost as surprised as he was that she offered to help in the first place. She was obviously freaked out when they'd woken up together a few mornings ago. She was clearly embarrassed that she'd been all snuggled against him, but Mac had been relieved that it hadn't been the other way around. If he had been the big spoon, it would have been all too clear what he had been dreaming about right before he woke up. And he was pretty sure that waking up with his boner pressed against her ass would have been a surefire way to never see Annie ever again. And at this point he was positive he wanted to keep seeing her.

'How about we take a break?' he suggested.

Annie looked at him, her cheeks rosy above her scarf,

and his mind returned to mulling over his new plan. The one in which he kissed Annie, preferably by the end of the day. It had taken precedence over figuring out his cross-country plan. That one seemed significantly less important at the moment.

He still wasn't quite sure how to go about it, though. He had wanted to kiss her when he rolled over and saw her next to him in bed—like his dream had somehow come to life. But kissing her in bed seemed like way too much of an escalation, and one that Annie would not have appreciated, especially after he mentioned brushing her teeth. That was a dumb move. Now they were out of bed, and he still wanted to kiss her and he still couldn't figure out how to do it.

'Yeah, a break sounds good. It's freezing out here.' Annie rubbed her mittened hands together.

'We can grab hot cocoa in the warming hut,' he said.

'Perfect.' She smiled at him, and he wanted to do it right then. He wanted to take her face in his hands and press his mouth to hers until they were both warmed up, no cocoa required, but they were in the middle of the crowded path and Annie was moving toward the hut before he could do anything about it. He followed her through the other Christmas shoppers into the little makeshift cocoa cabin. It was more of a tent than a cabin, and it wasn't much warmer inside than outside but at least they were protected from the wind.

They went up to the table and got their cocoa and found a seat at a picnic table in the back corner. An older man with a guitar was playing Elvis Presley Christmas classics in the other corner and two of the tables were filled with a mix of kids and their parents. It wasn't exactly a romantic setting, but Annie was cozied up next to him, so Mac was feeling pretty good.

'You warm enough?' he asked.

Annie laughed. 'I'm sure I'm warmer than you,' she said. Mac still couldn't bring himself to put on a hat.

He lifted up his hands. 'Hey, at least I'm wearing gloves today.'

Annie nudged him with her shoulder, snuggling in closer. 'Well, I guess that's progress.' She took a sip of her cocoa and gave a little sigh of contentment. Mac wondered if she would make a noise like that if—no, *when*—he kissed her.

'So,' Annie said, 'your mom...'

And that killed any thoughts of the noises Annie would make.

'... what else does she like?'

So far, the only things Mac had come up with for possible gifts had to do with cooking—which Annie immediately vetoed, saying he could not get her something chore-related for Christmas—or a new scarf, which they had seen at every other craft table and Annie vetoed as being too impersonal.

'She likes...' He was stumped. Annie sighed like she was disappointed in him, and Mac hated that. He thought harder, racking his brain for something else his mom might like. Now he needed this gift not only to soften his mother up to his drive-cross-country plan, but it was becoming more and more important in his impress-Annie-enough-to-kiss-her plan.

'She likes to read, I guess,' he said.

'Okay, that's good. We can work with that.' Annie perked up and Mac's chest swelled with pride.

She was fully leaning against him now, her arm pressed against his and it reminded him of the way her body felt wrapped around his, so warm and soft. She took another sip of her cocoa clearly deep in thought about things other than Mac, even though all his thoughts seemed to keep circling her.

'I think I saw e-reader covers at Bernadette's stand. We could look there,' she said.

'Right, yeah, that's a good idea.' But neither of them was in a hurry to leave the protection of the tent. They sat pressed against each other. The warmth of Annie's thigh against his took up all of his attention. He barely heard the man crooning 'Blue Christmas' or noticed when the families traipsed back outside. They were alone in their own little corner of the tent, and it felt like how the past few days had felt, like he and Annie were the only two people that mattered.

Eventually, Annie shifted next to him as she finished her cocoa. She turned to face him on the bench and Mac thought maybe now was his moment.

'I have to ask you something,' she said.

'Okay, anything.'

He leaned in a little closer and took Annie's glance down at his mouth to be a promising sign.

'I just...' She started and then shook her head like she was being silly. 'I just...'

'You just what?'

Annie's cheeks flushed pink. 'I was just wondering if you had ever woken up next to a girl before? I mean it was new for me, and I felt awkward about the whole thing, and I was just wondering if you felt the same.' She shook her head again, clearly embarrassed by the whole situation. 'Sorry, it probably doesn't matter. I don't know why I said anything.'

'There's been a few girls…' he started.

'Right. Of course. Of course there has been. I shouldn't have asked.'

'No. No, I mean, I dated some girls, but I've never stayed up half the night talking to any of them.'

'Oh.'

He couldn't help but grin at the way her cheeks reddened even more at that. 'And I liked waking up next to you.' He leaned in even closer.

'You did?'

'Of course I did. What's not to like?'

'I don't know, I thought maybe you found the whole thing weird, especially when I was clinging on to you. I want you to know that I totally understand what this is, and I get it. You're leaving soon and this is just…' Her voice trailed off.

'This is just what?'

'This just isn't a thing. *We're* not a thing. I didn't want you to think I was getting weird romantic ideas about us.'

Mac smirked. 'Romantic ideas?'

'Oh God.' Annie put a hand over her face. 'I made it worse, didn't I?'

He took her wrist and gently pulled her hand away. He smiled at her. 'You didn't make it worse. And *you* might not be getting romantic ideas about us, but who says I'm not?'

Annie's eyes widened in surprise.

Now was definitely his chance and he wasn't going to blow it. He leaned in close enough to hear Annie's breath hitch. Her blue eyes were bright with anticipation. He reached out and tucked a wisp of hair behind her ear, letting his fingers brush along her pink cheek and there was that little sigh he'd been hoping for.

'Annie, I—'

'Sullivan! Sullivan, is that you?'

The booming voice of one of his former teammates crashed through the tent.

Mac winced, squeezing his eyes shut as though he could block out the voice and the person and the whole disastrous moment, but Sean wasn't having it. He headed straight for them, completely oblivious to the fact that he was destroying Mac's entire life. Or at least that was how it felt to Mac.

Annie had straightened and moved away from him on the bench so quickly that, by the time Mac opened his eyes, she was already practically at another table.

Damn it.

'Hey, man, what are you doing here?' Mac tried his best to sound friendly and not like he wanted to murder his old buddy. In fact, if this had happened a week ago, he would have been thrilled to see somebody back in town. But right now, he wanted nothing more than for Sean to disappear. He glanced over at Annie who was pretending to be very interested in the musical performance and wouldn't meet his gaze.

'You know me, I'm here for the food.' Sean held up a bag of kettle corn and a box of chocolate fudge. He was a big guy, known by everyone on the team as someone who's real joy in life was eating. Mac's mother, as someone who's real joy in life was feeding people, absolutely loved it when he came over. Sean devoured everything she made. Mac couldn't help but laugh, seeing the man now piled high with Christmas snacks.

'Glad to hear you haven't changed.'

'Not a bit.' Sean grinned. 'What about you?'

'Christmas shopping.'

Sean's attention skittered over to where Annie was picking at the edges of her paper cocoa cup. Mac didn't know why, but he felt reluctant to draw attention to the fact that he was here with Annie. Not that he was ashamed of it or anything, but there was something unsettling about seeing these two together. It was like Sean was reminding him of who he had been in high school and *that* Mac never would have been this close to kissing Annie. He wasn't sure he wanted to be reminded of that guy, especially not right now.

Mac cleared his throat. 'You know Annie. She was … uh … helping me.'

Annie looked up and gave Sean a terse smile. Sean looked confused like he had never seen her before in his life, but he politely smiled back.

'We had Biology together,' Annie reminded him.

And Sean laughed. 'Biology, right, right. I didn't always attend that class.'

Mac could feel Annie resisting an eye roll.

'Yeah well, it's been fun reminiscing, but I should be going anyway.' She stood up and Mac wanted to stop her, but he couldn't think of any reasonable way to do it other than grabbing her and throwing her over his shoulder, which he obviously wasn't going to do. Although he had to admit the idea did hold some appeal.

'You don't have to go,' Mac said but Annie was already up and moving, tossing her cup in the trash and heading for the tent exit.

'I really have to get home,' she said.

Before Mac could go after her, Sean was already patting him on the back and telling him about the plans to hang out with other members of the team tonight and all Mac could do was watch Annie walk away. Even though that was the last thing he wanted to do.

Chapter Fourteen

Now

Annie should have been relaxed. This was after all the most relaxing part of her day, mani-pedis with the bride. And even though her feet were in the tub, bubbles at full tilt, and the massage chair she was sitting in was doing its best to work out the tension in her neck, Annie was not relaxed in the slightest. Mainly because her attention was still back in the parking lot with Mac. She'd felt like a complete idiot when she realized her appointment was right there at the inn and she'd had to get back out of his car and storm into the spa with Mac calling after her. He'd texted several times asking if she needed a ride home which she'd diligently ignored.

But here she was now, doing her best to be in the present moment, when all she could really think about was the devastated look on Mac's face when they talked and the way he felt pressed against her and, most concerningly, how badly she wanted him there.

She shook her head. She was supposed to be celebrating with some of her most favorite people in the world and she was not going to let Mac ruin that for her.

'So, Haze,' she said, turning to her friend beside her. 'Do you regret skipping all of this before your big day?'

Hazel smiled, taking another sip of champagne. 'I'm having a great time,' she said. 'But my wedding was exactly what I wanted.'

'Well, in that case I guess I forgive you for ditching us.'

'I didn't ditch you. We were being spontaneous.' And that was honestly why Annie hadn't been more upset about missing her friend's wedding. Hazel being happy and spontaneous was worth it.

'Tell us about it,' Kira piped up from where she was having her fingernails painted. Next to her was Jeanie, who looked much more relaxed than she'd sounded when Annie had been hiding in the closet. But Annie wasn't thinking about the closet incident, either. And she was certainly not thinking about how it had felt to rest her cheek over Mac's rapidly beating heart.

Nope. She was focused on the lovely bride, decked out in her white, pre-wedding, sweat suit. A gift from the book club, it had *Bride* bedazzled across the back of it.

'It was really romantic,' Hazel said, getting all dreamy-eyed like she always did when she talked about her wedding day. 'We were on vacation in Aruba, and Noah had just asked me to marry him the day before. He had it all planned out, with an officiant and everything. We went into town, and I picked out a white sundress that we found at one of the little shops. The front desk arranged for flowers to wear in my hair and Noah looked so gorgeous in his linen button-down with his hair all windswept and his cheeks freckled and sunburnt. Then it was just us on the beach at sunset telling each other how much we loved each other.'

Every woman in the room, including the nail technicians, sighed at Hazel's story. Annie had heard it before, but she had to admit it got her every time.

'That sounds perfect,' Kira said.

'And then they spent the rest of the week holed up in their hotel room sealing the deal,' Annie chimed in, and Hazel's cheeks flushed pink.

'And that was perfect, too,' she said.

'Yeah, I bet it was!' Kira said and all the ladies laughed.

'And what about you? When do you plan to make an honest man out of my brother?' Jeanie asked, turning with a raised eyebrow to Kira.

'Wouldn't he have to ask her first?' Iris asked from the seat beside Annie. Jeanie had insisted that Iris came, even though she wasn't in the wedding party. She'd also invited her mother, several cousins, her employee, Crystal, and Lyndsay and Alex from the bookstore. They'd taken over the entire spa for the afternoon. Maybe Dot and Estelle were off in a sauna or massage room somewhere? Annie should probably check on that before she left.

'Well, technically—' Kira started before Jeanie chimed in.

'He's asked her multiple times,' she said.

'He has?!' Annie nearly jumped up out of her seat. How did she not know this?

Kira shrugged. 'Yes, technically he has asked. He has a

weird habit of saying *marry me, peaches,* whenever we're just having a really great day or something.'

Kira's impression of Bennett's deep voice had everyone giggling again.

'But I don't think he means it.'

'He means it.' Jeanie was adamant.

'I'm not even sure I *want* to get married!' Kira insisted.

Iris ran a hand over her belly. 'I don't think it's necessary. If you two are happy together, that's all that matters.'

'Right,' Kira said with a nod and then she gave a little shrug. 'Maybe one day I'll say yes and see what he does then.'

Annie shook her head with a laugh. 'Poor Bennett.'

Kira waved a hand, careful not to mess up her nails. 'Oh please, that man is fine.'

'Well, married or not, he'd go to the ends of the Earth for you,' Jeanie said.

Kira smiled. 'Yeah, I know. He's a keeper.'

'Okay, I want to hear more about *this* wedding,' Iris said. 'Obviously, I know all about the food. Archer's been talking about it for months. But what else have you guys planned? Everyone's dying to see the barn all done up, Kira! It already looked amazing at the rehearsal dinner.'

'I know! I can't wait to see it tomorrow!' Jeanie jumped in.

Kira smiled, but Annie could see the nerves on her face. She knew how hard her friend had worked over the past six months to get this plan up and running. Ever since she and Bennett had found a stash of secret treasure on the farm, they'd put all their effort into transforming the barn into an event space. And now the wedding of the season was her first real event. Annie knew how important it was to her to pull it off.

But she would. Annie didn't doubt it.

'It's going to look gorgeous,' she said. 'The barn is so much bigger than I originally thought, and Kira did an amazing job overseeing the remodel. We have all white linens, white candles, white lights. It's a winter wonderland with pops of red flowers… What were those flowers you picked, Jeanie?'

'White anemones and red peonies. And then Daisy is going to add pine boughs to the tables as well.'

'Right,' Annie said. 'The vision is completely on point.'

Kira smiled at her in thanks. 'Yeah, it's going to be perfect.'

Iris leaned back in her chair and closed her eyes. 'That sounds beautiful.'

'And the dress,' Hazel added. 'How did the last fitting go?'

'It went really well. My mom was able to come, and we only cried a little.'

'You sure about that?'

'Okay, we cried a lot, but it was everything I'd dreamed of!'

Jeanie handed her phone to Iris so she could see pictures of the dress. Annie had been with her when she found it, a gorgeous frothy confection that made her look like a winter princess with a fitted top and a deep V in the front. Lace vines and flowers ran down the bodice and onto the skirt, as well as down the long sleeves. Logan was going to absolutely lose his mind.

'Damn, Jeanie, you're going to look amazing in this,' Iris said, and Annie agreed.

'She does.' Annie could already feel herself getting choked up. Hazel reached over and gave her hand a squeeze.

'You can't start crying yet.'

Annie shook her head. 'I've been crying for weeks.'

'Are you bringing a date?' Francine, the woman currently working on her toes asked, bringing everyone's attention back to Annie. 'Because my nephew—'

'I'm going to stop you right there, Fran. I'm not looking for a date.'

Four heads turned to stare at Annie as Jeanie, Hazel, Kira and Iris looked at her in disbelief.

'What?'

'You're going to show up to an event without a date *and* Mac will also be without a date,' Jeanie pointed out.

'I don't see why that's relevant.' Annie refused to engage in this line of questioning or to think about Mac charging across the parking lot to get to her. Or how it would feel to see him in the sexy suit she was sure he'd be wearing.

Jeanie gave a little shrug like she wasn't going to push the matter, but then she went ahead and pushed it. 'I'm just saying it's rare that you're both unattached at these things. Seems like it might be a good opportunity...'

'A good opportunity for what, Jean Marie?'

Jeanie wrinkled her nose at the use of her full name. 'I don't know. A good opportunity to bury the hatchet.'

'There *is* no hatchet. We don't need to bury anything, and we certainly don't need to be near each other any more than is strictly necessary. Like I promised you, I've been on my best behavior, but that's *all* I can promise.'

'Okay, okay.' Jeanie put up her hands with her newly painted nails in surrender. 'I appreciate it.'

Jeanie let it drop, and the girls turned their attention back to more pressing matters, like was it really bad luck to see the bride before the wedding because Jeanie had no intention of sleeping away from her groom tonight.

'I don't think it matters,' Iris weighed in, and Kira agreed.

'As long as he doesn't see you in your dress,' Hazel added.

'Says the woman who shopped for her dress with her groom,' Jeanie said with a laugh.

Hazel shrugged. 'He helped pick it out, but he didn't see me in it until we were on the beach together. It's nice to have it be a surprise, don't you think?'

'I do think that's romantic. To have his first look of you in the dress as you walk down the aisle,' Kira said, blowing on her fingernails.

'Logan is going to cry so much,' Annie said.

Iris looked at her in surprise. 'You think so?'

'That guy is all gooey inside. He's for sure going to cry.'

'Did Noah cry?' Iris turned back to Hazel.

'There were tears,' she confirmed, and everyone sighed again. What was it about making grown men cry that was so damn satisfying?

'Okay, so we're all agreed. I can sleep with Logan tonight, but he can't see me in the dress.'

'That's right,' Kira said. 'That feels like a good compromise.'

'We clearly don't believe in following tradition anyway,' Iris said, gesturing to her belly and smiling at Hazel and Kira.

Hazel laughed, raising her glass of champagne in cheers, but Annie knocked on the wood table beside her. She didn't need anyone jinxing the wedding or anything else for that matter, babies and relationships included. She still hadn't found Estelle or finished the secret wedding dessert. She didn't have time for any more bad luck. As soon as her nails were dry, she was going back out there, this time by herself. She didn't need a certain someone distracting her from more important things, like her friends' happiness.

'Aren't you not supposed to see the bride the night before the wedding?' Bennett asked, stepping up to take his turn at the dart board. They were at the pub doing what the groom had requested for his last night of bachelorhood: eating burgers, drinking beer and playing darts.

Logan scoffed. 'I'll be damned if I'm not going to sleep with my fiancée tonight.'

Noah patted him on the back. 'That's right. Who needs those old traditions, anyway? You two have been shacking up together for a year so that ship has basically sailed.'

'Says the man who barely left his hotel room long enough to get married before hauling Hazel back to it.'

'Hey, there was no hauling. She came willingly,' he said with a smirk.

Mac laughed, taking another pull from his beer. He was glad he'd come out. He needed a distraction. Annie's words had been tormenting him all day. *I faked a lot of things.* And then she'd gone off to get her nails done, like it was nothing.

Not to mention he'd failed to find Estelle and he didn't really know what they were going to do about it. A little detail he had no intention of telling the groom.

Despite all that, he was happy to be out with the boys. He'd lost touch with most of his friends from high school and, much to his surprise, it had been Logan who reached out first when he'd moved back. It was nice to have solid friends again now that he was settled in one place, even though he knew it pissed Annie off having to see him all the time. Or maybe *especially* because it pissed Annie off. For a while, he'd deluded himself into thinking that simply being around her would be enough to soften her feelings toward him, get her to see that he was different than the boy who had left her, but Annie was stubborn as hell.

Could he have pushed the matter? Probably. Over the years, there were plenty of times he could have forced the issue and demanded that they get all their bullshit out in the open. But then he would have had to face the fact that she really did hate him and that she would never forgive him. So, he hadn't pushed it, at least not until today. She'd made it so that they couldn't ignore their history anymore: because she'd altered it.

I faked a lot of things.

'Mac?'

'What?' He shook his head trying to rid himself of thoughts of Annie and her soft hand on his mouth in that dark closet and everything she'd said afterward.

'You're up,' Bennett told him.

'Right.' Mac got out of the booth and took the darts from

Noah. They were in the back corner of the pub, away from the crowded main dining room where a group of teachers were having their end-of-year party and were engaged in a rather contentious round of secret Santa, along with the volunteer fire-department's annual celebration and awards ceremony. It was nuts in here. He made a mental note to give Amber a raise in the new year.

He tossed his first dart and missed the board completely.

Noah and Logan both turned to stare at him. 'Dude, what was that?'

Mac shook his head. 'A shit throw.' He tossed the next dart, which barely made it onto the board, hitting the outer ring.

'Everything okay?' Logan asked, a look of actual concern drawing his dark brows together.

'Everything's fine.' Mac chucked the last dart, and it bounced off the wall.

'Holy shit,' Noah breathed. 'I've never seen you play this bad before.'

Mac tried to shrug it off. 'It happens.'

'Not to you,' Noah insisted, and unfortunately, he was right. If there was one thing Mac had gotten good at while spending years of his life in his father's pub and so many others, it was darts. And he'd spent far too many nights kicking Noah's ass at the game to try to claim that he wasn't any good.

'Forget it,' Mac said, heading back to the table. Bennett had just returned with another round of beers and Archer had joined them.

'Hey, what'd I miss? I had to wait for the babysitter.'

'Logan's going to sleep with Jeanie the night before the wedding and something's very wrong with Mac,' Noah reported.

Archer raised an eyebrow. 'Wow.'

'Nothing's wrong with me,' Mac insisted, except he felt like everything was wrong with him at the moment. He'd lived so many years convincing himself that there was nothing between him and Annie. That it had all been some teenage fantasy, blown way out of proportion. And then he'd moved back here and he was screwed, because Annie was exactly as perfect as he'd remembered. But she didn't want him, and he'd done his best to move on. He'd set up a life here. He'd dated other women, grown his business. He'd made fucking *friends*. And then he'd spent one morning with her, and she'd destroyed his resolve to stay away.

He couldn't think straight.

And he certainly couldn't play darts.

'He spent the morning with Annie,' Archer reported, and if he didn't have a baby on the way, Mac might have punched him in the face.

'Really?' Noah said 'Interesting...'

'Who told you that?'

'Iris. She said you and Annie stormed the Y this morning.'

'You were also spotted together at the café,' Ben added, taking a slug of his beer. These grown men, his alleged friends, were worse than the book club with their gossip.

'Jesus. You can't do anything in this town without everyone knowing about it.'

Archer chuckled. 'It's the truth, but what were you guys doing together? I thought she didn't let you near her.'

Mac shook his head, downing more of his beer. That was more true than he wanted to admit.

'I was at her apartment this morning,' he glared at Noah before the man could jump in with questions about things that definitely didn't happen, 'fetching Logan's cufflinks. And her car was out of gas. I helped her run a couple of errands. That's it.'

'That's it?' Bennett asked, skeptically.

'Yeah, that's it. Errands.'

Nobody looked like they were buying it, but Mac must have had a threatening enough look on his face that they let it go.

'Okay, man, whatever you say.'

'We're not here to talk about me, anyway,' Mac said, gesturing to Logan with his bottle of beer. 'We're here for our friend on his last night of freedom.'

Logan rolled his eyes. 'Last night of freedom is a bullshit thing to say,' he said. 'We're here because I wanted a pub burger and a beer and you're just lucky I let you tag along.'

Mac shook his head with a smile. There was the grumpy bastard they all knew and loved.

'To Logan and Jeanie,' Archer said, raising his bottle and the others followed suit.

'To Logan and Jeanie!' they all said.

'Congratulations, man.' Mac clapped his friend on the back.

'Thanks,' Logan said. 'I *am* glad you guys are here.'

Noah pretended to wipe his eyes. 'Don't get all sappy on us now. You're going to make me cry.'

Bennett laughed and Mac got up to grab some more food for the table. By the time he got back, Iris was perched on Archer's lap.

His heart rate picked up speed. Were all the girls here?

'Hey Iris, what are you doing here?' he asked, sliding a plate of fries in front of her.

'Perfect,' she said, with a little sigh. 'I was having a craving.'

'I can make you fries,' Archer grumbled.

Iris pressed a kiss against his temple. 'I love you and I love your cooking, but you can't *deep fry* me fries at home and this is exactly what I wanted,' she said, popping one of the crispy fries into her mouth.

Archer kissed her shoulder. 'Okay, sweetheart.'

'Jeanie wanted me to tell you she'll meet you at home,' Iris said, turning to Logan. 'She was grabbing dinner with her parents first.'

Logan nodded.

'So, I guess you don't think it's bad luck, either,' Iris said. 'Sleeping together the night before the wedding.'

Logan shook his head. 'Of course I don't think it's bad luck. Jeanie is it for me and I'm not going to spend the night away from her because of some ridiculous superstition.'

Iris smiled. 'She feels the same way.'

Logan dipped his head in acknowledgement, a happy smile tugging at his lips. And for a minute, Mac couldn't identify the sensation in his gut, until he realized it was jealousy. He was jealous of his friends. Jealous of Logan for being so sure about Jeanie. Jealous of Archer for having his beautiful and pregnant girlfriend in his lap, and of Noah, who'd already married the girl of his dreams; and then there was Bennett, who spent his days so wrapped up in Kira it seemed like he required nothing else.

On the night before his friend's wedding, it hit Mac like a ton of fucking bricks. Maybe this was what he wanted, too.

After years of trying to convince himself otherwise.

He wanted what his friends had.

And unfortunately, he knew exactly who he wanted it with.

Chapter Fifteen

Then

'Annie!' Her sister, Charlotte, burst through the bedroom door breathless with excitement.

Annie looked up from her book with a sigh. 'Don't you ever knock?' The idea was laughable in a house filled with as many siblings as Annie had, but it would be nice if her sister would respect her privacy. Not that she was doing much that required privacy. Ever since being pushed aside by Mac this afternoon at the market, she had retreated to her room for a cozy evening by herself. She was prepared with a stack of books, plenty of Christmas cookies, and a room to herself, thanks to the fact that her older sister had finally moved out.

Charlotte rolled her eyes and tossed her long blonde hair over her shoulder. She was Annie's youngest sibling, but at thirteen she already thought she was painfully cool.

'This is too important for knocking! *Mac Sullivan* is at the door.' The way Charlotte said his name you would have thought Mac was her latest K-pop obsession. How did her little sister even know who he was? Sometimes this town was far too small for its own good.

But the mention of his name certainly got Annie's attention. 'He's at the door right now? *Our* door?'

'Yes! He's at our door. Talking to *our* dad.'

Annie's blood went cold. 'He's talking to our father right now?'

'Yes, this is what I am trying to tell you! It was too important for knocking!'

Annie jumped up off her bed where she had been happily reading her latest mystery novel and glanced down at what she was wearing. She was dressed head to toe in a holiday onesie complete with a full-length zipper and front pocket.

'I can't see Mac looking like this!'

Her sister crinkled up her nose in disgust, confirming for Annie just how bad the outfit was. But then she shrugged like there was nothing to be done about it. 'Well, you don't have time to change unless you want Dad to keep talking to him.'

Annie groaned. That was not what she wanted at all. She loved her dad, she really did, but the man had a tendency to talk anyone's ear off and, after the week's multiple embarrassing events, the last thing Annie wanted was for Mac to have to enter a full and awkward conversation with her father.

'What are they talking about?' she asked, looking frantically around her room for something, anything to throw on that wasn't reindeer themed.

Charlotte gave a little shrug, plopping down on the end of Annie's bed. She was already losing interest in this particular drama. 'I don't know. When I left them, they were discussing all the possible ways for the Pats to make it to the playoffs.'

'Okay, that's not too bad.' Football was safe. Although how long had Mac been here and no one told her?! Sometimes there were so many people in this house that visitors simply got absorbed into the chaos.

Charlotte gave a little smirk like she knew something that Annie didn't.

'What is it?'

'Oh,' Charlotte said, twirling a long blonde lock around her little finger, 'did I forget to mention that Madison is down there, too?'

'Oh God!' Annie groaned. Mac, talking to her sixteen-year-old sister was far worse than Mac talking to her father. She needed to get down there ASAP before Maddie had the chance to tell Mac every embarrassing thing Annie had done for the past decade.

She hurried out of her room with Charlotte tagging along behind her, the tin of cookies she'd swiped from Annie's room tucked under arm. Annie was going so fast she nearly tripped and fell headfirst down the stairs but luckily caught herself at the last minute. Instead of falling, she skidded down the last two steps and landed abruptly in front of Mac.

'There she is,' her dad said, as though they had all been searching for her for hours when really no one had bothered to let her know that she had a guest.

'Here I am,' Annie said. 'But what are you doing here?'

She directed the question at Mac, deciding to ignore his amused perusal of her jammies.

'Annabelle, don't be rude. Mac here stopped by to say hello and wish us a merry Christmas!' her dad said.

She raised an eyebrow at Mac, and he grinned. 'Yeah, Annabelle, I came by to wish you a merry Christmas.'

'And I was just telling him the story about the Christmas you tried to climb the tree and the whole thing fell over on you,' Maddie piped up from her perch on the sofa, wearing the exact same onesie as Annie. They looked like crazy people. Thank God her father wasn't wearing his. Instead, he'd gone with an understated sweater. The one with a giant Christmas tree on the front that, if he turned on the switch in his pocket, would light up with real twinkle lights. If she was right and Mac really had been leaning in to kiss her that afternoon, he certainly wasn't going to try again. Not after this little visit.

'You weren't even born that year,' Annie said.

Maddie shrugged. 'I've heard the story enough times and it's a funny one.'

'I have to agree with her on that,' Mac said, chuckling, and Annie made a mental note to borrow and never return that sweater of Madison's she'd been eyeing.

'Okay, well, story time is over. Now that you've wished everyone a merry Christmas, I think you can head on home.' She took Mac by the hand and dragged him to the front door.

'You don't have to kick him out. He's welcome to stay,' her dad said, but Annie had had enough of Mac for one day.

'Yeah, I didn't even get to tell him about the time you

peed on Santa's lap,' Maddie said with an evil glint in her eyes.

Annie gave her best I'm going-to-kill-you-later scowl. Forget the sweater she had her eye on, she would now be donating the majority of Maddie's closet. To a good cause, of course.

'Out!' Annie said, slipping her feet into the closest pair of boots and grabbing a coat as she pushed Mac out the door, making sure to glare at her sister one more time on her way out.

'Bye, Mr. Andrews. Bye, Maddie,' Mac called over his shoulder as Annie slammed the door behind them. He was still chuckling as she spun to face him.

'What are you doing here?' she hissed.

'Besides enjoying seeing you in that onesie?' he asked with a smile. 'And hearing so many nice stories about you?'

Annie refused to be embarrassed any more today. She rolled her shoulders back as though she was proud of her current ensemble and not at all horrified by what her sister had told him.

'It's cozy,' she said. 'And those stories are wildly exaggerated.'

'It looks cozy.'

She was going to tell him to go to hell, but he seemed sincere, and he wouldn't dare say a word about her peeing on any beloved holiday figures. So, she didn't immediately shove him off her front porch.

'It is cozy, but really, what are you doing here?'

'I wanted to see you.'

Annie blinked. 'You saw me already today.'

'Is there a limit? Am I already filled up on my Annie quota for the day?'

'No...' There had to be a catch. It was one thing when they were both bored or when Mac needed help with something but why would he want to see her now? 'I figured you would be out with your friends tonight.'

Mac shrugged. 'I'll probably see them later. But there was something I was meaning to do earlier and didn't get a chance.'

'Are you still looking for a gift? We could go back out tomorrow and keep looking, I guess, if you still need my help...' Annie trailed off as Mac stepped closer to her.

'No, it's not about the gift.' He cupped her face in his hand, running his thumb along her cheekbone.

'Oh,' Annie breathed out as she realized what was happening. Macaulay Sullivan was about to kiss her. Even after meeting half of her insane family. Even though she was dressed like a holiday reindeer.

He dipped his head to hers until his lips brushed against her mouth. She was almost embarrassed by the little sigh that escaped her, but then she remembered she was done being embarrassed today. She wrapped her arms around Mac's neck and pulled him closer. She could feel him smile.

'I thought this could go either way,' he said, not pulling away but speaking softly against her mouth. 'I thought you would either be into it or punch me in the face.'

Annie's smile met his. 'I'm into it.'

Mac groaned before deepening the kiss. His lips pressed against hers, his arms wrapping around her waist and Annie melted into him.

Fantasies don't often live up to the hype. Kissing Mac was not like that. Kissing Mac far exceeded the fantasy.

The December air was cold around them, but Mac was warm. Warm lips on hers, warm tongue sliding along hers, warm hands clinging to her hips. Annie couldn't feel the cold anymore. All she could feel was Mac. The kiss had started off gentle like he was expecting her to change her mind. But now the kiss was slow and deep like Mac wanted to get his fill, like he'd been thinking about doing this and now that he had the chance he wasn't going to waste it. By the time he pulled away, Annie was breathless.

Mac's lips tipped into a lopsided grin. 'Well, I feel better,' he said.

Annie ran her fingertips over her lips. Still there. Still her lips even though they felt altered by the experience.

'Can I see you again soon?' he asked, when Annie still hadn't managed to formulate a sentence.

'Sure,' she said, her voice nothing more than a weird, choked whisper that made Mac's smile even bigger.

'Great. I'll text you later. Good night, Annabelle,' he said, turning and leaving her so stunned that she forgot to tell him not to call her that. She'd just had the best kiss of her life with the boy she thought she hated. What was she supposed to do now? She turned back toward the house to find the smug, grinning faces of her sisters watching from the window. They'd seen the whole show and were never going to let her live this down. She put up the hood on her onesie and trudged back into the house. And even though she knew she would spend the rest of the night being tormented by Maddie and Charlotte, she couldn't seem to keep the smile off her face.

Chapter Sixteen

Now

Damn snow, damn royal icing that wouldn't harden, damn best friend who decided to get married in the middle of freaking December!

Damn George for getting the flu and not being here to help her.

Annie took a deep breath, the snowflakes swirling in front of her as she stood in the open door of her bakery. The snow had been coming down hard for nearly an hour. The light flurry from earlier had turned from scenic to a mess. It was dark already, which seemed impossible because she had only stayed a little late to put the finishing touches on the gingerbread house she was making in lieu of a wedding cake for Logan and Jeanie—and now, somehow, it was very late. And dark. And snowy.

It had been hours since Mac left her at the spa, hours after the *incident*. The orgasm admission had been a low blow. She knew that but he deserved it. She didn't need his half-assed apologies, and she certainly didn't need him knowing how much he had hurt her back then or how much it still hurt now. She didn't need anyone knowing that. It was far too humiliating that as a fully grown adult she was still devastated by something that happened when they were teenagers.

After she hadn't answered his texts and got a ride from Hazel instead, Annie hadn't heard from him. She was assuming he hadn't found Nana, either. And that was the real problem here, not Mac and his apologies but the still-missing Nana and her possible accomplice, Aunt Dot. Annie had searched all the favorite senior locations in town and the ladies had been at none of them; and now she really didn't know what to do.

And she had to get this damn gingerbread house up to Kira's farm. She'd promised she'd help with the set-up at the barn tonight.

She took another deep breath.

Annie was not going to panic because Annie was a competent and successful businesswoman perfectly capable of balancing her bakery and her friendships and her need to be perfect.

She slammed the door and stormed back into the warmth of the shop. She could do this. She could very carefully carry this monstrosity of a gingerbread house out to her delivery van and not slip and fall on her ass and then she could just as carefully drive it up to Kira's farm on roads that were probably not at all treacherous and potentially deadly.

It was fine.

All she needed was a teensy, weensy Christmas miracle.

She circled the house where it sat on her worktable in the back of the bakery. She'd built the house on a wooden platform so she could lift it and move it wherever it needed to go, but it was clearly a two-person job. She made another circle. This house was huge. An exact replica of Logan's farmhouse made from gingerbread and royal icing. How in the hell was she going to carry it on her own? And in the snow?

The gingerbread-cookie versions of Jeanie and Logan looked at her with skeptical expressions.

'I can do it,' she told them. 'I just need to figure out the right angle.' And yes, it was normal for bakers to speak to their creations. Perfectly normal.

'I just need to…' Annie was about to attempt to wrap her arms around the house without knocking off a roof piece when a bang on her front window startled her out of her concentration.

'What the hell was that?' She sighed and stomped back to the front of the store. Her windows were fogged over from the heat of the ovens and the cold outside, so all she could see beyond the glass was a dark figure.

'Oh good, a mysterious stranger, just what I need.' She used her hand to clear a small circle on the glass. The dark figure was much worse than a mysterious stranger.

It was a very familiar pain in her ass.

Mac smirked at her through the glass.

So much for Christmas miracles! Annie stalked to the bakery door and flung it open.

'Did you find her?'

'Unfortunately, no. I stopped up at Logan's farm to talk

to Henry. He seemed to think Nana and Dot had gone to visit a cousin or something. But with this snow I don't think they're coming back tonight.'

Annie blew out a frustrated breath. She had no idea what Estelle and Dot were up to, but unfortunately Mac was right. With this snow, nothing was getting accomplished until the roads were cleared.

'Then what the hell are you doing here?'

'I was leaving the pub, and I saw your lights were still on.'

'So?'

'So, the whole rest of the street has closed up shop.'

'Well, thank you for the local business report, but I already knew they'd closed up.' Leaning in the open doorway, she crossed her arms over her flour-covered apron. Mac stood in the glow of the streetlight, the snow dusting his dark hair and broad shoulders.

He tried to peer past her. 'What are you doing in there that's so important?'

'Bakery stuff.'

He raised an eyebrow. 'Bakery stuff?'

'Yes. This is a bakery.'

His laugh sent a puff of breath into the cold air. She was not going to invite him in. She'd been doing too much of that already, letting Mac get close to her again. She had to draw the line somewhere: it might as well be the threshold of her bakery.

'I like the name-change by the way,' he said, gesturing up to the new sign.

Annie gave him a begrudging thank you. The bakery had gone through many changes over the years; the new name was the most recent one. She'd gone from her little table at the Christmas market to an online shop, sharing the kitchen with her parents and siblings and still managing to get her orders filled. When she got approved for the loan to lease this shop five years ago it had been one of the best days of her life. But Mac wasn't here for any of that.

She wasn't about to discuss with him why she thought The Gingerbread Bakery was a better name for her business.

'What's so important that you're here late on the night before your best-friend's wedding?'

'Well, we were kinda busy all day, remember? And besides, it's *for* the wedding.'

'The cake?' he asked, his interest piqued. Annie had kept her plans for this house completely under wraps. Only the bride knew that they'd replaced the cake with a gingerbread house, a gift for the groom, who had an aversion to frosting.

'Let me see it,' he said, inching toward the door.

'No way.'

'Come on, Annabelle. Let me see it.'

'Don't call me Annabelle, *Macaulay*.'

It was his turn to frown and Annie laughed at the reaction.

'As the best man, it's my duty to check the cake in advance.'

'You're still not the best man. And that is definitely not within the realm of groomsmen duties.'

Mac shrugged. 'Logan didn't want strippers so what else am I supposed to do?'

'Of course he didn't want strippers. The man didn't even want frosting. It's like he's allergic to joy.'

Mac's eyes lit up and Annie realized too late that she'd given away a vital piece of information.

'Logan doesn't like frosting?' He stepped closer until they were both crowded in the doorway. 'What did you make, Annie?' Their breath mingled between them, creating their own little steam cloud. 'Let me in.' He held her gaze and it felt like he was asking for so much more than entrance to the bakery. His offer from earlier to *try again* ran through her mind.

'Please,' he added, his gaze flicking to her lips and back. Annie hesitated, her resolve weakening like it always did around this infuriating man.

The problem was, Annie hadn't been lying earlier, not exactly. So maybe he hadn't given her an orgasm but that didn't mean the sex hadn't been good. It didn't mean he hadn't been sweet and tender with her for her first time. It didn't mean she didn't think about what sex could be like between them now. It was like her body had had sex with him eleven years ago, and her brain had kept it up ever since.

His head dipped closer to hers, his breath a welcome warmth on her face. Her eyes fluttered closed.

'Please, Annie.'

She put a hand on his chest and relished the small hitch in his breath as she opened her eyes and saw it, the hunger in his eyes. Hunger mixed with hope. And she almost felt bad before she pressed that hand harder and shoved.

Mac skidded back in the snow, slipping and sliding but, much to Annie's dismay, remaining upright.

The obnoxious smirk was back on his face by the time he

got his footing, but the earnestness with which he'd said *please* was long gone.

'Sorry, Mac, no strippers and no sneak peeks for you tonight. You should probably head home. Drive safe!' Annie wiggled her fingers in a wave goodbye and was turning toward the door when Mac's words stopped her in her tracks.

'How are you going to move it into the van?'

Shit. He had her there.

'You don't want to ruin whatever it is you made, Annie. I know you don't want to disappoint the bride and groom.'

Double shit.

Of course she didn't want to disappoint the bride and groom. She'd spent the whole day trying desperately to make sure this wedding would go smoothly. What kind of monster wanted to disappoint the bride and groom? Annie quickly assessed her options. She could tell Mac to go to hell, which was what she really, really wanted to do, and then wrestle the very large, very delicate gingerbread house into the van herself and risk dropping the whole damn thing and ruining Jeanie's secret gift to Logan or … she could let this asshole help her.

Ugh.

'Fine,' she said over her shoulder as she strode back into the bakery. 'But I'm only doing this for Jeanie.'

She didn't bother to turn around and heard Mac's footsteps behind her as he followed her to the back room.

'Shit.' She rushed over to the gingerbread house. 'These damn gables keep sliding off. I must have mixed the royal icing too thin,' she muttered to herself as she went to repair the damage. 'I just need to … a little bit more…' She piped on more icing and almost had it … there. She stepped back to assess her work and collided with Mac's firm chest.

He grabbed her upper arms, keeping her clutched tight against him.

'It's beautiful,' he whispered. His voice was low and admiring in her ear.

Oh no, you don't. Not 'sweet' Mac again.

'Yeah, well,' she said, squirming from his grasp. 'The damn roof keeps falling apart.'

'It doesn't have to be perfect.'

She spun to face him. 'Ha! It's like you don't even know me.'

Mac's gaze bore into her, his eyes flicking down to her mouth again as though he was thinking about all the ways he did in fact know her. Annie's face heated under his stare.

'Of course I know you, Annabelle,' he said, and she knew immediately that she was in danger. That was the worst part about all of this. He *did* know her. And that was the problem. He smiled smugly as he went on. 'You've been working for days to get this house exactly right because you want it to be special for the people you love. And you've been doing it all while filling Christmas cookie orders for the entire town and fulfilling your bridesmaid duties which somehow included a manhunt, and if I know you, and I think I do, probably babysitting for half your nieces and nephews while your sisters go Christmas shopping. And every single one of these tasks you've put your whole heart into. And you want things to be perfect because you think being perfect shows people that you love them, and a little piece of you believes they would love you less if you weren't.'

Annie swallowed hard. Damn it.

This was what she got for never leaving this town, for hanging out with the same people since she was five, for showing this man too much of herself back when she thought it was safe.

Mac stepped toward her, tipping her chin up to meet his gaze.

'I also know that by this time of the day your head hurts from having your hair pulled back too tight and your feet hurt from standing for hours but you never, ever complain.'

Annie couldn't breathe. This little speech had literally stolen the air from her lungs.

'*And* I know that a part of you wants to forgive me but you're too damn stubborn to do it.'

That cocky grin spread across his face at her wide-eyed expression. He leaned in closer, so his words brushed across her lips. 'But lucky for you, I'm just as stubborn. And I haven't given up yet. Your little admission earlier today gave me even more motivation. I'm not nineteen anymore, Annie, and I don't leave women unsatisfied.'

Annie swallowed hard. *Holy shit.* She forced herself to take a step back, to step away from this man and his smirk and his alarmingly accurate knowledge of her inner workings. Because he was right on all accounts, but especially the fact that she had not and would not forgive him. And it was *that* and not his very appealing offer that she had to focus on.

'Just help me get the damn thing in the van,' she ground out.

Mac chuckled, knowing exactly the effect he was having

on her. 'Of course, darling. Anything for you. But you're not taking the van.'

'Why wouldn't I?'

'Because I'm driving you.'

'No, you aren't.'

'Yes, I am. The roads are terrible, and I have snow tires.'

Annie nearly growled in frustration. '*Fine*.'

If this man was her Christmas miracle, she would like to file a complaint with Santa or the baby Jesus or whoever was in charge, because the only miracle here would be if she didn't kill or kiss Mac before the wedding was over.

And either option felt equally ill-advised.

Chapter Seventeen

Then

'What do you keep looking at?' Charlotte said, apparently catching Annie glancing to the back of the auditorium for the twelfth time since they arrived.

'Nothing.'

That was a lie. Annie was fairly certain she'd seen Mac back there, but maybe she was hallucinating. Ever since he kissed her, she thought she'd seen him everywhere. She could have sworn she'd spotted him at the grocery store when she went to grab milk, and then she really could have sworn he was in front of her in line at The Pumpkin Spice Café, and she was absolutely positive she'd seen him out for a run one morning down her street, but none of those men had turned out to be Mac. She was clearly losing her mind over this boy, which was really not something she did. But everything with Mac felt different. This whole December felt different.

She glanced to the back of the room again and Charlotte huffed a little laugh. 'If you're looking for your boyfriend,' she said, 'that's definitely him back there sitting next to his mom.'

'It is?' Annie whispered, trying not to disrupt the concert. Her older sister was playing the cello tonight as part of the town Christmas concert, but frankly Annie had more pressing issues than to ooh and ahh over her sister's musical abilities.

'Yep,' Charlotte said smugly. 'That's him. I spotted him as soon as we sat down.'

'Well, you could have told me sooner.'

Charlotte rolled her eyes. 'I thought you saw him. Isn't he your boyfriend? Why don't you just text him?'

'He's not my *boyfriend*,' Annie hissed. No, that wasn't what was happening here, just because they had kissed and she couldn't stop thinking about him. She wouldn't call him her boyfriend, right? Right.

'I'm going to go get something from the concession stand,' she said in between songs.

Charlotte smirked. 'Yeah, okay, that's what you're doing —"getting a snack".' The way her sister did air quotes around the words made Annie want to smack her, but she didn't have time for that before the next song started.

'I *am* getting a snack.'

Her baby sister winked at her like she knew exactly what was going on.

Annie shook her head and got out of her seat, signaling to her parents where she was headed. She walked down the aisle of the auditorium, passing former friends and teachers along the way, but she was single-minded in her pursuit of a 'snack'. She caught Mac's eye before exiting the auditorium and it didn't surprise her when he appeared behind her in the concession line a minute later. In fact, it filled her with relief that he wanted to see her, too.

'Hey, Annabelle,' he said, his voice beside her ear. 'Enjoying the show?

'I am. What are you doing here?' She didn't turn around. Just kept her eyes on the snack choices, trying to play it cool. They'd texted a few times since the kiss, but neither had made the next move. They could hang out, or not, whatever, she thought even as her heart picked up speed.

'My cousin's in the show this year and Mom wanted to come.' He had stepped closer; his chest brushed against her back. 'I've been waiting for you to come say hi,' he said. 'I saw you looking at me.'

Annie shrugged. 'I was just taking in the crowd.'

Mac chuckled as she made her snack purchase. 'Come on,' he said, grabbing her hand. 'Let's take a break from this concert.'

He led her through the empty halls of the high school, stopping alongside a row of lockers.

He pulled her closer, not wasting any time now that they were alone. 'Can I kiss you?'

Annie's breath caught in her throat. Kissing Mac was all she had thought about for the past five days.

She nodded. Mac seemed to be the only person on the planet that was able to leave her speechless.

He grinned and cupped her face with his hands, kissing her gently on the lips.

His smile grew and Annie couldn't believe that the cutest boy in school was kissing her. For a minute, standing in the dark hallway of their high school, she forgot that they weren't students here anymore, that they were technically adults. All she felt was the giddy joy of her crush liking her back.

'What d'you get?' Mac asked, pulling away and gesturing to the candy she still had clutched in her fist.

'Peanut M&Ms,' she said, sliding down to the floor. Mac joined her, their backs pressed against the lockers.

He put out his hand and she poured some candy into his palm. He tossed them all into his mouth at once, crunching happily.

'So,' he said. 'What have you been up to this week?'

Besides thinking about you?

Nope, don't say *that*. 'I helped my mom decorate the house and I took Charlotte to her basketball practice and I did a lot of baking. I actually had a few people place orders for Christmas.'

'That's awesome. You're like a real business.'

Annie beamed. She *was* like a real business.

'What about you? What have you been up to?'

'Mostly spent a lot of time thinking about wanting to kiss you some more,' he said with a grin.

Giddiness raced through her. She felt like she might float away. Mac was thinking about her while she was thinking about him!

'You can,' she said. 'I mean you can kiss me some more if you want.'

Mac leaned toward her and this time the kiss was less gentle. By the time they pulled apart again, Annie was breathless.

'Pretty fun doing that here and not having teachers split

us up,' Mac said with a laugh, and Annie could not imagine any version of herself that would have done this during school hours.

'Yeah, that never happened to me,' she said.

Mac looked at her, studying her like he was trying to figure her out.

'Never got detention, either, I guess.'

'Nope.'

'Skipped class?'

'Never.'

'Faked sick so you could stay home?'

Annie thought about that one for a minute. Had she? 'No, not that either. I didn't want to get behind.'

Mac tipped his head, considering her. 'What would have happened if you did get a little bit behind? Like what's the worst outcome?'

Annie shrugged. 'I would have ruined my perfect GPA.'

'Right. Failure.'

'Exactly.'

He looked at her for another minute and nerves fluttered in her belly. Maybe now was when he remembered that they didn't really make sense together. There were reasons they had spent the first thirteen years of knowing each other *not* hanging out.

'Just so you know...' he said, and Annie braced herself for what came next.

Just so you know, I'm tired of hanging out with you.

Just so you know, this has gotten weird.

Just so you know, I remembered I have other people I'd rather be friends with — people that aren't so ... intense.

But he didn't say any of those things. He smiled at her

and said, 'Just so you know … I would still like you even if your GPA had dipped a little.'

Annie laughed, the sound echoing through the deserted hallway.

'That's good to know,' she said.

'I'm having a lot of fun with you.' He leaned closer again, running the tip of his nose along her cheek.

'Me too,' she whispered.

'Want to hang out tomorrow?'

'Definitely,' she breathed as his lips brushed against hers.

'Cool.'

Very cool.

He kissed her and he tasted like chocolate and crushes and like the best December of her life.

Chapter Eighteen

Now

They were making the treacherous drive through the snow up to Kira's farm in silence. The gingerbread house was safely in the back of his Bronco and Annie in the passenger seat beside him, but Mac might as well have been alone with his thoughts. And his thoughts were mainly consumed with the fact that everything he'd thought about his time with Annie had been a lie.

If their experiences of that month had been so different, then maybe it really was time to let the whole thing go. Maybe that month hadn't been some magical Christmas moment between them. Maybe he had been the only one who had fallen in love.

Or maybe it was all just about an orgasm. And if it was just about an orgasm, *that* he could remedy. In fact, *that* he would love to remedy. And maybe that would help everything. Maybe one more time with Annie and he could finally put her in the correct category. In his mind, she could go from being the girl he never got over to being just another ex. An ex that he could move on from, a woman that he slept with; and then maybe they could actually be friends, or at least civil to each other. Maybe a decade was way too long to replay a memory and the whole thing had become distorted over the years. Maybe it hadn't all been as magical as he originally thought. What he and Annie needed was a night together to have closure once and for all.

He'd been losing his mind about it all day and then it had started snowing harder and he saw the bakery light still on and was at Annie's window before he could stop himself. He couldn't leave her there in the snow, knowing she'd put herself in a dangerous situation to make sure she didn't let anyone down. So here he was giving her a ride, and she hadn't said a damn word to him since they got in the truck.

'You know you could thank me,' he said, glancing over to the passenger seat. He took his eyes off the road just long enough to catch Annie glaring at him.

'I could,' she said, 'but you basically forced me into accepting the ride.'

'Only because I knew you would do something stupid if I didn't.'

'Stupid? Excuse me?'

Mac huffed a laugh. 'Yeah, something stupid. Like try to drive on these snowy roads up to Kira's farm in that old delivery van that handles horribly and end up in a ditch somewhere instead.'

'Really, Mac. I don't know when you became so dramatic.'

'Stop calling me that.'

'Then stop acting that way.'

'I'm not acting any kind of way, Annabelle. I'm trying to keep you alive for some reason that I really can't remember at the moment.'

She scoffed and sat back in her seat, staring out the window at the snow. It was really coming down now and Mac hoped his snow tires were as good as he said they were, or they would both end up in a ditch.

His plan to have one more night with Annie had made perfect sense when he was alone, but all Annie wanted to do when they were together was fight. He wasn't sure how he would convince her that what they really needed was to fuck.

The lights from the farmhouse appeared ahead on the dark road and Mac let out a sigh of relief. At least they weren't going to die on the side of the road sexually frustrated. That would be a tragedy. He pulled the Bronco up the driveway to the barn. Annie hissed as they went over each and every bump.

She gasped after they went over a particularly big rut. 'The gingerbread house!' she squeaked.

'I'm going as carefully as I can.' Mac assured her. 'It'll be fine.'

They hit another dip in the road and Annie gripped tight to his forearm.

'Careful!' she gasped, her fingers digging into his flesh.

Mac kept the truck at a slow crawl all the way down the road to the barn. Annie didn't take her fingers off his arm until they pulled up safely in front of the barn doors. It made him wish the road was longer.

She immediately hopped out into the snow and ran around to the back to check on the house. They'd buffered it on all sides to keep it from sliding around and it was at least relatively in the same place they'd left it. Annie let out a sigh of relief.

'It might have a few cracks,' she said when he joined her behind the truck. 'But it looks like it survived.'

'Good,' Mac said, relieved that he hadn't let her down for once.

She looked at him in the dim light from the trunk. 'Thank you,' she said.

'Yeah, no problem.'

'No, really. Thank you. As much as it pains me to say it, you were probably right about the whole me-ending-up-in-a-ditch thing, so I really appreciate the ride.'

The snow swirled in between them, and Annie's cheeks were red with the cold. Mac ran a hand down the side of her face.

'You drive me nuts, but I don't want you dead in a ditch.'

Annie's lips tipped into a begrudging smile. 'That's the sweetest thing you've ever said to me.'

It wasn't. He'd said plenty of sweet things eleven years ago. Or maybe he'd misremembered that too.

'I could probably come up with some other things if you want me to.'

There were a million things he could think to say about Annie. He could tell her how much he admired her or how proud he was of what she'd accomplished. He could tell her how gorgeous she was and how over the years he'd compared every other woman to her. He could tell her that she felt like home, even after all this time. Or he could tell her he was dying to know what she tasted like between her thighs and that he regretted not finding out when he'd had the chance. Mac could go on and on if she'd let him.

Annie's full smile was a lovely and rare thing in the cold night. It reminded Mac of the night he first kissed her, and he wished he could do it again. She'd liked him that night. She still thought he was cute and charming. He'd made her laugh. He hadn't broken her heart yet.

'Remember when we made gingerbread cookies together?' he asked. And he knew he was grasping at straws, looking for any evidence that they'd had the same experience.

'I do,' she said. 'I remember you ate about a dozen in one sitting.'

'They were small!'

Annie laughed, the sound so bright and beautiful that Mac could hardly believe she was letting him hear it.

'They weren't *that* small and that was after half a bag of sour cream-and-onion chips.'

'Well, we had worked up an appetite.'

Annie's cheeks flushed a deeper red and Mac felt vindicated. She did remember. And she felt it, too. The pull of that time, the need to find out if it was still there, that thing between them. If he kissed her right now, what would she do? Would it feel like the first time? Better? God, he wanted to find out.

He wrapped his hand around the nape of her neck, his fingers putting pressure on the tension there. Annie's eyes fluttered closed. He leaned forward and she didn't stop him, didn't knee him in the groin. He tightened his grip, just a little, just enough to have Annie melting toward him, her lips a hair's-breadth from his.

'Annie, is that you?' Kira called from the barn.

Annie's eyes flew open, but she stayed frozen in place. He could still kiss her, but it would have to be rushed, and the next time he kissed Annie, he sure as hell wasn't going to rush. Not after waiting over a decade.

He dropped his hand from her neck. 'Next time,' he whispered.

Annie blinked, swallowing hard. 'Yeah, it's us,' she called, her eyes still on Mac. He'd left her wanting, but this time he'd done it on purpose.

'I brought the dessert,' Annie said, taking a step back and then another, finally returning to herself.

Kira trudged around the side of the SUV with two dogs jumping around her in the snow. Mac found it impossible to keep all of her animals straight, so he had no idea which two these were, but one was huge and one was small and white with a Christmas bow tie affixed to his collar.

'You didn't have to come up here in the snow,' Kira said.

'I promised I would help set up,' Annie said. 'And besides I wanted to get the house up here before tomorrow.'

'House?' Kira asked.

'Gingerbread house. In lieu of a wedding cake.'

Kira nodded. 'Right. Of course. The groom hates frosting. Makes perfect sense. Okay. Well, let's get it inside.'

Bennett came out to help and between the four of them they were able to carefully move the gingerbread house onto a table in the barn. Annie needed to do a few repairs with the extra icing she'd brought, but overall, she seemed pleased that they made it with the house intact.

'Okay, Kira, what else do you need help with?' Annie asked, looking around the barn for her next task, studiously avoiding catching Mac's eye. He had her flustered now and he liked it. Let her spend some time feeling as keyed up as he always did around her.

'We were going to set up some Christmas trees on that end with white lights to serve as a backdrop for the altar.'

'I can help with that,' Mac offered, and Annie immediately turned to argue.

'You don't have to stay.'

'How are you going to get home if I don't stay?' he asked. If she thought she was getting rid of him now, she was very, very wrong.

'Bennett has a plow. I'm sure he could get me home or I could crash here, right?'

'Sure, of course,' Kira said. 'Whatever you want to do.'

'I'm staying,' Mac said. 'I want to help.'

He held Annie's gaze, daring her to challenge his willingness to help his friend, but she let it go with a raised eyebrow.

'Okaaay…' Kira said, her eyes flicking between them. 'So, Mac, you can help Bennett haul the trees in and get them dried off, and Annie, you can help me and Daisy from the flower shop set up the flowers and place settings on the tables. Hazel and I got a lot done earlier, so that's all we have left to do!'

'Sounds easy enough,' said Annie.

'Great! Because there's one more thing,' Kira said, walking toward the corner of the barn. She came back with a cardboard box in her arms and an apologetic look on her face.

'So ... we found these.' She held the box out in front of her and two small faces appeared over the edge.

'Kittens!' Annie squealed. 'Oh my gosh, Kira! They're so cute!'

The kittens were perfectly normal but what was really cute was Annie's reaction to them.

Kira sneezed and the two furry faces disappeared back into the box. 'Yes, they are very cute,' Kira agreed. 'However, I am very allergic to them.' She sneezed again, as though to put a point on the matter.

'Where did they come from?' Mac asked, reaching out to rub the little orange kitten between its ears. It nuzzled against his hand.

'We found them curled up together in the pile of tablecloths,' Kira said, sniffling. 'We're not sure where the mother is, but we can't have them in here for the wedding and I can't bring them in the house.'

She sneezed again three times in rapid succession. Bennett had appeared at her side at this point, and he draped an arm over her shoulder, shaking his head. 'It's one of the great tragedies of Kira's life. She can kiss reindeer but she's allergic to cats.'

'Reindeer, dogs, bunnies...' Kira listed on her fingers. 'I can do them all, but I get within a few feet of a cat, and I can't breathe.'

Mac took the box from her hands looking down at the two little kittens inside, one orange and one black and white. They peered up at him with big green eyes. Annie came closer and looked into the box as well. A small crease appeared between her eyebrows.

'What are we going to do with them?' she asked.

'I was hoping you would be able to take them at least for a few days until we can find them a home.'

'I can't,' Annie said, shaking her head. 'My landlord won't allow pets.'

Kira sneezed three more times and Bennett dragged her away from the box of kittens.

'I guess maybe if we kept them in one of the guest bedrooms away from me then it might be okay,' Kira said, rubbing her eyes but Bennett was already shaking his head.

'Babe, if we bring these into the house, I'm afraid you will actually die. And I prefer that not happen. I kinda like you.'

Kira looked up at Ben, her eyes already more puffy and swollen than when they started this conversation. 'We can't just put them out in the snow!' she wailed.

Annie was wringing her hands next to him, and Mac knew it was killing her that she couldn't do something to fix the situation. But he also knew that she loved that little apartment of hers and she couldn't do something that would jeopardize her lease.

'I'll take them,' he said, and Annie's gaze snapped to his.

'You'll take them?'

'Yeah, I've been meaning to get a pet anyway.'

'You have not,' said Annie.

Mac crossed his arms over his chest. 'Do you want to put the kittens in the snow?'

'No, of course not.'

'Okay, then let me take my kittens in peace.' He put

down the box and took a kitten in each hand. They greeted him with eager meows of thanks. Annie was right. He'd had no intention of having pets, but they were pretty darn cute. And as he tucked one in each of his coat pockets, he caught Annie smiling at him.

'Let's go get those trees,' he said to Bennett, leaving a slightly stunned, still smiling Annie to help with the flowers.

Chapter Nineteen

Then

Annie was making out with Mac. There was no other way to describe it. His mouth was on hers, his fingers raking through her hair. They were making out. And Mac was really damn good at it.

Annie pulled back a little so she could see him in the soft glow of the Christmas lights. She'd strung several strings over his bed for ambiance, and now they were curled up together just like they had been that first night she stayed over, except this time Mac was not keeping his hands to himself. And Annie liked it just a little too much. He smiled at her, the skin crinkling at the corner of his eyes.

'Hey,' he said. 'Everything okay?' He'd been doing that all night. Checking in when he kissed her, when his hands found their way to her ass and squeezed. He'd asked all along the way if she liked it, if she was okay, if she was comfortable. It was unexpected and thoughtful. Apparently, she was still underestimating Macaulay Sullivan.

'Yeah, everything's great,' she said with a dopey smile she couldn't seem to stop. She'd done a lot of dopey smiling today as she and Mac had scoured the mall for a gift. They'd found quite a few contenders, but Mac had vetoed them all. She was starting to get the feeling that he was rejecting gifts just so they could keep looking.

'Good,' he said. 'Everything is good for me, too.' His smile turned mischievous as his hands roamed over the curve of her hip and back again. Annie scooched closer to him on the bed, marveling at the fact that only a few weeks ago she had fantasized about doing this, and now she got to. She laid a hand on his chest, feeling the strong beat of his heart beneath her palm. He was firm and solid, and she liked touching him. His smile grew.

'I'm glad you were bored enough to hang out with me this month,' he said.

'Now that I know you better, I might even consider hanging out with you when I'm not bored.'

'Wow,' Mac raised his eyebrows in mock surprise. 'That is a high compliment coming from you.' He leaned forward and pressed another kiss to her lips. Annie couldn't help the curve of her smile against his mouth.

'Well, I do have very high standards,' she said with a soft laugh.

'I'll try my best to live up to them.' He used the arm he had draped over her to pull her closer, tucking her tight against his body as he deepened the kiss. His tongue slid against hers and she found herself making needy little moaning sounds and arching against him. Things she had never done in her entire life but that felt right with Mac. She wanted more. More kissing, more pressure, more everything. His hands were moving faster now. Firmer. Never dipping beneath her clothes but tracing every curve and inch of her. Their kissing became more frantic, sloppier. Their hands, grasping and groping. Annie was *burning*, wanting things she had never really wanted in any concrete way before, wanting this man in ways she had never wanted anyone else, and she felt like she might actually combust if he didn't do something to *fix* it, to ease the ache inside of her. She was counting on Mac here because she felt completely out of her element. Unmoored by the intensity of her feelings. For the first time in her life, Annie's body didn't feel like her own. She didn't recognize it like this. And it was both exhilarating and terrifying.

'Wait,' Mac gasped, pulling back.

His hands were on either side of her face holding her in place. His eyes were dark, his lips swollen from kissing her.

'What's the matter?' she asked, her breath still coming in short spurts. Had she done something wrong? Judging by the erection pressed against her belly she'd assumed she was doing okay but, again, she was out of her element. A few hurried orgasms alone in her shower with one or two siblings banging on the door hadn't exactly made her an expert.

Mac squeezed his eyes shut and then opened them like he was trying to get his bearings. He tucked a piece of her hair behind her ear, brushing his knuckles along her cheek. 'Nothing's the matter. I just thought maybe now would be a good time to make some cookies.'

Annie blinked. Had all the kissing given her some sort of brain injury? 'You want to make cookies?'

Mac swallowed hard, clearly still trying to regroup. 'Yeah, I thought you could teach me how to make those little gingerbread men.'

'Right now?' Annie didn't understand what was happening. Her thoughts were still filled with *want* and *need* and *Mac*.

'Yeah.'

'You want to stop what we're doing and go make cookies?'

Mac nodded, his hair crackling with static against the pillow. 'I thought it might be a good time for a break.'

'Oh,' Annie cringed at the sound of disappointment in her own voice. He wanted to stop.

'If we don't take a break now,' he said, pressing his forehead to hers, his fingers still playing in her hair. 'Then we might make decisions we'll regret, and I really don't want to do anything that you'll regret, Annie.'

The reality of the last few minutes slowly started to seep into Annie's kiss-addled brain. In the heat of the moment, she had definitely been on the edge of making decisions she wasn't sure she would make when Mac's tongue was not in her mouth.

'Right, good idea,' she said, still marveling at his restraint. She had been about two rolls of his hips against her from giving it all up and maybe she still wanted to. But Mac was right. She didn't want to do anything she would regret later. Sure, she fully believed that virginity was only a social construct, but her first time was still her *first time*. It was still a big deal.

'But for the record,' he said. 'I don't regret any of that.'

Annie smiled. 'Me neither.'

Mac pressed one more kiss to her lips before rolling over and staring at the ceiling. 'I'm going to need a minute or two to think about baseball, or that time I reached into my cereal box and pulled out a dead mouse.'

'Ew, God.'

'I know, very traumatic. But it works. You can feel free to head up to the kitchen and rummage around for ingredients. My mom's on the night shift tonight, and Dad's at the pub so we'll have the kitchen to ourselves.'

Annie didn't think thinking about baseball would do much to help her and she certainly wasn't going to think about dead mice in her cereal, but a few minutes away from Mac would probably be a good idea. She hurried upstairs leaving him on his bed with an arm draped over his eyes. The bottom of his T-shirt had ridden up just enough to give her a glimpse of tan stomach before she left. That definitely didn't help.

Alone in Mac's kitchen, she took some deep breaths, pressing the back of her hand to her cheek. She was still burning hot. What had that boy done to her? Whatever it was, she didn't hate it.

But she needed to calm down. It was time to bake cookies, not tackle Mac onto his kitchen floor. She took the opportunity to snoop around the kitchen a bit. It was a decent size with honey-colored cabinets from the nineties just like her parents had before they'd finally redone it last year. Plenty of counter space with a table tucked in the corner where she and Mac had had breakfast a couple of weeks ago. From the window over the sink, Annie could look out at the driveway and the neighbor's house. To her surprise, she found Mr. Prescott, the mailman, at his sink waving to her. She had the bizarre impulse to duck down, like she needed to hide this visit to Mac's house, but it was probably safe for the mailman to know. She gave him a little wave back before stepping away from the window, making a note to herself that if she was going to jump Mac's bones, she probably shouldn't do it there.

The old linoleum creaked under her feet as she opened a few cabinets trying to figure out where the baking supplies were kept. Instead, she found a cupboard full of souvenir mugs and an alarming amount of potato chips in every flavor imaginable.

'Big chip fan?' she asked, hearing Mac's footsteps behind her.

He chuckled. 'No, but my mom is. It's her only vice. She gets home from a long shift and can devour an entire bag of those things by herself.'

'Wow, that's impressive for such a tiny lady.'

'She really packs them away.'

'Your mom's a nurse, right?'

'Yep. NICU nurse. She basically saves little babies.' The pride on Mac's face when he talked about his mom was too adorable to face head-on, so Annie continued browsing his cupboards.

'Where do you guys keep the baking supplies?' she asked.

'That's an excellent question, Annie, and one that I feel I should have the answer to. However…'

'It's your own house, Mac. How do you not know where the baking supplies are?'

'This might surprise you,' he said, 'but I'm not exactly a big baker. Which,' he continued with a grin, 'is why I need these lessons.'

'It's a good thing I'm here, then,' Annie said, turning to face him.

He grinned. 'It's a very good thing.'

The look on his face sent a multitude of inappropriate thoughts racing through her head. She turned abruptly and opened the freezer, sticking her head inside, desperate for anything that would cool her down.

'I don't know if you're going to find what you're looking for in there,' Mac said with a laugh. She felt him come up behind her, his head joining hers inside the freezer. 'I'm pretty sure we don't keep the baking supplies in here.'

'It was worth a look,' Annie said. 'And I was feeling a bit overheated,' she admitted.

'Did you try thinking about dead rodents in your breakfast?'

She grimaced. 'I most certainly did not. And I will be spending a lot of time erasing that image from my mind, actually.'

Mac laughed as they both exited the freezer, closing it behind them. 'That image has saved me from a lot of embarrassing moments,' he said, stooping down to rummage in some of the bottom cabinets. Annie forced herself to not check out his ass as he did so or think about the embarrassing moments he was talking about it.

'Bingo!' he said, holding up a cookie sheet in one hand and a big metal bowl in the other.

'Great! Now we just need ingredients.'

'That one, I know.' He got up from his crouch and

opened a door beside the refrigerator, revealing a small pantry. He pulled out flour, salt and sugar and then looked to Annie for guidance. Lucky for him, she happened to have her gingerbread-cookie recipe memorized and his mom had a well-stocked pantry. Before long, they had everything they needed laid out on the counter and were working side by side to measure and mix.

It was nice, peaceful even, except for when Mac's arm would brush against hers, sending electricity tingling through her body all over again, but other than that disconcerting side effect, baking cookies with Mac was fun.

'You've really never made gingerbread men before?'

'No, my mom's not much of a baker and my dad pretty much never comes in here unless it's to eat. I used to bake with my grandfather sometimes. Actually,' he said, his voice suddenly dipping quieter. 'I'd forgotten about that.'

'You two were close?'

'Yeah, he lived with us for a bit before he...' Mac cleared his throat, 'before he died.'

Annie let her shoulder brush his and kept it pressed to his side. It felt like she'd done the right thing when Mac leaned back against her.

'My grandpa was one of my first customers,' she said.

'You charged your grandfather for cookies? That's pretty ruthless, Annabelle,' he said with a smile in his voice.

'He insisted! He loved my thumbprint cookies and told me I should sell them. So I did, and he was the first person to come to the little stand I had set up in front of our house.' It was the first time she had felt like she was really good at something, and it was the first time she'd made someone else feel good by making them something. She'd loved the feeling. It snowballed from there. She begged her mother to let her bake any chance she got. She worked hard at it, wanting to give her family and friends the best. She still did.

'He gave me twenty dollars for that first cookie.'

'Damn.'

'I know, he really set my expectations for the profits I could make far too high,' she said with a laugh. 'Okay, now we add the most important ingredient.'

'Love?' Mac asked, wiggling his eyebrows.

Annie shook her head in amusement. 'No! Ginger.'

'Right, of course that makes more sense.'

He dumped in the spice and mixed per Annie's instructions.

'Your grandpa's gone too?' he asked as the dough came together.

'Yeah, for a few years now.'

'That sucks,' Mac said, and oddly it was the most comforting thing anyone had said to her about the death of her grandpa. It *did* suck.

Annie dumped the dough out onto the counter and started rolling. 'It does,' she said. 'He was one of the few people who really got me, you know?'

'All those siblings, and your grandpa was the only one who got you?'

'That's the thing,' Annie said, handing Mac a cookie cutter. They were making gingerbread hearts and stars because those were the only cookie cutters they could find. 'There's so many of us. You kind of get pigeonholed. Like we each get our one thing that defines us, and no one really focuses on anything else.'

'That makes sense,' Mac said, pressing hearts into the dough. 'What's your one thing?'

Annie shrugged. 'Somewhere along the line, I became the smart one, I guess. The one who was good at school. Maddie's the athlete, Charlotte's the baby, Brian's the only boy. Evelyn's the oldest, so she gets to be the leader, and Natalie is the musician, the *sensitive* one.'

'Being good at school is not the worst thing.'

'It's not a bad thing at all, but it's not the only thing and, I don't know, my grandpa was the one who paid attention to the other stuff like baking.'

At least he was until Annie took over her parents' kitchen. There was no ignoring her baking anymore. Her grandpa's joy over her cookies had started her down this road but it was all Annie now. She was determined to be the best baker in town.

Mac nudged her shoulder and this time Annie leaned into him.

'Okay, what now?' Mac said, assessing all the hearts and stars filling the cookie sheet.

'Now we bake.' Annie slid the baking sheet into the oven while Mac grabbed a bag of potato chips from the cabinet.

'A snack for while we wait,' he said with a grin.

Annie joined him at the table, reaching into the bag.

'Sour cream and onion. My favorite.' She popped a chip into her mouth with a smile. 'I guess we're done with the kissing part of the evening.'

'Oh yeah?'

'Well, sour cream and onion... Our breaths aren't exactly going to be fresh after this.'

Mac grinned. 'I would still kiss you even if your breath was a little sour-cream-and-onion-y.'

Annie scrunched up her face in disgust even as she secretly thought that was very cute of him to say.

'What? Is sour-cream-and-onion breath a deal breaker for you, Annabelle?' Mac teased.

'I don't know. Probably!' she said, although at this point, she would kiss Mac even if he had a horn growing out of his head, but he didn't need to know that.

'Well, what is a dealbreaker for you?' he asked, leaning back in his chair, studying her with dark eyes under those pretty eyelashes.

She shrugged, not able to come up with anything clever under the intensity of his stare.

'Okay, what about this?' he said, leaning forward, really getting into it now. 'Let's say you really like a guy and things are going well, but then you go to the beach, and it turns out he has gross feet. Dealbreaker?'

'Gross feet?' Annie asked with a laugh.

'Yeah! Like gnarled toes with weird toenails.'

'Ugh, gross. Is this your way of telling me that you have weird feet?'

'No way! I have very pretty feet,' he said, plopping them in Annie's lap. 'Go ahead, pull off a sock and find out.' He wiggled his toes, and Annie couldn't help the giggles spilling out of her. She couldn't remember the last time she had laughed quite so much.

'I am not pulling your sock off!' she said, trying to push his feet off her.

Mac leaned forward and yanked off his sock like he was revealing a prize she had won in a very strange game show.

'See? Very pretty.' He wiggled his toes some more and Annie ran a finger up the arch of his foot.

Mac squealed and pulled his foot back.

'You're ticklish!' Annie exclaimed like she had revealed some deep dark secret, but she liked learning new things about Mac.

'Of course I'm ticklish on my feet! Who isn't? And let's just pretend I never made that noise.'

Annie shook her head, laughter bubbling out of her. 'Oh no, I'm going to remember that high-pitch squeak for the rest of my life.'

'Shoot.' Mac put his head in his hands. 'That plan really backfired.'

'And what plan was that? To seduce me with your pretty feet?'

He looked up at her with a wicked grin. 'That was exactly my plan,' he said. 'Until you foiled it with those sneaky fingers.'

Annie scoffed. 'You were the one putting your feet in my lap! What was I supposed to do?'

Mac shook his head with a smile, grabbing more chips. 'Seriously,' he said, 'dealbreakers?' He asked like he really wanted to know, but what did it matter what Annie's dealbreakers were?

'I don't know. I guess I would want someone who was there for me. Someone to count on.'

Neither of them brought up the fact that Mac was still planning to leave at the end of the month. The ultimate dealbreaker.

'And they can't cheat at board games. That would be a huge problem,' Annie added.

'Ooh … I guess that takes me out of the running. I'm a notorious cheater,' Mac said, the playfulness back in his voice.

'Well, that settles that, I guess,' Annie said. 'What about you? What are your dealbreakers?'

Mac shrugged. 'Probably the foot thing.'

Annie tossed the dish towel at his head with a laugh before getting up to pull the cookies out of the oven.

Mac followed her, trying to grab a cookie straight off the tray. Annie moved it out of his reach.

'They need to cool,' she said. 'You're going to burn yourself. Not to mention they don't taste as good when they're hot.'

Mac put his hands up in surrender. 'Okay, okay. I'll wait. You're the cookie boss.'

Annie moved the cookies from the tray to the cooling rack and as soon as she was done, Mac had her pinned against the kitchen counter.

'What are you doing?' she asked with a breathy laugh.

'I wanted you to know I don't have any dealbreakers with you, Annie.' His voice was a whisper against her cheek and suddenly it didn't matter that she was still wearing his mom's plaid oven mitt or that maybe her breath had a hint of sour cream and onion. All that mattered was that Mac kissed her. Immediately.

His lips met hers and Annie sighed in relief.

'I love that little noise you make when I kiss you,' he said, running the tip of his nose along her cheek.

'You do?'

'Oh yeah. You might remember that embarrassing

squeal I made but I'm never going to forget your little sighs.'

It felt like they were talking about the end of all this, and Annie didn't want to talk about that. Not yet. So she wrapped her arms around him and kissed him again and again, sure that she would never get her fill because somehow the boy she'd thought was just a dumb jock was actually a sweet man who could make her laugh and who loved his mom and memories of baking with his grandpa and who still had a stuffed polar bear on his bed. Everything she learned about Mac made her want to hold on to him for a little bit longer.

Chapter Twenty

Now

Annie's hands were putting flowers on the tables, and her head was nodding at whatever it was Kira and Daisy were talking about, but her eyes were tracking Mac's movement through the barn. He'd put his brand-new kittens back in their box, tucking them in with an extra tablecloth when he went outside to help Bennett haul some fresh-cut Christmas trees, but now that the trees were in position and dried off from the snow, he had one kitten tucked in the crook of his arm and the other peeking out from his coat pocket. It was absurd in its cuteness. He was up to something. That much was obvious.

Mac laughed at something Bennett said, the rich sound echoing through the barn. He stopped his work on the lights to pet the head of the orange kitten, opening his pocket a little to check on it. He was really laying it on thick today. First, insisting on driving her up here, and now adopting kittens?! It was diabolical. Not to mention his threat about not leaving women *unsatisfied*. The memory of the way he'd said that continued to send shivers through her body.

He'd nearly kissed her by the truck. She could still feel the imprint of his fingers on the back of her neck. Mac was making his move, and she wasn't sure if she wanted to stop him.

Even though she should. She definitely should.

'Annie, you think that's a good idea?'

'Huh? What? Yeah, that's a great idea,' Annie answered, her eyes still on Mac until she heard Kira and Daisy giggling beside her.

'What?' she snapped.

'I asked you if you thought it was a good idea for us to cartwheel down the aisle tomorrow instead of walking,' Kira said.

'That was low.'

'You've been stalking that man with your eyes all night. I feel like I'm watching a nature documentary and you're about to pounce,' Kira said with a laugh.

'Oh, shut up,' Annie said, giving her friend a playful shove. 'It's not my fault! The damn man has kittens in his pockets!' Kira laughed harder and Annie snorted as she tried to stifle her own laughter. It didn't work.

'What *is* going on between you two?' Daisy asked.

'Nothing.' Annie knew her answer was too quick and too sharp to be believable.

Daisy raised her eyebrows. 'Really? Because we have a bet going at the flower shop and I would love to have the inside scoop.'

'A bet? I want in on that action! I bet the whole farm that these two end up in bed together by the end of this wedding,' Kira said.

Annie shook her head. 'You're going to lose that one. There's no way.' Even as she said it, Mac's words echoed in her ears. *I don't leave women unsatisfied.* A threat and a promise all in one.

'But seriously,' Daisy said, 'there's history between you two, right?'

'It's all very mysterious,' Kira said, arranging the plates on the table. 'She doesn't talk about it.'

'It's not mysterious,' Annie said with a huff. 'It's ancient history and it doesn't matter anymore.'

'If it doesn't matter, then why is that man looking at you like he wouldn't mind being your prey?' Kira asked with a grin.

Daisy sighed. 'He really is. But that's the sort of look that's gotten me into trouble twice already. If I was you, I'd look away.'

'You can't give up on love forever,' Kira said, her gaze lingering dreamily on Bennett across the room. He was currently explaining to Mac why it was impossible to have too many lights on a Christmas tree.

'My attempts at love have hurt not only my heart but my business, so I'm done trying,' Daisy said, thumping another arrangement of flowers on the table. The cream and maroon flowers that Jeanie had picked were artfully arranged in low vases, so they didn't obstruct conversation across the table. They were gorgeous.

Daisy was incredibly talented.

And a teensy bit cursed. Or at least according to the

town she was. Annie happened to know, as did everyone else, that Daisy had not only an ex-husband but an ex-fiancé. It didn't help matters that the last three weddings she'd provided flowers for led to marriages that had ended within a year.

'Are people still refusing to use your shop for weddings?' Kira asked.

The three of them had moved on to the next table and were arranging tall white candles around the pine boughs and flowers.

Daisy let out another exhausted sigh. 'It's been only funerals for me for the past six months and frankly not enough people are dying around here.'

'That's ridiculous.' Daisy lamenting the lack of death in Dream Harbor had Annie biting down on a smile, but it was obviously a serious problem if it was hurting her business. The funny thing was, the woman looked perfectly suited for the funeral business. Annie had never seen her in anything but black, even down to her fingernails. It was like she was trying to appear as opposite from her sunshine-y name as possible.

Daisy shrugged. 'I thought so at first, but I don't know. Maybe it's true. Maybe I am cursed, and now it's rubbing off on everybody else.' She glanced around the room, apparently remembering what they were in the middle of doing. 'I'm sure it's nothing, though. I mean, I'm sure Jeanie and Logan will be fine.'

Annie rolled her eyes. 'Those two are obsessed with each other. There's no way even a curse would pull them apart. I'm not worried.'

Daisy gave her a weak smile. 'Well, I do appreciate you recommending me to Jeanie.'

If Annie could help the fools in this town see that Daisy was talented and in no way responsible for the end of other people's marriages, then she was happy to do it.

'Of course! Your flower arrangements are the best. It's silly to waste them on dead people.' A laugh burst from Kira's lips at that remark and all three women were quickly giggling again.

'What's so funny over there?' Bennett asked from across the barn.

'Just the usual girl talk,' Kira called back. 'Nature documentaries and funerals.'

To his credit, Bennett didn't even look surprised at that answer. 'Come over here and let us know what you think.'

The three women finished up the last table and joined Bennett and Mac. They'd managed to arrange a half dozen fresh Christmas trees to create a backdrop for the ceremony. They'd covered them in white lights and, when Bennett flipped off the overhead lights, the effect was magical.

'It's beautiful,' Daisy whispered.

It really was.

Annie looked around at the work they'd done tonight. The wood rafters of the barn were covered in white, twinkle lights. Annie was pretty sure there were even more than there had been the night before and they made the room glow with golden light. White chairs stood in rows flanking the aisle and at the end of each was a white lantern with candles inside. On the other side of the barn were a dozen round tables, each draped in a cream-colored tablecloth with Daisy's beautiful centerpieces in the middle, moody reds and dark greens; like Christmas but sexier.

The gingerbread house was on a table in the corner with a curtain in front of it, to keep it a surprise for the groom and the guests. Tomorrow, the table beside it would be filled with cookies and cupcakes fresh from the bakery.

Everything looked perfect.

Jeanie was going to love it. Annie wiped her eyes with the back of her hand.

'Crying already?' Mac asked, appearing beside her.

Annie sniffled. 'I can't help it. It's just ... I love those two! And I'm really happy for them.'

'So, are you ready to go?' Mac's voice was a low rumble in her ear. When had he gotten so close?

'I should probably make sure Kira doesn't need anything...'

'Kira is just fine,' Kira said, butting into the conversation. 'You are free to go.' She gave Annie a devious smile. Annie would remember this. She'd make sure Kira got stuck talking to whatever offensive relatives Jeanie and Bennett happen to have in attendance tomorrow.

'See, there you go,' Mac said. 'We're dismissed.'

And there was that hand again on the small of her back leading her toward the door. She should really tell him to knock that off. She wanted to protest but she also didn't want to inconvenience Bennett and Kira by sticking around.

'Daisy, do you need a ride?' she called, in a last-ditch effort to not be trapped alone with Mac.

'No, I'm good. I drove my truck and I'm not far from here.'

Damn Daisy and her four-wheel drive. Mac was

smirking at her when she caught a glimpse of him from the corner of her eye. Definitely up to something.

Bundled into the passenger seat with the box of kittens on her lap, Annie felt like when they were teenagers all over again. She felt out of control, her body feeling things she had never given it permission to feel.

But also like when they were teenagers, she felt ready to give into it all. Give it all up to Mac, consequences be damned.

'I thought we could go to my place first and get the kittens settled in. It's closer,' he said, getting into the truck. It was a stupid excuse and made no sense, but Annie found herself agreeing. The kittens needed settling. Obviously. They'd had a traumatic few days.

She needed to go back to Mac's for the kittens' sake.

Chapter Twenty-One

Then

'I think we should have sex.'

Mac nearly choked on his French fry.

'You think we should...' He couldn't bring himself to finish the sentence. He had clearly misheard her.

'Have sex,' Annie helpfully supplied, stealing a fry from his plate. She had ordered the chocolate-chip pancakes, but somehow in the weeks that they'd been hanging out, it had become normal for her to steal some of whatever he had ordered. Like it had become normal for them to meet in this same booth at the diner to make their plans for the day. Somehow, in just a few weeks, he and Annie had become normal.

'Shh...' Mac said, glancing at the other diners. 'You can't just say things like that!'

Annie laughed. 'What? Are you afraid of the town elders hearing or something?'

'Kinda, yeah.'

She shook her head like he was being ridiculous, but the last thing he needed was for his mother's mah-jongg group to hear him discuss his sex life out in public.

'Hear me out,' she said, as though he needed to be convinced to have sex with the girl he couldn't stop thinking about, the girl he loved kissing and hanging out with. Of *course* he didn't need convincing, but Annie was already in full argument-mode. It made Mac think that if this bakery thing didn't work out, she should consider lawyering.

'First of all, I think we have established that we are physically compatible,' she said, laying the arguments out on her fingers. Mac grinned. They had proven that several times over the past week. Making out with Annie had become his new favorite thing to do. In fact, his whole drive-cross-country-to-find-himself plan would be unnecessary if the thing he could be was the guy who kissed Annie.

'Secondly,' she went on, 'I know you were worried about making rash decisions in the heat of the moment that I might regret, but this is something I have given a lot of thought to over the past few days and I have decided it's a good idea.'

Mac's brain tripped over the image of Annie thinking about them having sex. Sure, he had been thinking about it pretty much nonstop, but to know she had been thinking about it, too, was a whole new level of hot.

'And third,' she said, ready to drive her argument home as though Mac wasn't ready to drag her out of this booth and back to his bed already. 'We are working with a limited timeline, and if we only have a few more days together then this is what I want to do.'

Mac felt himself deflate. She'd brought up the one thing they had been avoiding, the fact that he still planned on leaving after the New Year. Not that he'd managed to tell his parents yet but that was another thing he was very specifically not thinking about.

There was a ticking clock on this thing between him and Annie, and he knew that, but more and more, Mac found himself wondering what would happen if there wasn't? What if he stayed? Would he and Annie continue on like this? Would she still want to see him?

'What do you think?' Annie asked, stealing another fry. She wasn't meeting his eye anymore. The bravery she'd had during her fully planned argument seemed to have left her for the moment and now she looked nervous. And what was Mac supposed to say? No, I don't think we should have sex because I'm worried that, if we do, I'll get even more attached to you, and then how will I leave?

Or yes, we absolutely should, because I have also been thinking about it nonstop and I know that I will one hundred percent regret it if I leave town without being with you in every way possible?

Neither option sounded like the response of a sane and reasonable person. This thing between them was supposed to be to kill some time before the holiday. He couldn't go saying crazy things like that. And he really didn't know how Annie would react to any of it. All he knew was that Annie was a woman with a plan and, if this was how he fit into it, then who was he to turn it down?

Sex with a beautiful, funny, smart girl? Mac never

claimed to be the brightest bulb in the box, but even he could figure out the answer to this one.

In the end he was saved from having to say anything at all.

'Annie, there you are!' A girl with curly hair and glasses who looked vaguely familiar to Mac came up to the table. 'People that are alive answer their texts!' she said. 'I've been trying you all morning. I ended up stopping by your house and Charlotte told me you were here with your new boyfriend.' It was then that the girl's attention switched from Annie's surprised face to Mac.

'Hey,' he said, fairly sure he was supposed to know who this girl was. They'd probably gone to school together, but he honestly couldn't remember, which was probably part of why Annie always thought he was an asshole.

'Hi,' the girl said, looking confused and then turning back to Annie. 'What's going on?' she whispered, as though Mac couldn't hear her.

Annie gave a strained smile. 'Hazel, you're back! I was just grabbing some breakfast, and I ran into Mac. Remember Mac?'

Hazel's gaze flicked between the two of them like she was still trying to figure out why Annie would be sitting with him. She looked like she would have been less surprised to see Annie eating with a chimp.

Mac thought maybe they'd had Art together for a semester or maybe English? He still couldn't quite place it. The whole thing reminded him that, apparently, he and Annie had attended entirely different high schools.

'Of course I remember Mac,' Hazel said. 'We had PE together for three years.'

'That's what it was!' he said, smacking a hand on the table. 'PE!'

Hazel blinked and Annie cleared her throat, giving him a pointed look to shut up. 'Right, you're old PE buddies. Anyway, what are you doing here?'

'I came to find you. We were supposed to go Christmas shopping today. Remember?'

Annie winced and Mac thought she must be so tired of Christmas shopping at this point. He had dragged her to every shop, mall, and Christmas fair within a fifty-mile radius, all just so he could spend more time with her.

'I'm so sorry, Hazel. I completely forgot, but we're about done here anyway, right, Mac?' she said, her eyes pleading with him as though he might reveal to Hazel everything they'd been up to for the past month.

'We're all set here,' he said, giving Annie a smile he hoped showed no hard feelings. He got it. Their temporary bubble had burst. Fun was over.

'Oh, good!' Hazel said with a relieved smile. 'Because Logan's on his way, too.'

Annie was looking more uncomfortable by the minute as though she'd been caught doing something she shouldn't have. It kinda sucked to be the thing she shouldn't have been doing.

'I have to get going anyway,' he said, grabbing his jacket and sliding out from the booth.

'You don't have to go,' she said, but he did. Annie didn't want to explain this temporary thing to her friends, and he didn't want to force her hand. There was really no need to. Why explain a thing that was ending?

'No, I really should go, but thanks for breakfast,' he said. 'Have fun shopping.'

'Yeah, okay,' she said, her gaze holding his even as Hazel slid into the booth beside her.

'Oh, my gosh,' Hazel said as he walked away. 'What on Earth were you doing here with Mac Sullivan?'

Mac paused on his way to the door, dying to hear Annie's answer.

'We kind of bumped into each other,' Annie said.

'Wow! I'm surprised you even talked to him.'

'Why would you be surprised about that?' Annie asked, and Mac strained to hear the rest of the conversation over the clang of dishes and conversation around him.

'Well, you never liked him,' he heard Hazel say and, even though he already knew that, it still stung to hear, especially now that so much had changed. 'You always said he was overrated.'

Mac nearly laughed out loud. That certainly sounded like something Annie would say.

'Turns out maybe he's not so bad,' Annie said. It wasn't exactly a declaration of love, but it was something, being not so bad. Maybe that was all he was going to get.

'But I'm so glad you're home.' Mac glanced back one more time to see Annie's arm slung around Hazel's shoulder, the two girls' heads tipped together. Her people were back. Maybe Annie didn't need him anymore.

Maybe that was for the best. He needed to start his life. He needed to get out of here before he ended up pouring pints at his dad's pub for the rest of his life and never figuring out what he actually wanted.

It was time to move on.

From Annie. From Dream Harbor.

Mac needed to go.

'There's Logan,' Hazel said, waving him over to Annie and Mac's table, except it wasn't hers and Mac's table anymore because he had left and she had let him. She didn't feel good about that, but she had been caught totally off-guard by Hazel. She'd completely forgotten her friend had come home yesterday. They'd been texting all month, of course, but somehow the days had gotten away from her. It was like her two worlds collided and suddenly she was back in reality. The reality in which she and her friends had never once hung out with Mac and his friends. She could tell by the look on his face that he had no idea who Hazel was, despite the fact that they had all gone to school together for the past four years, because guys like Mac didn't notice girls like Hazel and Annie.

But he had noticed her. And it was nice, and she *liked* him now.

What the hell had she done?

'Hey,' Logan said, plopping into the seat across from them.

'You're back! How was the cruise?' Annie asked, pushing her confusion about Mac aside. Now was not the time to sort that out. She was finally reunited with her two favorite people in the world.

Logan grimaced 'Well, it was far too long to be trapped on a ship with several thousand senior citizens.'

The sunburn across his nose and cheeks had started to

peel and his normally brown hair had taken on golden highlights.

'Quit complaining! While you were lounging in the tropical sunshine, I've been here freezing my butt off.'

Logan's frown deepened. 'There were nightly events,' he said.

'Sounds fun.'

'With themes.'

'I love a good theme.'

'And dress codes. People wore costumes.' He said it like there were nightly, virgin sacrifices or something.

'Did you dress up?' Annie asked, knowing damn well there was no way Logan put on a costume or remotely theme-appropriate outfit.

'Of course not.'

'Of course not. That would be too fun.'

'Fun for children and criminals on the lam.'

'Do you think criminals on the lam are having fun?'

'Until they get caught, maybe.'

'You're a good grandson,' Hazel cut in, knowing from experience that this conversation could go on and on for hours and get them absolutely nowhere. 'I'm sure you made Nana very happy.'

Logan grimaced. 'She had to argue my way onto the boat in the first place.'

Annie laughed. 'What do you mean?'

'It was a senior's cruise. No one under the age of fifty-five was supposed to be on board. We showed up with our tickets and Nana had to fight with the captain to let me on.'

Now Hazel was laughing, too. 'She did?!'

'Yeah,' Logan said, shaking his head, a smile slipping

onto his face. 'She started by trying to convince him that I just looked really good for my age.'

'No!' Annie squealed, delighted.

'Yes,' Logan groaned at the memory.

'Then she threatened to go to the media and accuse the cruise company of ageism.'

'Ha! Incredible. Nana is a queen.'

'She ended up telling him that I needed to be there to make sure she took her meds on time. Which is hilarious considering she is healthier than I am. But the captain just wanted her to stop causing a scene at that point.'

'I bet. Nana causing a scene is a scary thing,' Annie said.

'For the rest of the trip she called me "Nurse" any time there was a staff member nearby.'

The image of Logan as a nurse sent Annie and Hazel's giggles into full-blown, side-splitting laughter.

'Ha. Ha. I'm so glad you find my pain hilarious.'

'We really do. Thanks for the laugh,' Annie said, wiping the tears from her eyes with the back of her hand.

'Anytime,' Logan said dryly.

'And what about you, Haze? How did the semester go?'

'It was good, but I'm happy to be home.'

'And we're happy you're back.' Annie pulled her in closer.

'What have you been up to while we were gone?' Logan asked and Hazel's face immediately lit up.

'I caught Annie having a romantic lunch with Mac Sullivan,' she said.

'First of all—' Annie started, and Logan rolled his eyes.

'Here we go,' he muttered.

Annie ignored him. 'First of all,' she said again. 'There

was nothing romantic about it. We're at the diner, for goodness' sake. My dentist is sitting two booths over.'

'What? Dentists can't go to romantic places?' Logan asked.

'And, secondly,' Annie went on, ignoring him again. 'Am I not allowed to hang out with other people when you two abandoned me?'

'Abandon you?!' Hazel gasped in mock horror. 'Is that what we did?'

'I'm pretty sure you were the one that told me I had to go on this cruise, or I would break my grandmother's heart.'

'Yeah, and you told me I had to get out and explore the world. You filled out the paperwork!'

Annie took a sip from her third mug of cocoa of the morning. 'Whatever, we're back together now.'

'And what about Mac?' Hazel asked.

Annie shrugged. 'What about Mac?'

'Well, are you two going to keep seeing each other?'

'You're blowing this way out of proportion. We weren't *seeing* each other. We were just, you know, seeing each other around while our friends were out of town. You know, pre-holiday boredom and everything.'

Hazel looked highly suspicious, and Logan looked completely disinterested scratching at the peeling skin on his nose.

'It's irrelevant anyway,' Annie said. 'Mac is leaving soon.' She shrugged it off like it didn't matter, like she didn't care where Mac went or what he did, because that was how she should feel. It was true what she told Hazel; they had just been hanging out while they waited for life to get back to normal. But, somewhere along the line, being with Mac had started to feel normal and it had Annie wishing for things that couldn't be.

It had her thinking about what she'd been asking him for right before Hazel showed up. He hadn't answered her. Maybe she'd taken things a step too far. But … she found herself wanting it anyway.

'Okay,' Hazel said. 'If you say so. He is really cute, though…'

Annie shrugged like she hadn't experienced that cuteness up close and personal for the last few weeks, as though she hadn't gotten to kiss and touch that cuteness and she really wanted to have even more of it. 'Yeah, I know.'

'Wait,' Logan said, looking up from his omelet. 'Mac's cute?'

Annie nodded. 'Some might even call him hot.' Someone like her.

Logan frowned. 'But not as cute as me, right?'

She and Hazel both groaned, chucking straw wrappers and balled-up napkins at Logan as he swatted them away, a stupid grin on his face. God, she'd missed these two.

'All right, that's enough discussing Macaulay Sullivan for one day,' Annie said. 'Let's go shopping. And we need more details, Haze. I want to know everything!'

Unfortunately for Annie, not talking about Mac didn't mean she wasn't thinking about Mac. As she roamed the stores with her friends, all she could think about was the time she had spent doing the same with Mac. About the way he had put his hand on the small of her back to guide her through the crowds or the time he had her giggling so hard she nearly peed as he recreated the terrified face he'd made in nearly every picture he'd had taken with Santa as a child. Or how he would kiss her goodbye when he dropped her off at her house at the end of the night. Somehow it wasn't *nothing*. Hanging out with Mac had turned into a big giant something and Annie didn't know what to do about it.

All she did know was that she had to see him. She had to see him and tell him that the past few weeks had meant something to her. Even if he was leaving. She wanted him to know.

And she wanted to apologize for ditching him today.

And she wanted to kiss him.

And more.

Chapter Twenty-Two

Now

Somehow, Mac had convinced Annie to come back to his place to settle in his new pets. He wasn't really sure how he'd managed it. Frankly, Annie had been more agreeable today than she'd been in the past three years, but Mac wasn't about to question it.

He glanced over at the passenger seat to where Annie was sitting with the kittens on her lap. She was talking to them in a voice he was sure she only used on fluffy animals and babies. He'd certainly never heard it before.

'Now don't you worry,' she was saying. 'This is just temporary. We'll find you a good home soon.'

'Who said it was temporary?' Mac said and Annie looked up at him in surprise.

She rolled her eyes. 'You can stop playing the hero now,' she said. 'We're the only ones here.'

Mac scoffed. 'Why do you always assume the worst of

me? What did I ever do that makes you think I would abuse kittens?'

'I never said you would abuse them! But you can stop pretending that you're going to adopt these cats. Kira and Daisy aren't around anymore, so I'm just saying you can drop the animal rescuer act.'

'I'm keeping those cats,' he said more forcefully than he was expecting to. Sure, he'd said he'd take them in some ill-conceived plan to get on Annie's good side, but he'd be damned if she was going to know that. 'They're my cats now.'

He could feel Annie's stare boring into the side of his face, but he kept his eyes on the road. He was tired of her always thinking the worst of him. He knew he'd hurt her, but he was done being the villain in Annie's story.

'Well, what are you going to name them, then?' she said after a minute. 'If these are your cats, they'll need names.'

'Easy. I'll name them … Bert and Ernie.'

'Bert and Ernie, no way.'

'Why not?! That's a classic duo name.'

'No. Veto that.'

'And why do you get veto power over my pets' names?'

'I'm looking out for the best interest of the cats; and Kira says one is a boy and one is a girl. She's practically a vet at this point, so I think we can trust her.'

'I highly doubt the cats care if their names match their sex assigned at birth, but if you insist, how about Sonny and Cher?'

'Nope, try again.'

'Adam and Eve.'

Annie burst out laughing at that one. 'You're going to

call this adorable little kitten Adam?' she said between giggles.

Mac smiled at the sound.

'Well, what do you suggest since you're such a pet-naming expert, despite the fact that you currently have zero pets?'

'I don't think you need a duo name just because there's two of them,' she said, humming a little as she thought. 'Christmas-y names would be cute.'

'Like what? Rudolph and Frosty?'

'No, something a little less on the nose. Oh, I got it!' she said. 'How about Holly and Claus? Get it?! Claws like cats have claws, and Santa Claus.'

Mac couldn't help his laugh. 'That's actually pretty good,' he said.

Annie sat back in her seat pleased with herself. 'Well, there you go, Holly and Claus. At least your pets have good names now.' He wasn't sure which one she'd named which.

'See,' he said, 'I'm not all bad.' He meant to say it teasingly, not really wanting to get into it with her again, but the words hung heavy between them.

'I know you're not. I'm sorry I do that. I'm sorry I still assume the worst about you. It's an old habit,' she said quietly, petting Holly or Claus's little head.

'Maybe we need a fresh start,' he said.

'How do we do that now? I've known you since I was five years old, Mac, and the one time I opened myself up to you, I got crushed in the process, so I'm not really sure how we start over. Or if we can.'

Mac swallowed hard. That was more than Annie had said about what happened between them the whole time since he'd been back. Just this morning she told him she wasn't hurt, that she didn't need his apologies. It had been the same for years.

Crushed. She said she'd been crushed by what he did. It was so much worse than her pretending she was fine. To hear her admit how he'd made her feel, to have it out in the open, what was he supposed to do now? Who was he to ask for a second chance?

This day had completely fucked with his head, and he didn't know anymore if he was asking for a second chance or for hate-sex to end this once and for all.

'Do they still do the light tour?' he asked instead.

'Yeah, of course. It's one of the biggest fundraisers of the year,' Annie said, sounding relieved at the change of topic. 'I haven't had a chance to go this year though.'

'Why not?'

'Been too busy.'

Too busy doing things for other people. He knew that was the case. He took a left into one of the neighborhoods before his.

'Where are we going?' Annie asked, looking up from the kittens in her lap.

Mac shrugged. 'I thought we could take the scenic route instead, you know, so you can see some of the lights you missed.' He hated that she'd missed one of her favorite traditions.

A pleased smile crossed her face in the darkness, and he thought, between this mini light tour and the kittens in her lap, maybe he was making some progress. While he had her trapped here with him in the car, he was damn well going to take the opportunity to show her how much he still cared about her. For all he knew, after this weekend she could go right back to avoiding him like the plague.

God, he hoped that wasn't what happened.

'Oh, that's new!' Annie said, pointing to a particularly garish light-up snowman display.

'It's certainly bright. You can probably see it from space.'

She laughed and he wanted to bottle the sound.

'Oh, look at that one.' She pointed across his body to a house on the left and it reminded him of when they were kids on that tour, the way she'd leaned into him, the way he hadn't wanted it to end.

She didn't move all the way back to her side of the car and instead stayed close to him, her shoulder nearly pressing against his. She smelled like frosting and ginger and Mac barely contained his groan. He *wanted* her.

Whatever she was willing to give.

He wanted it.

The snow was still falling in thick white flakes and Nat King Cole crooned a Christmas classic on the radio. The truck was warm, the windshield fogging over in between swipes of the wipers. They drove slowly around the block, admiring the light displays as they went. It had been years since Mac did anything like this. He slid his gaze to Annie's face, watching her delight in her neighbors' efforts.

She was so fucking beautiful.

'How about that one?' He pointed to a house with white icicle lights on the porch and a candle lit in each window.

'Understated. I like it.'

Mac smiled in the darkness.

'How about that one?' Annie pointed.

'Too blue for me.'

'You've gotten picky with lights in your old age,' she teased, nudging him a little with her shoulder. The warmth of her seeped into him. He wished she would stay pressed against him in the dark.

'I learned a lot about myself while I was away,' he said. 'But one of the main things was that I like my Christmas décor understated.'

'Wow, you really did some deep thinking out there on the road. It's a good thing you stayed away for so long, I guess.' And just like that the mood in the car shifted again. Annie moved away from him, back to her seat, and turned her gaze out her window.

Would they ever be able to be near each other without digging up the past?

He'd been joking about the Christmas decorations, but it *was* a good thing that he'd been gone so long. He sorted out a lot of stuff while he was away. Learned a lot about himself, what he wanted from life. When he came back to Dream Harbor, it was because he wanted to, not because he was born here, not because he was stuck here, or because it was his only option. He needed to experience life outside of Dream Harbor before he could appreciate life in it.

But if he said any of that, he knew it would come out wrong. That all Annie would hear was that he was glad he left her.

They drove the rest of the way without speaking. The only sounds were the quiet mewing of the cats and the windshield wipers pushing the snow from the window. Sometimes, he wondered that if he had done things differently, would there still be a chance for him and Annie? He didn't regret leaving but he hated the way he'd left.

Chapter Twenty-Three

Then

'I 've gathered you here today to discuss an important matter,' Mac said, glancing from his mom to his dad. He hadn't actually gathered them anywhere. He'd waylaid them at the dinner table.

'Mac, what is this about?' his dad said, already looking impatient. His father was not a man who liked to be waylaid. Mac rarely ever even saw him sit down.

Mac folded his hands on the table in front of him and then unfolded them and then folded them again. His palms were damp. He'd had a whole speech planned but now, with his mother 's worried face and his father already looking antsy, Mac's preparedness went right out the window.

'But first, a gift!' He was totally stalling but he and Annie had finally tracked down the perfect gift for his mom and now felt like the right time to give it to her. He set the gift bag on the table.

'An early Christmas present?' his mom asked. She looked skeptical which, after the gifts he'd given her over the years, she had every right to be.

'Yep. For you.' He pushed the bag toward her.

She pulled out the tissue paper that Annie had insisted he put in, saying it didn't count as wrapping without it, until she got to the hand-carved Nativity scene he'd found at a craft fair. It was Annie who'd noticed that his mom had several scenes around the house, and when he saw this one, he knew it was the perfect gift.

'Mac, it's lovely,' his mom said. 'Thank you.'

Mac breathed a sigh of relief. He'd nailed it, which was good because now was the hard part.

'I also wanted to talk to you about … you know … the future. Uh … my future, specifically.'

His mom looked hopeful at that. 'Have you finally decided to enroll at the community college? They have a great nursing program.'

Mac sighed. He was positive he would be a terrible nurse. He didn't have his mother's patience or her iron stomach.

'No, that's not really what I was thinking…'

'Well, we could use you for more hours down at the pub,' his dad said, and the suffocating feeling in Mac's chest grew. He knew his dad would love it if he worked more hours pouring pints or serving food and eventually take over more of the business side of things, but the pub was his dad's dream. Not his. At least he didn't think it was.

Mac shook his head. That was the whole problem.

He still didn't know *what* he wanted and, faced with the expectations of his parents, he already felt himself slipping into old habits. It would be easy to make his mom happy and enroll in school or to take some of the workload off his dad. Mac liked easy. He liked being liked. He liked it when his parents were happy with him, and his teammates were cheering for him, and his buddies were congratulating him on a game well-played. But this wasn't some stupid lacrosse game and Mac couldn't keep picking the easy thing.

He thought of Annie and how hard she was working on getting her business started, how she told him she was taking classes and trying out new recipes and setting up a table at every farmers' market, festival and fair in the county on the weekends. Mac had never worked that hard on anything in his life.

'No, that's not what I was thinking, either,' he said and now he really had both parents' attention.

'What did you have in mind?' his mom asked.

And he knew he owed her an explanation. He owed her a plan. He owed her everything, really, for raising him, taking care of him and making his life incredibly easy for nineteen years. His dad, too. He'd given Mac his first job. He would have given him a job for the rest of his life if Mac wanted it.

But Mac didn't want it. Not yet anyway. He needed to go somewhere else, *anywhere* else. He would never grow into the person he was meant to be if he continued to let his parents do everything for him. He needed to grow up. And he couldn't do that here. Not with his kindergarten teacher still watching his behavior or his mom's friends reporting back to her on who he was dating. Or girls like Annie thinking he was just some dumb jock. He was pretty sure he'd changed her mind about that, but still.

The town already thought they knew who Macaulay Sullivan was but he'd kinda like to figure it out for himself.

'Actually, I am going to do some traveling.'

His father scoffed like Mac had suggested space exploration. 'Traveling?'

'What do you mean? You're going on a trip with some friends?' his mom asked.

'No.' Mac squirmed in his seat. No was not a word he liked to say to his mother. 'No, I plan on traveling for a while across the country. I need to figure some things out. I have money saved up and…'

'What the hell do you need to figure out?' his father barked.

'I need to figure out what I want. What I'm doing with my life.'

'College is a great place to figure things out,' his mom chimed in, and Mac felt like his head might explode. They'd had this conversation so many times.

Mac shook his head. 'College isn't for me, Mom. I need to get out in the world, you know?'

'Everything you have here isn't enough for you?' his dad said, his voice rising.

'That's not what I'm saying.'

'It sure sounds like it's what you're saying. After everything your mother and I do for you, it's not enough.'

'That's not it! I just need to be on my own.'

'And you need to travel across the country to do that? There are plenty of apartments right here in town.

You could stay close and work at the pub and be here for your mother.'

'Mom doesn't need me!'

'The hell she doesn't!'

They were both standing and yelling now. Mac's plan for a rational discussion was long gone.

'I need to get the hell out of this town!'

'Running away doesn't make you an adult.'

'I'm not running away,' Mac said, the fight going out of him. Was his dad right? Was he running away? Should he stay? Is that how he became an adult? He didn't know anymore but, when he took a breath and looked down at his mom, the tears in her eyes had him ready to scrap the whole idea.

He dropped back down to his seat and put his head in his hands. 'I just thought it would be good for me to be out on my own for a while. That's all. Mom?'

She gave him a weak smile, wiping the tears quickly from her face. 'Okay, baby,' she said. 'We'll talk about it more later. I need to get to mass.'

And with that she got up from the table and left Mac alone with his father. The older man let out a long sigh. 'She's going to miss you like crazy if you go,' he said.

'I'll miss you guys, too. But I feel like it's what I need to do.'

His dad gave a brusque nod. 'If that's what you feel like you need to do, I can't stop you.'

He gave Mac a rough pat on the back before heading out to work, leaving Mac drained and confused about whether his parents were angry with him or just sad to see him go. He didn't know anymore if this plan was worth it.

He took the torn piece of paper from his pocket that he and Annie had scribbled some ideas on at the diner that first day they hung out. He'd felt hopeful that day, like maybe this was something he could actually do, but maybe he'd been wrong. Maybe he should stay here in Dream Harbor. There were worse places to be stuck. He knew that he should be grateful.

But at the moment he only felt confined.

Trapped.

And more lost than ever.

Annie found herself on his doorstep that night full of nerves and excitement and uncertainty.

She was certain about only one thing.

'Mac,' she breathed when he opened the door, looking surprised and a little rumpled. His hair was messy like he'd been running his fingers through it. He had on a pair of old sweats and a stained lacrosse T-shirt which should have been good payback for him seeing her in her reindeer onesie, but of course he still looked far too hot and not at all ridiculous.

'Hey, Annie.' He winced a little. 'I wasn't expecting you.'

'Yeah, sorry, I probably should have texted you. I just…' She paused, sucking in a deep breath of cold night air, stealing herself with what little courage she had left. 'I just really wanted to see you.'

His face softened and he didn't say a word, just stepped out onto his cold front porch barefoot and messy, and wrapped his arms around her, lifting her off the ground.

He nuzzled his face in the crook of her neck, his breath warm on her skin.

'I really wanted to see you, too,' he said.

He held her like that for a long time like he needed to be close to her.

'Is something wrong?' she asked after a while, not wanting to break the moment but starting to get worried.

Mac sighed, setting her down. 'Not really. But I finally told my parents I'm leaving.'

'How did it go?'

He laughed a little, though there was no humor in it. 'Not great. My mother basically told me I was breaking her heart, and now she's at church, probably praying for me to change my mind.'

Annie winced. 'Yikes.'

'Yeah,' he said, 'but I'm really glad you're here.'

'You're not mad at me?'

'Should I be?'

'I kind of ditched you today.'

Mac shrugged. 'I guess we're even. I ditched you at the Christmas market.'

'True,' Annie said with a smile. 'So… Can I come in or are you going to make me stand out in the cold all night?'

Mac grinned 'You can come in. I've been thinking about your idea.'

'My idea?'

'Don't pretend you already forgot, Annabelle. You propositioned me for sex this morning.'

Annie's face got hot. 'That's not why I came. I really did just want to see you.'

She followed Mac into the house through the kitchen and down to his basement bedroom.

'So, the offer is off the table?' he asked, turning to face her.

'I didn't say that.' Her voice lowered to a whisper. 'I still want to do that with you.'

Mac blew out a sigh of relief. 'That's good.'

'It is?'

'Yeah,' he said. 'I haven't been able to stop thinking about it all day.' He stepped closer, putting a hand on her cheek, his thumb sweeping across her cheekbone. 'I haven't been able to stop thinking about you at all.'

'That sounds very time-consuming.'

Mac's lips curved into a smile. 'It is, but there are worse ways to spend my time.'

'And better ways,' Annie said, tipping her face up to his.

'Much, much better ways,' Mac agreed, lowering his lips to hers. 'Are you sure about this, Annie?' he asked.

She didn't know what would happen after this. She didn't have a plan for how to handle Mac or her feelings for him or him leaving. She didn't know about any of that.

But she was sure about this.

'Yes,' she whispered, and Mac kissed her again.

Chapter Twenty-Four

Now

Annie knew that Mac had bought his parents' old house, but somehow pulling up in the driveway still felt disorienting, as though she'd gone back in time.

'I was half expecting your mom to greet us when we came in,' she said as they shucked their boots and coats by the door.

Mac huffed a laugh. 'Yeah, I half expect it sometimes, too.'

'Do you miss them?'

'Yeah, of course I do. But it's my own fault. I guess I made traveling sound too good. Once I bought the pub, they got an RV and never looked back.'

'Never looked back, huh?' She knew that couldn't be true. He and his mom had always been so close.

'Other than the phone call I get from my mom every other day,' he said with a self-deprecating smile.

They walked through the entryway into the kitchen where Mac set the box of kittens on the island.

'Wow!' Annie said, spinning in a small circle. 'It looks really good in here.' The kitchen had been completely redone. It was sleek and clean, white cabinets and granite countertops. It helped her feeling of déjà vu subside. This was a new house and she and Mac were new people. They weren't kids anymore.

'We might have kitty litter out in the garage,' he said, rubbing the back of his head. 'I think my dad kept some in case we got stuck in the snow.' He moved around setting up things for the cats while Annie focused on petting them and not thinking about everything else she wanted to do with Mac in this shiny new kitchen. She was fifty-fifty on wanting to bake something and wanting to tear his clothes off with her teeth. Maybe they had time for both?

He set out a little dish with water and another with some tuna for the cats and Annie set them down on the floor. They immediately raced to the dishes, mewing happily and scarfed down their dinner.

'It was good of you to take them,' she said as they watched the little kitten's feast.

Mac shrugged. He wasn't watching the cats. When Annie looked up, his gaze was all for her.

By the time the kittens had eaten their fill and curled up in a little pile together, Annie thought she might need to spend some more time with her head in the freezer.

'Annie,' Mac's voice was gruff when he spoke. He was close to her again and she wished he would touch her.

'What are we doing?' she asked, desperate to get a handle on the situation, on herself, on anything. She was slipping again, falling for Mac, and last time it had taken her so long to get back up. Did she really want to do that again?

Mac's hand slid to the nape of her neck, his fingers strong and firm. She wanted to tell him to squeeze tighter, to hold onto her this time.

'Let me make it up to you,' he whispered.

She *wanted* to. She wanted him to make it up to her. All the years she hurt, all the years she missed him. She wanted him to make it up to her.

'What's it going to take, Annie? Do I need to get down on my knees for you?'

The question sent a shiver down her spine. Mac felt it and his eyes darkened. 'Is that what you want, Annabelle? You want me on my knees?'

She couldn't speak, her voice trapped in a throat that was tight with emotion and desire and fear.

'If that's what it takes,' he said, dropping to his knees in front of her. Annie sucked in a breath. She looked down and found him staring up at her. It was everything she had wanted for ten years. Mac begging for her forgiveness, Mac *wanting* her. The fantasy in her mind had gone back and forth between her rejecting him and Mac pleasuring her until she forgave him. It depended on her mood, and which mood was she in now?

Should she walk away like he had? Did she have it in her to reject him?

For so many years, she had thought she'd fallen in love with Mac and that he had fallen in love with her, but she'd been foolish and young and the whole thing had just been sex.

But she was older now. She knew sex with Mac didn't have to be anything other than that. It wouldn't mean love, but it didn't have to. Maybe she could finally get what she wanted from him.

She held his gaze, letting her fingers run through his hair, savoring the deep groan that rumbled through him. She gave a little tug. 'And how exactly are you going to make it up to me?' she asked.

A wicked grin crossed his face, his hands lifting to her hips. His fingertips dug into her flesh. 'I thought I would start by licking you until you scream.'

Chapter Twenty-Five

Then

Annie was in his bed, sweet and soft and naked. Trusting him, making those breathy little sighs.

She was here and he couldn't believe it.

She was here and he didn't want to let her go.

Mac was on top of her, surrounding her, his face above her so tender and worried, his forehead crinkled in concern. So, she kissed him and told him it was good.

She liked it.

Keep going.

Keep going.

It was perfect.

She pressed the words into his skin, his shoulder, his chest, his lips. She told him until he believed her.

It wasn't like his first time. That time felt like fooling around; this time didn't. This time felt like Annie had split him open, like she held his heart in her hands. It felt like he would gladly give it to her.

She wrapped her legs around his waist gazing up at him with big blue eyes. He didn't want to hurt her. Ever.

'You sure?' he asked her again.

'Yes,' she whispered. 'Yes, keep going.'

She murmured it over and over. *Keep going* and *yes* and *it's good* and *she liked it*. And he did. He pushed into her as gently as he could, holding himself back, going slow even though he felt like he might die from the effort.

Her little gasp stopped him in his tracks, but she smiled up at him, pulling him down for another kiss, whispering that she was okay against his mouth.

He hadn't hurt her. He wouldn't hurt her.

Ever.

Mac gasped her name in her hair, against her neck, his body moving with hers. She held on tight, loving the feel of him, firm and hot and strong on top of her. Inside of her.

She knew she could never regret this moment. It was too perfect.

Mac was too perfect.

She didn't want to let him go.

Chapter Twenty-Six

Now

Mac was on the ground in front of her, waiting. Waiting to see if Annie would reject him, push him away like she had every other time since he'd been back. He knew a little part of her wanted to. He knew Annie wanted revenge, but she had been punishing him for years and Mac was ready to repent for his sins.

The porcelain tile he'd chosen for his fancy new kitchen was digging into his knees and Annie's fingers were still tangled in his hair pulling just enough to sting. He waited, barely breathing, for her to turn him away.

'Okay,' she said, her voice a throaty whisper that made Mac's heart race and his cock stiffen.

'Okay? You're going to let me eat you out?' he asked, needing confirmation before he did something insane and ended up getting his ass kicked.

Annie clapped a hand over his mouth. 'Don't say it out

loud!' She gasped and Mac laughed, barely believing what he was hearing.

'I can do it, but I can't talk about it?'

'Yes, exactly. We don't need to talk about it.' She held his gaze. She didn't want to talk about any of it. She never did.

Mac would take it. He didn't know if this was a second chance or one last time or an apology, but he wanted it whatever it was. He wanted this moment with Annie.

No regrets this time. He wasn't going anywhere and, if Annie still wanted him after this, he'd be ready.

He leaned his forehead against her hip bone, breathing her in. Her little moan when he reached around and grabbed her ass made him glad he was already on his knees. That sound had haunted his dreams for over a decade.

'This ass is still perfect,' he said, his voice a low rumble.

'Mac.' Annie's voice was nearly a whine. Her legs were already trembling, and he hadn't even unbuttoned her pants yet.

Mac chuckled, looking up at her.

'Just do it,' she bit out, and it was so different from the last time when she had been gentle and nervous. When she'd kissed him and trusted him.

But this felt more honest. There would be no kissing this time. She didn't trust him anymore. He hadn't earned it yet. This time was to exorcise their demons. He undid the button on her jeans, tugging down the zipper, urged on by Annie's harsh breathing and the feel of her fingers digging into his scalp. He pushed the pants down over her hips and groaned at the sight of her tiny lace panties. A pale blue that left nothing to the imagination, a string of satin over her hip and around to a little lacy triangle in the back nestled right between the delectable curves of her ass.

'If you had been wearing these the first time, I wouldn't have made it past getting your pants off.'

'If this whole thing is going to be a compare and contrast to the last time...' Annie's voice trailed off as Mac kissed and nipped the flesh of her thighs.

'It's not,' he said. 'It won't be. But you should know you were perfect that first time and somehow, you're even better now.'

Another little gasp as he licked along the string over her hip. And then it didn't matter anymore what she had been like then because he was here with her now.

Annie wriggled the rest of the way out of her jeans. Mac helped tug them over her feet and toss them aside before going back to his task. He didn't know if he was a better man now, but he knew he was better at this than he was at nineteen. And, if nothing else came from this night, he was damn well going to settle the score.

'Hold on, darling,' he said, looking up at her one more time before he pushed those absurd panties aside. 'Jesus, Annie, you're so beautiful.'

Annie tugged tighter on his hair, little whimpers escaping her. He knew he was teasing her, but he didn't mean to. He had two regrets in his life: one was leaving this woman the way he had, and the other was not doing this the first time around. He wanted to savor it, now that he'd been granted a second chance.

He dug his fingers into her thigh and hooked her leg over his shoulder, opening her up to him.

'Mac,' Annie groaned, and the sound was so aggrieved

that he was smiling when he finally let his mouth dip to her center. One lick had Annie gasping and Mac groaning. Another and Annie's legs were shaking, and Mac thought he might die here on his kitchen floor with his head between her thighs.

But now was no time for dying. Mac was a man with something to prove.

Annie had thought about Mac a lot over the past decade, far too much, actually, and she had imagined similar scenarios to this one more times than she would ever admit. The fact that Mac was a frequent star in some of her most favorite fantasies was certainly not something she had ever said out loud. But this, this moment right here far surpassed anything she had imagined.

At some point she'd ended up with her back against the wall, her leg still draped over Mac's shoulder and his face still buried between her legs. He was licking and sucking and groaning like a man possessed. From somewhere outside of her body, Annie vaguely considered that his knees probably hurt from those tiles and that his scalp probably hurt from the way she was using his hair as reins to move his head where she wanted it. But Mac was undeterred.

Worship was the only word to describe what he was doing.

And he had been right. He was very good at this. She fully believed that he did not leave women unsatisfied. Annie felt a brief stab of jealousy at the thought of the other women he'd practiced this skill on, but mostly she was just thankful that he had.

'Mac,' she gasped, the pleasure building and he looked up at her, his eyes dark, his hair a mess beneath her fingers. He looked as wrecked as she felt. Unraveled. Unmoored. Maybe this was a mistake? How would they ever come back from this?

'Take it,' he said. 'Take what you want, Annie.' Mac's desperate plea brought her back to the present.

Take what you want. She wanted this, didn't she? Mac on his knees for her. She rolled her hips using Mac's tongue to get the exact pressure she needed. Mac groaned, the vibration adding to the sensations rioting through her.

'Do that again,' she bit out, unable to stop. She couldn't. Not now.

He did what she demanded, sending pleasure coursing through her body. His voice rumbled against her. Her heel dug into his back. Her toes curled. She was going to come like this, with Mac's mouth on her clit and his hands on her hips and her back against his wall. She was going to come with her heart a confused mess and Mac looking up at her like he wanted more. Like he was here, and he wanted everything.

'Again.' Annie rocked against him. And the pressure and tension and heat built inside of her. Another groan, another rock of her hips against Mac's perfect tongue and Annie was unraveling, the orgasm rolling over her in waves so intense she couldn't stand. She couldn't see, she couldn't think. Mac held her up, pinning her to the wall as he lapped every bit of pleasure from her body.

She was boneless, sliding down the wall as Mac was standing, scooping her up on his way.

'God, Annie,' he was saying, his voice next to her ear, but Annie could barely take it in. 'That was so amazing … so fucking beautiful,' he murmured against her skin as he lifted her up.

'What are you doing?' she asked even as she snuggled her face against his neck as he held her. 'I'm not staying here for the night,' she said as Mac carried her out of the kitchen.

'Okay, darling,' he said.

'I'm serious. I'm not staying.' Annie's voice was drifting closer to a whisper, exhaustion overtaking her. She'd been working so hard on this wedding and on her business and on resisting Mac. She didn't think she could do it all anymore. And it was so *nice* in his arms. Maybe she could give in just for tonight.

Even as she claimed she wasn't staying, Mac was carrying her upstairs. She'd never been upstairs, and her curiosity woke her up a bit. He carried her into the first room on the right.

'Is this your parents' old room?' she asked as he lowered her onto the bed.

'No, I turned two of the smaller bedrooms into one bigger one for me. It seemed too weird to take my parents' room.'

Annie nodded. That would be weird. The room was a good size, but Mac's enormous bed took up most of it.

'This bed is huge,' she said, running a hand over the plaid bedspread.

Mac shrugged. 'I like to spread out.' He turned and started rummaging through his closet.

The rest of the room was tidy but lived in, a leather chair in the corner was draped in a small pile of shirts and the dresser had a coffee mug from this morning still sitting on it. Little details of Mac's life that Annie never thought she'd see. The walls were a moody, navy blue, but one was covered in colorful framed postcards and travel posters, reminders of all the years he was gone. Annie refused to think about the packet of postcards she still had under her bed, the ones she should have gotten rid of a long time ago.

Mac emerged from his closet and tossed Annie a pair of sweatpants and an old lacrosse T-shirt. 'You can wear these.'

'I'm not staying,' Annie repeated, tugging on the pants. She couldn't cram herself back into her jeans at this hour.

'Okay,' Mac said, still looking at her like he wanted to keep her. It was unnerving.

'I'm glad you moved out of the basement.'

'Yeah?' he said.

'Yeah, I mean it was cool when we were teenagers, but a grown man living in the basement would be kind of creepy. Wouldn't be a great place to bring women.'

'I'm glad you're concerned about where I might bring women,' Mac said with a smirk, leaning against the door frame of the closet.

'Turn around,' Annie said, holding up the shirt. She resisted the urge to bury her face in it and inhale.

'Why?'

'So I can change.'

Mac stared at her. 'Annie I was just face to face with your—'

'Do not finish that sentence.'

Mac let out a low laugh of disbelief.

'Turn around,' Annie insisted.

He shook his head but complied, turning to face the wall.

'Just because we did *that*,' Annie said, 'doesn't mean anything else changes between us.'

'Oh, really?' Mac said, addressing the wall.

'Yeah, really. We were only blowing off some steam, relieving tension. It was basically like doing yoga or going for a run.'

Mac scoffed. 'Wow, Annabelle, you sure know how to make a guy feel good.'

Annie pulled the shirt over her head, relieved to be out of her sweater and bra. It had been an incredibly long day and Mac's shirt was soft and worn and smelled just like him.

'I'm not here to make you feel good.' She said it to remind herself as much as him.

Mac snorted. 'Well, joke's on you because that made me feel pretty darn good.'

Annie felt the heat rise to her cheeks and was glad Mac was still facing the wall. She was sure her face would give away exactly what she was feeling. And what she was feeling was highly ill-advised.

'And it sure sounded like it made you feel good, too,' he said, running a hand through his hair. Annie took the opportunity to *really l*ook at him. She spent a lot of time avoiding looking directly at Mac. It was always far too dangerous.

But now here she was in his bed, wearing his clothes, and looking at him seemed like the least of her worries. She took in the breadth of his shoulders and the flex of his forearms as he stood there. *Waiting* for her. She took pleasure in the fact that his hair was a mess because of her fingers, and she wondered if he was still as hard as he was while he was going down on her.

God, what was she doing here?

'I should probably go,' she said, snapping out of it.

Mac turned around. 'You sure?' he asked. 'You're welcome to stay the night. I'll sleep in the guest room.'

Sometimes Annie thought about that day at the Christmas market when Mac asked her to hang out and she wondered what would have happened if she had said no. Maybe she would have been able to have a healthy, lasting relationship in the eleven years since then. Maybe she wouldn't still be caught up in some stupid teenage fantasy. This moment felt similar to that one, like there was a fork in the road and Annie's life would change entirely depending on which path she took.

She should go home. She'd gotten what she came for. She got her orgasm. She got Mac wanting her. If she left now they could maybe go on as friends. Or something similar. People that got along, at least.

Mac was watching her from his place propped up against the wall. He looked tired, too, and maybe Annie was tired of punishing him.

'It's probably cold outside,' she whispered.

'It definitely is,' he said with a knowing smile. 'And it's still snowing.'

'And it's late,' she murmured.

'Really late.'

'So maybe I'll just sleep for a bit?' Annie whispered, and Mac's smile grew but he didn't say anything. He nodded and headed for the door.

'Where are you going?'

'The guest room.'

'No,' Annie said, taking a sharp turn down the wrong path.

Mac froze. 'No?'

'No.' Annie held his gaze, laying it all on the line again, just like the last time. Just like the last time Mac held her heart and tossed it away. 'Sleep here with me. Please.'

'Annie, I—'

'Just for tonight, Mac, please,' she said again, and he wavered. She could see it on his face. The indecision, the questions about what this meant. But Annie didn't want to think about what this meant. She just wanted Mac next to her.

'That's what you want?'

'Yes,' she said. 'I just want a break. With you. Okay?'

Mac nodded 'Okay, Annie.'

He didn't ask her to turn around as he pulled the shirt over his head, and he grinned when he caught her looking.

'Don't worry,' he said, 'I'll sleep with clothes on tonight. I don't want to find you gazing at me longingly.'

Annie rolled her eyes but couldn't help the laugh that escaped her, happy for a break in the tension. 'I will try my best not to stare at you all night.'

'Good,' he said, shucking his jeans with the same lack of

embarrassment as he did his shirt. 'I wouldn't want anything to change between us. You know, just because of this…' he said, gesturing to his body.

Annie bit down a smile. He looked damn good standing there in only his underwear, but that wasn't the reason she felt everything shifting beneath her feet.

She'd let her defenses down today. She'd let Mac be nice to her. Or maybe she'd finally noticed that Mac *was* nice to her, that he took care of her, that he knew her even after all this time.

But the way he looked in his underwear didn't hurt, either.

'Get in the bed,' she said. 'I'm tired.' She laid back in the pillows, tugging up the blankets so she could crawl under. Mac came around to her side of the bed and lifted the blanket, tucking it around her. He leaned down, a hand on either side of her head, the mattress dipping beneath his weight. Annie held her breath. She was surrounded by him, his heat, his scent, his stupid muscle-y arms, that damn way he kept looking at her. It was too much. If he kissed her right now, she knew she'd be lost. She'd give him everything again and be left to pick up the pieces when it didn't work out.

But he didn't kiss her, he just smiled and tucked the hair behind her ear, his fingers brushing along her cheek.

She let her eyes fall closed and bit back a whimper of protest when Mac stood up. She listened to the sound of him getting ready for bed and tried not to think about the consequences of what she'd done. Of what she was currently still doing.

The last thing she remembered before falling asleep was Mac crawling into bed next to her. He pulled her close, tucking her against him.

'I get to be the big spoon this time,' he whispered, and Annie fell asleep with a smile.

Chapter Twenty-Seven

Then

'Was it okay?' he asked. 'I mean, did you... I mean, was it...'

Annie smiled from her place next to him on the pillow. 'It was perfect,' she said.

He tucked a piece of hair behind her ear. 'So, no big regrets?'

'Nope, no regrets. What about you? You haven't actually gotten a good look at my feet. They might be gnarly.'

Mac laughed and it felt good. A whole other kind of release to be in bed with Annie naked and laughing. He thought it might be the best moment of his entire life. His legs were tangled up with hers under the blanket and her fingers toyed with the chain around his neck.

'Annie, you could have the gnarliest feet in the world and I would not care.'

She ran a toe along the back side of his calf. 'You sure

you don't want to check?' she said with a mischievous smile.

'I told you; I have no dealbreakers with you. You could have six toes per foot with talons on each one and I'd be totally cool with it.'

Annie giggled, the sound filling him up. The only light in the room was from the Christmas lights he'd let her string over his bed. They lit up her hair in red and green and gold.

'Maybe I won't go,' he blurted out, suddenly terrified of the thought of leaving. Leaving her, leaving his family, leaving his home. Maybe he'd been wrong about all of it.

But Annie was shaking her head, her blue gaze holding his. She dropped the chain, letting it fall back against his chest. She put her hand on his cheek.

'You have to go.'

'Maybe not. My mom's pretty upset about it, and I don't want to hurt her. I don't want to hurt you.'

'You have to go, Mac. You can't stay here for us. Your mom will be fine. I will be fine. You need to do this for yourself.'

He was shaking his head, wanting to argue with her, but Annie kept going.

'What happens if you don't go?' she said.

He opened his mouth to answer but then closed it, changing his mind. He wanted to say that he would be fine if he stayed. He wanted to say he and Annie could be together and they could see where this would go. He could figure out who he was here, couldn't he?

But when he really thought about it, he got that suffocating feeling he always had when he thought about spending the rest of his life in the exact same spot where he'd started. It made him itch. He thought about how everyone here had known him since he was a baby. They thought they knew everything about him, but he felt like he didn't know himself. If he stayed it would be too easy to just do what everybody else wanted him to do.

Annie was right. He couldn't stay. He would regret it if he didn't at least try. If he didn't at least go see something other than Dream Harbor's Main Street. If he didn't at least experience life outside of this small town.

'Give it a year,' she said as though she could tell what he was thinking, like she could feel his indecision, caught between his fear of staying and his fear of leaving.

'A year?'

'Yeah,' she said. 'Give it a year. A year to travel around, a year to figure it out, to decide what type of Mac you want to be.'

'And then what?' he asked, wanting more of Annie's plan for him, already feeling better now that she was putting parameters on this crazy idea of his.

'And then,' she whispered, moving closer, letting her fingers run through his hair, 'and then you come back to me.'

He sighed, relieved and happy that she wanted him to come back, that she wanted him at all.

'Where does that leave us in the meantime?' he asked, because they were definitely an *us* now. He couldn't pretend otherwise anymore. He and Annie were something. He wanted them to be something, and he couldn't leave without knowing what that something was.

She was pressed against him, her mouth nearly on his.

He was ready for a repeat of what they'd just done and the thought of not having this, of not having *her* for an entire year made him want to cry.

'You could send me postcards,' she said.

'Postcards? That's what you want us to be? Pen pals?' he asked, feeling Annie's lips curve into a smile against his.

'Pen pals. It'll be romantic,' she said.

'Can I text you?'

'Maybe.'

'Call?'

'I don't know.'

'What's not to know, Annie? I can't *not* talk to you for a year. I can't not hear your voice for three-hundred-and-sixty-five days.'

She kissed him, nibbling on his bottom lip. 'Until this month, you lived your entire life not caring at all about whether you heard my voice.'

'That was back when I was an idiot,' he said, and her laugh brushed across his face.

'I don't want to ruin your big year of adventure by being the thing holding you back. If the point is for you to get away from Dream Harbor, I can't have you calling here all the time.'

She was right. He knew she was. He knew if they tried to keep this relationship going while he was gone, he would always be looking back.

His arms were wrapped around her waist, and he pulled her closer wanting to feel the full length of her body against the full length of his.

'Okay, postcards it is,' he agreed, kissing her deeper

until she was moaning again, her hands clinging to his shoulders.

'What about other guys?' he said, coming up for air.

'You can see as many other guys as you'd like,' Annie said with a smile.

'Noted,' he said dryly, and Annie laughed.

'And what about you? Will you be seeing other guys while I'm gone?' He shouldn't have asked but he couldn't help himself. At this moment, with Annie in his arms, he absolutely hated the idea of her seeing other guys, even though he knew it was insane to expect her not to.

'How about this?' Annie said. 'If either of us gets serious with someone while you're gone, we'll be honest about it. Non-serious things don't need to be reported.'

'Is kissing a serious thing?' he asked, working his way down her neck.

'Probably not...'

'What about kissing here?' he asked, exploring places he hadn't gotten a chance to the first time around.

Annie gasped. Another sound he'd remember all year.

'That's a bit more serious.'

Mac smiled. 'Good to know.'

Annie tugged him up by his hair. 'I want you to do what you need to do, okay? Don't spend your time thinking about me.'

'I can't promise that. There's no way I can stop thinking about you, Annabelle,' he said, planting a chaste kiss on the tip of her nose.

'Okay, fine,' she agreed, like he was really putting her out. The big smile on her face told him otherwise. 'You can think about me the whole time you're away.'

'Deal,' he said.

'I *will* miss you while you're gone,' she said, 'but I'm excited for you.'

'Thanks,' he said, kissing her again. He wanted to say more. He wanted to tell her he was falling in love with her but that seemed unfair to say now. He would save it for when he got back.

Chapter Twenty-Eight

Now

'So much for being the big spoon,' Mac said, tugging Annie's arm tighter around his waist. Her fingers flexed, pressing into his skin. He could feel her groan rumble through his back, and he laughed.

'Damn it,' she said, pulling away.

'Where are you going?' he asked, rolling over to face her. 'That was cozy.'

Annie rolled her eyes, but she was smiling, and Mac thought this was his favorite morning in a long time.

'What time is it?' she asked and Mac glanced at his alarm clock.

'Just after six,' he said. Thanks to the tilt of the Earth that made December so grim in the Northern Hemisphere, it was still dark in his bedroom, although the streetlights hitting the snow outside gave the room an eerie glow.

He could make out Annie's gentle smile and her sleepy eyes, her gaze soft. For now, she wasn't scowling at him.

He liked it a lot.

'We should check on the kittens,' she said, even as she pulled the blankets up higher around her shoulders, clearly not intending to get up anytime soon.

'Already did.' Mac pointed to the side of the bed where he'd brought up the box in the middle of the night. 'Got worried about them downstairs all alone,' he explained.

Annie bit down on another smile.

'You really have to stop doing that,' she said.

'Doing what?'

'Being sweet.'

'I am sweet.'

That caused a little crease to form between Annie's eyebrows. She still didn't believe him. She still wanted to cling to her image of him as the villain.

'What do you think of me now?' he asked, echoing the question they'd asked each other all those years ago.

Annie sighed. 'I'm not really sure anymore.'

He'd take it. Anything was better than her thinking of him as the asshole who broke her heart.

'Okay, biggest fear,' he asked instead.

'That I like this a little too much,' she admitted, and hope flared in Mac's chest. 'What about you? Biggest fear?'

'That you'll never forgive me.'

The crease between her eyebrows deepened.

'What do you think of *me* now?' she asked.

Mac paused, taking her in, her bedhead and her sleepy face peeking out above his covers. He needed to get this exactly right.

'I think you're just as bright as when I left. I think you hold this town and your friends and your family together. I think you are still an over-achiever, but I think it's made your dreams come true and I think you're even more beautiful than the last time we did this.'

Annie held his gaze, not speaking, and Mac felt the world stand still as he waited. He'd wait for Annie forever.

'That was pretty good,' she said, after so long that Mac thought maybe she'd never answer. He couldn't help but chuckle. She was never going to make this easy for him but he didn't deserve easy so that was okay.

'Favorite movie?' she said.

'*The Muppet Christmas Carol*,' he said without missing a beat. Annie's laugh filled the quiet room.

'That cannot possibly still be your favorite movie,' she said.

'It absolutely can!' he countered.

'You're ridiculous,' she said, her nose crinkled in disbelief.

'So, what's yours, then? Has it changed in the past eleven years?'

'It's been a while since I've even had time to watch a movie,' she said. 'All I really seem to have the bandwidth for at the end of the day is reality TV.'

'Really? And you're going to make fun of me for loving the Muppets?'

'There's something relaxing about watching other people blow up their lives!'

At some point she'd reached out a hand beneath the blankets and was toying with the gold chain he still wore around his neck.

'What was the best place you lived?' she asked, her finger still looped through his necklace. He willed her to tug him closer.

'I liked anytime I was on the coast. Santa Barbara was cool. I really liked Chicago, too.'

She wanted to ask him more, he could tell, but she hesitated. The only sound in the room was her light breathing and the slow slide of his cross along the chain.

'Go ahead,' he said. 'I know you want to ask.' He'd been waiting years for her to ask. He'd been waiting years to explain.

Annie's lips tipped into a frown, and it took all his strength not to lean forward and kiss it off.

'Okay, fine,' she said, like she'd made a decision, like she was ready to meet the challenge he laid out for her. 'Why didn't you come back? Why did you leave me sitting in the diner waiting for you like an idiot.'

He knew the question was coming, and yet somehow he hadn't been prepared for how much it would hurt to hear it out loud. He wasn't prepared for all the hurt she'd say it with.

'I did come back,' he said, and Annie scoffed.

'Oh, you must have been invisible that day.' She dropped the chain.

Mac sighed. 'I did come back, and I saw you sitting in that booth and I couldn't do it.'

Annie rolled away from him, but he saw the tears in her eyes before she did. Damn it. He was screwing this up. He had to make her understand.

'I saw you sitting there, and I had been gone for an entire year, Annie, and I still knew nothing. I didn't know who I was or what I wanted to do. I was twenty years old, and I was still lost, and I saw you sitting there and what could I possibly have had to offer you?'

He remembered it like no time had passed at all. The feeling of looking through the diner window and seeing Annie sitting there, so poised and perfect. He'd thought about her the whole time he'd been gone but seeing her again in real life had made him doubt everything. It made him doubt his memories. It made him doubt himself.

He'd been miserable that first year he'd been away, but he'd done it to prove something to himself, to his family. That he could be on his own, that he could figure out his own life, and he hadn't figured out shit. He came home feeling like a failure. How was he supposed to walk up to Annie feeling like that? What was he supposed to say? I'm back but I'm still the same loser that left here a year ago.

He couldn't do it.

Annie sat up abruptly, taking half the blankets with her, leaving Mac in the cold. 'You didn't have to offer me *anything*. You only had to show up!'

Mac sat up to face her on the bed. 'I was scared,' he said, desperate for her to understand. He knew he didn't have to offer Annie anything concrete, but he at least needed to offer her some version of himself that he was proud of. 'I was scared that I wouldn't be what you remembered or what you wanted me to be.'

Annie shook her head. 'I sat there waiting for you all day. I felt like a complete fool, like some stupid lovesick girl who waits an entire year for a boy. I never wanted to be that girl and I haven't been her since.'

She got up, taking the blanket with her, looking around

his room for her clothes. 'This is why I can't do this with you, Mac. We can't do this again. You made me feel that way once and I won't let you do it again.'

'And what about you?' he said, getting up and following her around the bed even as the voice in his head was screaming at him to *retreat*. This was not how this was supposed to go. He was taking his one chance to fix things with Annie and ruining it. But he couldn't stop. If they had any chance of having a fresh start, they needed everything out in the open. 'I'm not the only one to blame in all of this.'

'*Excuse me?*' Annie said, her eyes going wide. 'What are you talking about?'

He'd had no intention of ever bringing this up, but now years-old hurt bubbled to the surface. 'I chickened out the day we were supposed to meet, but I came to Brandon White's party on New Year's Eve.'

Annie froze, the blanket wrapped around her shoulder. 'What are you talking about?' she whispered.

Mac stalked closer until they were toe to toe. 'I came to that New Year's Eve party looking for you. I had spent the week trying to figure it out and I realized that it didn't matter what I was doing with my life. I knew you would want to see me anyway. I knew we had something special.'

That's what he'd convinced himself of, anyway. That he could trust Annie to want him even if he was still incomplete. He'd gone to that party ready to apologize for standing her up but also so fucking hopeful that she'd forgive him. That they could finally pick up where they'd left off.

Annie swallowed hard. 'I didn't see you at that party.'

'You didn't see me because you were too busy.' He

stepped closer until Annie had to tip her face up to his. 'Do you remember what you were busy doing that night, Annabelle?' he asked, his voice a low rumble, every feeling he'd had when he'd seen her that night barreling back into him.

Annie faced him head on like she always had. 'Yes, I do. I spent that night *forgetting you*.'

Chapter Twenty-Nine

Then

Annie's second plate of pancakes was already cold. She'd given up looking busy about an hour ago and was now just staring forlornly into space.

It was December 23rd, the day she and Mac had agreed to meet back at the diner, nearly one year after Mac had taken off on his cross-country adventure. Annie had waited for this day with unrestrained excitement. She had two-dozen gingerbread cookies in a tin in her bag that she couldn't wait to give him. She'd barely sat still in the last two weeks.

She'd imagined being here in this booth with Mac so many times, it was hard to believe it hadn't already happened. She pictured them laughing and talking. She wanted to hear all about Mac's travels, about where he'd gone and what he'd seen, the things he liked best and the things he hated. She wanted to know if he was happy to be home and if he was going to stay and if he had gotten what he wanted out of the trip. She was so freaking excited to just see his face again and she really hoped she would get a chance to kiss it again.

All month she'd been nearly jumping out of her skin with anticipation. Mac had sent postcards over the year like he'd promised, but Annie had kept up her end of the deal, too. She hadn't wanted to hold him back. They'd done a little bit of texting and they'd only spoken on the phone once when Mac called to wish her a happy birthday, but she'd wanted him to have his year on the road. She didn't want to ruin that for him.

But maybe that had been a bad idea. Maybe over the course of this year Mac had turned back into a fantasy. Maybe Annie had blown their weeks together way out of proportion. Maybe Mac was as big of an asshole as she had always thought. Just because he was nice to her for a few weeks last year, and just because he had sent her a few postcards, didn't mean there was anything serious between them.

Clearly there wasn't, because he hadn't even bothered to show up.

She checked her phone one last time. She had two texts from Hazel about meeting up later. One from her mom to grab eggnog on her way home and that was it. No, *sorry I got caught in traffic*. No, *I can't make it today*. Not even a, *forget the whole thing. I'm not coming back*.

Nothing but radio silence from Mac.

Annie had restrained herself and sent only a single text to him. A simple, *I'm in our usual booth,* and now she hated that she had sent it. Their *usual booth*, like this was something they had done all the time when it had been just a few weeks. Here she was acting like they were something when clearly, they were nothing.

Over the course of the afternoon waiting for Mac, she'd pretty rapidly gone through the stages of grief.

Denial: she'd spent the first half hour questioning whether this was the right day and the right time, then thinking that obviously something had gotten in his way of showing up. He wouldn't stand her up.

Anger: after another hour had passed, Annie was blindingly angry. How could she have been so stupid to believe that this boy had changed? She'd known him forever and she'd never liked him. Why had she let him trick her? And why the hell hadn't he even bothered to break up with her like a man?

Bargaining: all she wanted was to see him one more time, mostly so she could throw her drink in his face. That always seemed satisfying in the movies. If she could only have that chance, then she would let it all go.

And now she had settled somewhere between depression and acceptance. She figured if she gave it another half hour or so, she could move on and live a fairly normal life.

After all he was just one stupid boy. There would be others. Hopefully some that were less stupid. Some that would actually come when they said they were going to. Annie was relatively certain that eventually she would meet someone that didn't make her feel as devastated as Mac Sullivan had made her feel.

She wiped her cheek with the back of her hand. Maybe she wasn't as close to acceptance as she thought.

'You almost done here, hun?' Gladys asked, coming up to her table for the tenth time today. The diner was closing soon. Annie really needed to go.

'Yeah, I'm sorry, Gladys. I'm just about done,' Annie said, trying to hide her sniffling. Unfortunately, Gladys didn't buy it.

She slid into the seat across from Annie, wisdom and sympathy on her face. 'It's a boy, isn't it?' she said, and Annie *hated* that, hated that the go-to thought was that a boy had made her cry. Didn't matter that it was true. She just hated it, like what else would make a girl cry? She could think of a hundred other things to cry about that were much more worthy than one stupid boy.

She wiped her eyes again. 'Actually, I'm pretty torn up about the polar ice caps melting,' she said, rolling her shoulders back. She would be damned if she ever got caught crying over a boy again. She certainly would never cry over Macaulay Sullivan again. Today would be the last day that Annie let Mac have any sway over her emotions. She swore it to herself.

Gladys smiled. 'Good for you,' she said, like she knew they weren't talking about polar ice caps at all. She patted Annie's hand on the table. 'You're a strong girl. You'll be all right.' With that, she got up, leaving the check behind, charging Annie for only one order of pancakes instead of two.

Annie paid the check, leaving the gingerbread cookies as a gift for Gladys, and marched out of the diner. She was proud of herself when she didn't even glance around the parking lot to see if maybe a certain car was pulling in. She was determined that this was the last bit of energy she would give to a certain someone. She was going to move on with her life. She was going to find better people to spend her time thinking about.

She glanced down at her watch.

Five twenty-four p.m. on December 23rd would be the last time she would think about Mac and their perfect month and all the feelings she thought she'd had about it. Clearly, she'd been wrong. Mac had used her. He'd lied to her and he'd ditched her. Frankly, she should have seen it from the start that this was exactly how he would behave. Mac was used to getting what he wanted, and she was just one more person that fell for his charm.

Even as she thought it, it felt like a betrayal, a betrayal of the Mac she had gotten to know. She *thought* she had seen the truth of him but, apparently, she'd been wrong all along.

Mac's hands were sweating despite the fact that it was freezing outside. He was standing outside of Brandon's house between an inflatable Santa and an enormous working snow globe, steeling himself to go in. A few party-goers wandered in and out of the house and there were plenty of cars parked in the quiet cul-de-sac, but so far, the party seemed pretty mellow compared to some he'd been to in high school.

Hopefully, that meant it'd be easy to find Annie inside. Her sister had said she'd be here, and Charlotte seemed to know everything about her older sisters, so Mac trusted her intel.

He knew he'd screwed things up. He knew Annie

would be pissed at him, but he was still holding onto a strange sort of hope that she would be happy to see him, that she would forgive him, and they could go back to how things were last year.

Last year, when Annie had warmed up his frozen fingers with her fuzzy mittens, when she'd kissed him, when she'd smiled at him. He wished he could go back.

He wanted to tell her that most of those postcards he'd sent had come from his first two months on the road. He'd spread them out to send them to her, but most of his traveling was done by March. He'd spent a lot of the year in a shitty motel not that far from Dream Harbor. Just waiting out the time, waiting to come back, bartending at bars that weren't his father's. It had been a waste of time. It was probably why he still felt like he was lost. He'd been too embarrassed to come back sooner even though he probably should have.

It was why he hadn't gone into the diner. Why he'd been too embarrassed to see her again, but he had to, even if it was just one more time. Even if it was just so she could tell him that she didn't want to pick up where they left off. He needed to hear it. He needed to know if the memories were real, if things between them really had been as magical as he remembered.

He blew out a long breath, watching it cloud the night air. It was now or never. He couldn't start a new year without knowing where he stood with Annie.

He walked into the house, heading to the back, following the sounds of the party. There were plenty of familiar faces, people that had stuck around in town, and some new ones. Honestly, he was surprised Annie was at this party. It didn't seem like her kind of thing. The thought caused a little seed of doubt to plant itself in his gut. Maybe he didn't know her that well after all or maybe she had changed in the past year.

He made his way to the kitchen where the drinks were laid out. He helped himself to one of the ubiquitous red cups, scanning the party for the one person he was looking for.

His heart kicked him in the ribs. She was here.

Annie.

The girl he'd been dreaming about for a year was here looking as gorgeous as she did when he left. She was here and she was real and she was smiling, a rosy blush on her cheeks. Mac nearly swallowed his tongue at the sight of her tucked into the corner of the couch, her attention on something out of Mac's line of sight. She looked … happy.

Mac hesitated. Maybe he should leave her alone, maybe he'd been right at the diner, and she was better off without him hanging around. But then her smile grew, her face lighting up, and the Christmas lights lit up her blonde hair just like they had that night…

He had to talk to her.

To apologize, at least.

He took a step in her direction and froze when he noticed the arm draped over her shoulder and the dude it was attached to staring at her like he'd won a prize. Who the hell was that guy and why was Annie looking at him like that?

She laughed at something the guy said, and Mac was unprepared for the immediate flash of rage coursing through his body. Why the hell was she laughing at that guy like that? Why was he *touching* her?

Mac had been wildly wrong about how this evening was going to go. He'd figured Annie would be mad at him or upset. He had never once considered the fact that she'd be here with someone else.

He needed to talk to her but before he could get two steps away from the kitchen counter it was Logan who he came face to face with.

'What are you doing here?' he asked gruffly as if Mac had offended him in some way.

'I need to talk to Annie.' Mac tried to move around Logan, but the guy moved to block him. He was bigger than Mac remembered. Apparently lifting hay bales was a great workout.

'I don't think you do,' Logan said.

'What the hell, man? Get out of my way. I need to talk to her.'

Logan stepped in front of him again, doubling down. 'She's clearly busy right now. You can talk to her tomorrow.'

Mac felt frantic at the suggestion. He couldn't wait another day. He couldn't start another year without her. 'I need to talk to her now.'

Logan shook his head.

'What's your problem?' Mac asked, straining his neck to see around Logan. It had been a while since he'd been in a fight but tonight seemed like a good time to get back into it. The guy with Annie had moved even closer and her face tipped up to his. Mac wanted to scream. He knew what it felt like to be on the other side of that look. He wanted to be back there.

'I don't know what's going on with you two,' Logan said, voice low, 'but this is what I do know: Annie's been weird all month. I've known her for a long time, and I know she's been keeping something from me, and then you get back to town and she gets really sad. I don't like it when my best friend is sad.'

Sad. Why hadn't he considered that Annie would be sad? 'What are you talking about? I didn't do anything.'

Logan shrugged. 'I didn't say you did. All I said was you got back, and she got sad, and I don't know why. But I don't like you being here right now, and I don't like the way you're acting. You can text Annie tomorrow and she can decide if she wants to talk to you.'

Mac opened his mouth to argue further but stopped when he saw Annie get up. A small bit of hope sparked and then immediately died when he saw the guy was still with her, their fingers intertwined like she was leading him somewhere. No, not *somewhere.* She was leading him *upstairs* and Mac had been to enough house parties to know what that meant.

'*Shit,*' Mac whispered under his breath and Logan turned, too. Annie had stopped a few stairs up. Smiling, she leaned down and kissed that guy, her hands sliding through his hair, and it was like Mac could feel it on his own head. Could remember the taste of her tongue on his own and now this guy, this *nobody,* got to have it and Mac *hated* it. His fists curled at his sides, the urge to fight rearing back up again.

'Looks like she already forgot about whatever was making her sad,' Logan said as they watched Annie lead that guy up the stairs.

For a split second, Mac considered following her. He imagined pulling that guy away from her and dragging her out of here. He wanted to tell her everything. He wanted to rip his heart out and lay it out at her feet.

But apparently Annie didn't want that. She'd already forgotten about him. He made one mistake, and she'd moved on. Just like that.

A humorless laugh escaped him. 'Yeah, I guess so.'

Logan almost looked sympathetic when he turned back around but not like he was about to give in and let Mac charge past him. Not that it mattered. Mac had lost the urge.

'Going to be back in town long?' Logan asked.

After all these months away, waiting to come back, Mac knew there was only one answer.

'No, I'm leaving again tomorrow.'

Logan's eyebrow rose.

'There isn't anything here for me,' Mac said, and Logan answered with a frown like he might disagree, but Mac didn't want to hear it.

He strode out of the party vowing to himself to not waste another minute thinking about Annabelle Andrews. It was time he did this traveling thing for real, and this time he'd have no one waiting for him back home.

This time he'd have no trouble staying away.

Chapter Thirty

Now

Mac flinched when she said it, like her words physically hurt him, like he couldn't bear the idea of Annie forgetting him.

'Did it work?' he asked, his voice choked. 'Did fucking that random guy at that party help you forget me?'

Annie's hand cracked across Mac's cheek so fast it surprised both of them. They stood there in shocked silence, her hand stinging from the impact, both of them breathless, like they'd just run a marathon.

She'd *hit* him. She'd never hit another person in her entire life. Yet one more example of Mac making her do things she would never ordinarily do.

'First of all,' she said, trying to regain her composure. 'He wasn't random. His name was Ryan and we had class together and he was nice to me. And second of all, it is none of your business who I *fuck*.' She tossed the blanket she'd wrapped around herself aside, her anger enough to keep her warm now.

How *dare* he? How dare he try and make her feel bad for that night? He had no right.

Mac stared at her, a hand on his cheek. His eyes were dark, hurt. 'I shouldn't have said that,' he ground out. 'But it sure didn't take you long to move on.'

Annie crossed her arms over her chest. 'Ha! I waited *a year* for you, Mac! And then you didn't show. How long exactly should I have waited? Should I have forsaken all other men until you came back? Did you think you had some kinda claim on me because you took my virginity?'

He stepped closer, grabbing her arms in case she might hit him again. 'Of course I don't think that. Christ, Annie. I didn't *take* anything. But I thought you'd give me more than one chance. It felt like I made one mistake, and you bailed.'

'You could have called! You could have texted! But you didn't. I couldn't wait around for you any longer.' She pulled out of his grasp. Maybe she would hit him again. Maybe he deserved it.

Mac slumped, the anger seeping out of him. 'You're right. I know you're right. But it still felt shitty seeing you with that guy.'

'Kinda like how it feels when you bring random women to Christmas at Estelle's?'

Mac grumbled. 'Don't think I've forgotten about Trent from Friendsgiving.'

'Trent was nice.'

'Fuck Trent.'

Annie's laugh burst out unexpectedly, and Mac smiled.

'It's been a long time, Mac. We both know we've been with other people.'

'I know. Talking about all this just brought back all those feelings, you know?'

'Yeah, I know. I probably shouldn't have hit you.'

Mac shrugged, a small smirk lifting the side of his mouth. 'I deserved it.'

Annie sighed, slouching back down onto the bed, the fight going out of her too. 'Anyway, it didn't work,' she said. 'I couldn't forget you.'

Mac dropped to the floor in front of her wedging his body between her thighs. She put a hand gently on the cheek she had smacked.

'I tried,' she said. 'I wanted to, but I couldn't do it.' She shook her head, biting back tears. 'And then you show up here and work your way into my life. What am I supposed to do?'

'I tried to forget you, too,' he whispered, leaning toward her.

'Why didn't you come talk to me that night at the party?'

Mac shook his head with a laugh. 'That would have gone a lot worse than this,' he said. 'I have a feeling I would have won the fight against Ryan, but you definitely would have kicked my ass.'

Annie's laugh mixed with the tears falling down her cheeks. Mac wiped them away with his thumb, cupping her face in his hands.

'I'm sorry I stood you up that day. I shouldn't have left like that. But in my defense, I was young and stupid, and I ran away. I bartended in Maine, and I painted houses in Tulsa, and I mucked stalls on a ranch in Texas and none of those places felt like home and no other woman I met felt like you. It's one of the biggest regrets of my life, leaving the way I did. I needed time away from this place, Annie, but I never should have left without talking to you.'

'I was young, too. I'm not sure that's a very good defense,' Annie whispered, leaning toward him until their foreheads touched.

Mac smirked and Annie was close enough she could kiss him if she were braver.

'You were young, but not stupid. Standing you up was just one of the many stupid things I was up to that year.'

'Really? What else you got?' she said, smiling again. She couldn't seem to help it around Mac anymore.

'Well,' he said, his smile growing to match hers. 'I got frostbite on my pinky because I was still refusing to wear warm gloves.'

'That's ridiculous!'

'I know. Then there was the time I drove a hitchhiker from Philly to DC, and I was only about seventy-five percent sure he wasn't going to murder me.'

Annie gasped. 'That is seriously dangerous.'

'That's kind of my point. Don't tell my mom. And then there's the tattoo I got.'

Annie raised an eyebrow. She'd never seen a tattoo on Mac before. 'What tattoo?'

'It's on my rib cage,' he said.

'Okay, so what is it? Plenty of people get tattoos.'

'But do plenty of people get tattoos of the name of the person they had just unceremoniously ditched and were pretty sure hated them?'

'You didn't.'

Mac leaned away from her and lifted his shirt. In tiny script on his left ribs was her name. It was so small she hadn't seen it last night when he undressed but there it was plain as day. *Annie* in black ink under his heart.

'You did,' she whispered, running a finger over the tattoo. Mac squirmed under her touch.

'I did. *See*, young and stupid. I wanted to keep you close even when I knew I didn't deserve to.'

She leaned forward and pressed her forehead into his chest. 'Oh, Mac,' she whispered. 'Why is this so hard?'

'It doesn't have to be. The first year I was away I was scared and lonely. The second year I did a lot of stupid shit to forget you. But after that, I really did figure some things out. I *studied* while I was out there, Annie. I worked at a lot of places, always thinking about what I could bring back here. What would make my dad's place even better.'

'That's great, Mac. Really, but—'

He shook his head like he didn't want to hear what came after that but.

'I know what I want now, Annie—'

Her phone rang, cutting him off.

'Shit,' she said. 'The only way someone's calling me this early is for some kind of emergency.'

'Maybe not,' Mac said, running his hands through her hair. Annie moaned. His fingers felt so damn good, being near him felt so damn good. 'Maybe don't answer it. Maybe whoever it is can figure it out themselves.'

He held her gaze, his breath warm on her face. He'd dropped his shirt, but her hands remained under it, roving over the expanse of his skin.

'Maybe it doesn't have to be hard for us anymore,

Annie,' he said, and she wanted to believe him. He traced his nose along her cheek.

The phone stopped and then started up again. She was sure something catastrophic was happening with either the wedding or the bakery or one of her nieces or nephews.

'I really have to answer that,' she said.

Mac sighed, leaning his forehead against hers for one more breath before he pulled away. He looked like he wanted to say more or maybe just to lean forward and kiss her and God, Annie wanted him to but...

'I'm sorry,' she said, and Mac nodded as she scrambled for her phone because he *knew* her. He knew she couldn't not answer. He knew she had to help. And that meant more to her than his apology.

She mouthed sorry one more time and Mac gave her a slow smile, and Annie briefly reconsidered her stance on answering the phone, before picking up.

She was who she was.

'Hello?' she said, not recognizing the number.

It was Estelle.

Chapter Thirty-One

Now

'What do you mean she's in New Hampshire?'

Annie huffed, continuing her search for her clothes. Mac wouldn't mind if she stayed in his lacrosse T-shirt for the rest of forever, though, so he wasn't being particularly helpful. Getting dressed was the last thing he wanted Annie to do.

He wanted her back in his bed.

He wanted to do everything they hadn't last night.

He wanted to kiss her *finally*. Again.

They were so damn close.

'I mean, Estelle and Dot are in New Hampshire, and they need a ride home.'

'What the hell are they doing in New Hampshire?'

Annie tossed aside his pillows and found the shirt and bra she'd apparently tucked under there last night and held them up triumphantly.

'Your pants are still downstairs,' he said with a smirk, and thanks to the fact that Annie had flung on the overhead lights as soon as she finished her phone call, Mac was treated to the sight of a delicious blush working its way up her neck and cheeks at the memory of what they'd done in his kitchen last night. He knew it was one he'd hold onto for a very long time.

'Right,' she said, clearing her throat, tucking her clothes under one arm and marching out of his room like a woman on a mission. Mac grinned and followed her downstairs. Sure, he was pissed that their moment had gotten interrupted. He hadn't felt that close to Annie in over a decade, but there was something about seeing her in her element that also got him off. So, he'd have to take that for now.

He found her in his kitchen scooping her jeans up off the floor.

'Can you drive me home?' she asked, turning to face him. 'I figure I have time for a quick shower before I drive up there to get them.'

'Wait, wait, wait. You're going to drive up to New Hampshire alone today?'

'Of course I am.'

'On the day of the wedding you've been helping to plan for months?'

'Someone needs to go get them, and it can't be Logan or Jeanie, obviously. So, I'll do it. Estelle called me.'

'I'll come with you.'

'That's unnecessary.' She didn't even pause, didn't take one second to consider that she didn't have to do this by herself, that she wasn't single-handedly responsible for her friends' happiness.

Mac stared her down. 'You have too much to do today, Annie. And your car is presumably buried under snow right now with an empty gas tank, so you can let me drive you around to do all the things I'm sure you have on your wedding day to-do list, or you can go attempt to dig your car out of the snow and add a drive to New Hampshire into everything else you have to do.'

'You can't leave the kittens.'

'The kittens will be fine. I'll put them in the bathroom with their cozy box and some food and water. They won't even miss us.'

Annie scowled, clearly dying to argue with him but he knew he had her. There was no way in hell he was letting her out of his sight now, not when they were so close to fixing things between them. He leaves Annie alone for a few hours, and she's right back to assuming he's plotting against her. No freaking way.

'When do you have to be back here to get your hair done?'

'Two o'clock,' she said slowly like she was suspicious of why he wanted to know.

'Okay, and what else is on your list for today?'

She was still looking at him like he was trying to get state secrets out of her, but she begrudgingly answered. 'I need to check in at the bakery. George is feeling better and is opening it up this morning and I need to make sure the other wedding desserts are ready to go.' Mac was sure George was capable of handling that himself or that a quick call would do the trick, but he knew Annie needed to see it for herself.

'Okay, what else?'

'I'm supposed to pick up the bouquets and boutonnières.'

'Hazel can do it.'

Annie paused like she didn't have a good reason to argue with him on that one. Good, he was making progress.

'We'll swing by your place for a change of clothes and then we'll go check in at the bakery. We should be able to get to Estelle and back before your hair appointment if we hurry. Unless you want me to do your hair,' he said with a wink, clearly joking, but Annie was staring at him like he'd grown another head.

'Why are you looking at me like that? It was a joke. Hairdressing is one of the few skills I don't have.'

'I just...' she shook her head, still not laughing, 'I just ... I don't know. Didn't expect the help, I guess.'

'Well start expecting it. Tea or coffee?' he said, leaving her standing there gaping while he went to the coffee maker.

'Coffee,' she said and when he turned back to look at her, she looked lost and a little confused like she was reworking who he was again. But this wasn't anything new for Mac. This was who he was now. He was a man. A man with a business and a house and a love for the woman standing in front of him that was too strong for him to ignore anymore.

He was done with the childish games he and Annie had been playing for years.

But he figured she'd need a minute to catch up.

He made the coffee and then came over to Annie, taking the clothes from her hands and replacing them with a mug.

'You might as well stay in my clothes for now,' he said, not able to resist the smirk on his face. 'You can grab fresh ones when we stop at your apartment.'

Again, the blush crawled up her cheeks and Mac could think of a million other ways he'd rather spend the day than picking up Logan's missing grandmother, but he knew Annie would never let it go. If she wanted this day to be perfect for her friends, then so did he.

But Logan owed him so much for this. At this point, he was basically the best groomsman ever. What was ice fishing with the bride's cousins compared with giving up sex with the woman of his dreams to go pick up two old ladies who'd gone rogue?

He was kicking Noah's ass at this.

Not that Noah knew they were competing.

But Mac was totally winning best groomsman.

'Do you want to tell me where they are in New Hampshire? And why exactly did Logan's grandmother and Jeanie's aunt take off to another state the day before their wedding?'

Annie blinked, coming back to the present moment and out of whatever memories of last night she'd been playing in her head.

'They're not that far, about an hour from here. Apparently, they went up there to visit some distant cousin of Estelle's or something like that. She said they needed something for the wedding and then they got stuck in the snow.'

Mac glanced out the window. 'It's not snowing now,' he

observed, still hoping for a last-minute reprieve from this errand. Annie looked so tempting sitting at his kitchen island, cradling her mug. He wanted her here every morning, just like this, talking over coffee as the sun came up outside.

He wondered how she'd react if he said so.

She'd probably tip right off the stool.

Annie blew out a long sigh and took a sip of her coffee. 'They left their headlights on last night and now the car battery is dead, and frankly, I don't trust those two to make it back in time for the wedding, not at this rate. They've proven to be entirely unreliable.'

'Well, that settles it. We're taking a road trip to New Hampshire. Do you want a travel mug for that coffee because we should probably get a move on. We want to make it back in time.'

Annie was staring at him again like she was waiting for the real Mac to come back. Like she was waiting for the irresponsible kid he was to walk through the door. Or maybe she was waiting for the guy she'd painted in her head all these years as the asshole that left her.

But he wasn't either of those guys and he had a new plan. He was determined to show Annie the man he was now, and she could decide for herself if she wanted to be with this Mac.

Because he'd already made up his mind.

He'd loved Annie then and he loved her now.

She was it for him.

Back at Annie's apartment, she was in the shower and Mac was sprawled out on her bed doing his best not to think about her in the shower. He'd suggested they shower together at his place to save time, but Annie had laughed in his face.

So here he was in Annie's tiny apartment, forced to listen to the sounds of the water and try not to imagine Annie naked and soaking wet. So far, he wasn't doing a great job of it. He put his hands behind his head and closed his eyes. Maybe he could get a few more minutes of sleep before they embarked on this ridiculous journey. The shower turned off and a few seconds later the bathroom door opened.

'Keep your eyes closed.' Annie's voice washed over him.

'Please tell me you're kidding.'

'I'm not kidding. I accidentally left my clothes out there. Keep your eyes closed.'

He heard her padding across the floor toward him, and he groaned. Clearly, he was being tested, by Annie or by God he wasn't sure, but his resolve to be a gentleman was rapidly weakening.

He could hear Annie rifling through her clothes in the dresser right next to his head.

'How about I open one eye?' he teased.

'Don't you dare.'

'Or…' he said, 'I could keep my eyes closed and just use my hands.'

Annie snorted. 'Yeah, that's not happening, either.'

He was going to go on teasing her but something about the fact that she trusted him to keep his eyes closed was more important.

Progress.

If Annie could trust him not to peek, then someday she could trust him with everything else.

Unfortunately, his cock didn't care as much about gaining Annie's trust and was pushing painfully against the fly of his jeans. Between tasting Annie last night and now knowing she was just a foot away from him completely naked, Mac wasn't sure he'd survive the day.

Even the sounds of her getting dressed were sexy. Was that the elastic of her absurdly tiny panties being pulled over her hips? The shush of her jeans as they were tugged up her long legs had him thinking about how it felt to peel them off. Seeing her like that, God he had dreamed about it for years, obsessed over this woman, and then there she was bare in front of him, finally letting him lick and suck and worship her. It had been perfect, and he wanted more, and lying here not being able to touch her or look at her was absolute torture.

She let out a small sigh.

'Christ, Annie,' he breathed, pressing his palm to his aching cock.

Her sharp intake of breath skated over his skin, letting him know she'd noticed what he was doing. He could feel her standing over him, her gaze lighting him up.

He pressed once more, savoring the sound of Annie's whimper. He was about to stop, to say they needed to go, to apologize, but then he felt the mattress dip beside him.

'Annie, what—'

'Keep your eyes closed,' she whispered.

The feather-light touch of her fingers under his waistband nearly had his back bowing off the bed.

'What are you doing?' he gasped.

'What I should have done last night,' she said, undoing his button. So business-like, so Annie.

He opened his eyes and found her leaning over him.

'Eyes closed,' she said.

And there was something in her gaze. She sounded like her usual confident self, but he could see it in her eyes. She was nervous, uncertain.

'Annie, you don't have to—'

'I want to,' she said, holding his gaze. She lowered her voice. 'Just close your eyes.'

This time he listened but Mac had so many questions. He wanted to know why she wanted to do this. Had she forgiven him? Did she want to *be* with him or was this just something she'd fantasized about over the years like he had? Was she simply getting it out of her system? Getting *him* out of her system?

They needed to talk about all of it, but Annie was slowly sliding down his zipper, and all Mac wanted, all he could think about in that moment, was her mouth on him. Everything else could wait. The entire world could wait.

'Can I?' she asked.

'Yes,' he rasped, his voice stuck in his throat. 'Annie, I—'

He didn't know what he was going to say, but he felt like he had to say something, until Annie cut him off.

'No, don't say anything,' she said. 'Please just let me…'

She was hiding from him. Still. Even after all he confessed this morning, she was still keeping her distance.

But her hands were on him, her breath coming in short little gasps, and who was he to deny her?

So, he let her. He let her wrap her hand around his

aching erection. He let her slide her mouth around him. He let her cross another thing off the list of things he'd thought about over the last eleven years. Annie's mouth around him, her tongue sliding over his length was as close to a religious experience as Mac had had in a long time.

Her hair brushed along his lower abs, and he gathered it in his fist making the ponytail she was so fond of wearing. He thought about how many times he'd resisted tugging it. He didn't resist now. He gave it a tug, gentle at first, but judging by the low hum Annie was making, she didn't mind at all.

Her hair was like silk between his fingers, and he gave it another pull. Annie groaned and the sound shot through him. He wasn't going to last long but who would blame him? He was living out his teenage fantasies. This moment was everything he'd wanted all those years while he was out on the road, or at least he'd thought it was all he wanted.

But somehow it wasn't enough. He wanted to hold her and touch her and *see* her. Somehow, even as pleasure barreled through him, even as Annie's sweet mouth worked him to the best orgasm he'd had in years, Mac felt like he was missing out, like he wasn't getting all of Annie. And after all this time, he wanted everything.

She sat back with a sigh, leaving Mac panting on the bed.

'You can clean up in the bathroom if you want,' she said. 'But we should probably get going soon.'

His eyes sprung open. 'You're kidding, right?'

Annie blinked back at him. Her flushed cheeks and messy hair were the only evidence that anything had even happened, that just a second ago his hands were in her hair and her mouth was filled with him.

'I'm not kidding. You know we're on a tight deadline.'

He ran a hand down his face in frustration. 'So, we're just going to pretend this didn't happen? What the hell are we even doing, Annie?'

She sighed, standing up from the bed. 'I don't know but maybe I'm not ready to forgive you yet.'

Well, this was a shitty way to come down from an orgasm.

'But I couldn't leave you like that all day,' she added, gesturing toward his lap. 'You *could* thank me.'

'Jesus, Annie. Is this seriously how it's going to be between us?'

'We don't have time to deal with this right now,' she said, hand on her hip. She was trying to get back to business, but Mac saw the fear in her eyes. She didn't want to get hurt again. 'Are you driving me, or should I go get my shovel to dig out my car?'

He tucked himself back into his pants and stood up. 'I'm still driving you,' he nearly growled. 'But this isn't over between us. I'm not letting it go this time. I'm not going to go from enemies to whatever this is.' He gestured between them in some futile attempt to explain what they were to each other at the moment. Exes who now orally pleasured each other? Friends who gave each other orgasms every once in a while?

He felt like he was losing his mind. A few days ago, Annie couldn't stand being in the same room with him, and then this morning it seemed like maybe she was about to forgive him, and now she was giving him blowjobs and trying to pretend it never happened. It was enough to make a man go crazy.

'Fine,' Annie ground out, like he was being the unreasonable one. 'But we really need to go.'

There was clearly no point in arguing with her any further, so he used the bathroom, they grabbed their things and headed for the door. But on the way out he spotted something on Annie's refrigerator. An old postcard, one he recognized from the Grand Canyon.

'Wait a minute,' he said, and Annie paused, glancing back at him. 'You kept it,' he said. It was one of the later ones he'd sent her, after he stood her up and went back out on the road. The Grand Canyon was supposed to be one of his original stops, one of the ones on the list they'd made at the diner. He never made it in that first year but when he finally did, he felt like he should let Annie know.

It had been the first time he'd reached back out to her. The first time he'd let himself admit that he missed her.

He'd kept the message simple. Something about the canyon being as cool as they thought it would be and that he hoped she was well.

She'd never written back but she'd kept it.

Annie's eyes flicked to the postcard and back to his face.

'Yeah, well you got my name tattooed on you, so I guess we're both idiots,' she said before heading out the door.

Mac couldn't help but laugh.

He took one last glance at the postcard before following Annie. Maybe there was still hope for them to get this right.

Chapter Thirty-Two

Now

In the course of three hours this morning, Annie had hit a man and made the very questionable decision to engage in oral sex with him, and she was now stuck in his passenger seat trying to pretend neither of those things had happened. To his credit, he seemed to be doing the same.

She wouldn't have done those things with anyone other than Mac, the man who seemed to be determined to make her act completely out of character.

Why could she not keep her damn emotions in check around him? She'd spent the last two days wanting to murder him or mount him and today had not provided any more clarity on which option she should choose.

Sure, he'd apologized, but what the hell good did that do her now? She'd spent ten years hating the man; could she really change her feelings for him just like that?

Maybe she should let it go. Maybe no one should be

held responsible for things they did before their brain was fully formed.

But every time she looked at him, she remembered how much it had hurt to sit alone in that diner. How was she supposed to forget about that feeling? The feeling of being abandoned by someone you considered a friend? Someone who was supposed to come back for you?

She'd been so convinced he would.

Until he didn't.

And then she was devastated. It was her dealbreaker, and he knew it and he broke it anyway.

And then she'd gone and put his dick in her mouth. When had that ever helped anyone find clarity about their feelings? She was pretty sure never.

Not that she hadn't enjoyed herself, because she definitely had. Mac had looked so delicious, so *tortured* lying on her bed, his cock straining against the front of his jeans. He'd looked like he was about to burst, all just from being in the same room as her while she was getting dressed. He hadn't even seen anything. She was sure of it. Just being near her had done that to him.

She'd have to be dead inside to not find that incredibly hot.

And besides, she couldn't have him driving her around all day with that erection between them; they'd never get anything accomplished. So really, the blowjob had been for practical purposes.

Or that was what she chose to tell herself.

The day was bright and sunny and nearly blinding with the snow covering everything. Annie squinted out the window at the white fields and coated trees. She spotted a few cows, a farmhouse in the distance. It would be easier to enjoy the scenery if she wasn't so confused about everything that had happened in the last twenty-four hours.

'Five more exits to go,' she said, breaking the silence they'd been driving in since they got in the car.

Mac grunted. You'd think he'd be in a better mood after the whole getting off thing, but he'd been pouty during their stop at the bakery and for the first half of the drive. He was probably regretting the offer to chauffer her around. In another first, she actually felt kind of bad about it.

'I bet you wish you had let me drive myself today,' she said, glancing at him from the corner of her eye. He kept his eyes on the road, but she could see the slight shake of his head.

'I don't wish that at all.'

'You could have fooled me.'

He blew out a long sigh like she was exhausting him. 'At some point we're going to have to talk about it, Annie. All of it.'

'Not today.'

'You can't keep doing that!' He actually sounded … angry? He was mad at her?

'You can't keep stopping me from telling you how I feel,' he went on. 'It's been hard enough these past three years but now it's impossible.'

She opened her mouth to argue but opted to pause instead. Is that what she'd been doing? Silencing him, shutting him down at every turn? *Of course it was*, but she'd only been trying to protect herself. Ever since Mac came back to town, she'd either avoided him or picked fights with him. Even before he moved back, she'd refused to see him any time he'd been back home to visit his family. She kept busy. She told herself she didn't need to see him, didn't want to talk to him. It was all ancient history. Anything to keep her actual feelings at bay. And now here he was, forcing her to face them.

Except now, for the first time, she saw that maybe she hadn't been fair to Mac. Maybe, by trying to protect herself, she'd been hurting him. And while that may have been the goal originally, she suddenly didn't want it to be.

She didn't want to hurt Mac anymore.

'One more day,' she said.

'One more day?' He sounded ready to shut that idea down. She had never seen Mac at the end of his rope before, but, apparently, they'd finally gotten there.

'Yeah, one more day. Just today. The wedding day. Let's get through today and then I promise we'll talk about everything.'

She waited, holding her breath. She still didn't even know what she would say when they did talk but she knew she owed it to him. She owed him at least the courtesy of telling him nothing was going to happen between them—if that was the case—instead of ambushing him with surprise blowjobs and telling him to shut up about it. It was possible that she'd been sending some mixed signals.

'Okay, I'll give you one more day. And then you're going to tell me where I stand with you, because I can't play games anymore.'

'Too old?' she teased, desperately trying to get back on some familiar ground.

Mac huffed a laugh. 'Too old to be chasing after a memory of you. I need the real thing. I need to know if we have any chance of working or if it's finally time for me to let you go.'

Annie's breath caught.

'But I'll give you till tomorrow,' he added, saving her from having to speak.

She still didn't know what she would say, but she knew she didn't want Mac to let her go.

And she knew it was about time she let him say his piece.

Chapter Thirty-Three

Three years ago

Mac stood outside of the brand-new bakery on Main Street. It was only his second day back in Dream Harbor, but this was his most important stop. The shop looked good. Its big front window was filled with delicious-looking treats and the bench out front made him want to sit and eat a cookie in the December sunshine. But he knew it was more than simply an inviting store. It was the culmination of years of work. This bakery was the end product of Annie's determination, and he was so fucking proud of her. So happy that she'd achieved what she wanted to all those years ago. He remembered it like it was yesterday, lying in his bed next to her talking about what they wanted from life. Annie had gone out and got it, worked for it, earned it. And it was incredible.

And it smelled delicious.

He'd been standing outside for far too long now, indecision and nerves keeping him frozen to the spot.

He caught a glimpse of Annie moving around inside and his breath caught in his throat. She was the same but different; older but still gorgeous; moving around with the same purpose she always did. He didn't know how she would react to him being back but, if they were going to live in the same town again, he had to face her. Might as well do it now.

He pushed open the door to the shop and a little bell tinkled overhead.

'I'll be right with you,' Annie said, not looking up from the tray she was sliding into the display case.

Her voice was enough to send his heart racing. He'd waited so long to hear it again. Too long. He'd been a damn coward for too long. As much as he'd loved his years on the road, he never should have waited this long to talk to her, to apologize. At first, he thought it was best to try and forget her, to put distance between them so they could both move on. And then years had gone by, and he hadn't known what to say or how to say it. He got the feeling she avoided him whenever he was back in town, and he convinced himself it was better that way.

But he knew this: no matter where he had gone or who he'd been with, he'd never been able to shake his feelings for Annie.

He was done running from them.

'Hey, Annabelle,' he said, and Annie picked her head up so fast she hit it on the counter.

'Ow,' she hissed, rubbing her head and standing up.

'Sorry, I didn't mean to startle you.'

She stared at him in disbelief. 'What the hell are you doing here?'

Mac's heart sank. He should have known this wouldn't be easy.

'I'm moving back to town.'

'No, you're not,' she said, so firmly that Mac nearly laughed.

'I am, actually.'

'You can't.'

'Annie, I'm pretty sure you don't have a say in that.'

She crossed her arms over her chest. 'Well, I do have a say in who comes into my bakery so you can get the fuck out.'

'Can I at least explain? I wanted to say I'm sorry for what happened.'

'I don't know what you're talking about.'

'Annie, come on…'

'Don't *Annie come on* me! I haven't seen you in eight years, Macaulay Sullivan.'

'I *tried* to see you.' He had tried. Several times over the past few years he'd stopped by her parents' house. Conveniently, she'd never been around, and no one had known where to find her. It was like she disappeared anytime he came back to Dream Harbor. Or her friends and family were instructed to make him think she had.

Annie scoffed. 'Look, we don't need a big reunion moment. You're moving back to town. That's lovely for you, but I don't need to interact with you, so please leave.'

'*I'm sorry.* For everything.'

Annie put her hands on the counter and leaned toward

him. 'I don't need or want your apology. We were children and it was just a silly fling between us.'

Mac swallowed hard. He understood her anger, but she couldn't erase what happened between them. It had been extraordinary. He hadn't found anything like it since. 'There was nothing silly about it,' he ground out.

Annie shrugged like none of it really mattered to her. She should have punched him in the face. It would have hurt less.

'I guess it meant more to you than it did to me,' she said, her words cutting him to the bone. A small part of him was glad. If she had welcomed him with open arms, he wouldn't have trusted it.

'You don't mean that, Annabelle.'

'Don't fucking call me that.'

'Sorry.'

She stared at him from across the counter. Those same blue eyes that had once looked at him so lovingly were staring daggers.

'Look,' she said, 'I've already forgotten about what happened between us and I don't need you coming here to *my* town and dredging it all back up again. So, as far as anyone's concerned, I don't like you, Macaulay Sullivan. I never have and I never will.'

He nodded, swallowing everything else he wanted to say to her; everything he'd never confessed. Clearly, she didn't want to hear it. And she didn't owe him anything. She didn't owe him forgiveness. Not after the way he'd treated her.

'Right,' he said. 'I'm sorry I came in.' He turned to go but looked back one more time. 'The bakery looks really great. You did an amazing job.' And for a brief second Annie's expression softened, a tiny glimmer of the way she used to look at him, before she shuttered it again with a scowl.

The Annie he'd known all those years ago was gone. This Annie wasn't his anymore. This was the Annie he'd hurt.

Now he had to figure out how to live in the same town as her and not lose his mind pining after her.

Because while Annie wasn't *his* anymore, he would always be *hers*.

Chapter Thirty-Four

Now

About a half an hour later, they pulled up in front of an unassuming ranch-style house at the end of a cul-de-sac in a town Annie had never heard of. The mailbox was in the shape of a largemouth bass.

'Where the hell are we?' Mac muttered from the driver's seat.

'We are at the address Estelle gave me this morning—the home of her cousin Sylvia—and those two runaways better still be here,' Annie said, hopping down from the truck.

Mac did the same and they made their way down the uncleared path to the door. Icy snow crunched beneath their boots.

There was a festive wreath on the door and a welcome mat that read, *Happy Holidays!* Annie found that encouraging. Someone was in there and they'd at least been around recently enough to decorate for Christmas.

She rang the bell, and they waited, crammed together on the small landing at the top of the cement stairs. Mac smelled like spiced sex appeal and mixed emotions. It was wildly distracting.

'Nobody's coming,' he hissed.

'They'll come,' she insisted. 'This is where they said they would be.' *They better come.* She did not have time to go searching any more small towns today. She rang the bell again.

Mac glared at the door like maybe that would make it open sooner.

Finally, it opened and revealed a very small, very old woman on the other side.

'Hello,' Annie said. 'Are you Sylvia? We're here to pick up Estelle and Dot.'

The woman blinked.

Dear God, she'd better know where they are.

'What was that, dear?' she said, cocking her head.

'Estelle and Dot! Are they here?!' Mac yelled loud enough that Annie was sure half the neighborhood knew who they were looking for. She jabbed him in the arm with her elbow. He jabbed her back while continuing to smile at the old lady.

The woman's face lit up. 'Oh yes, they're here. Come on in.' She opened the door, and Annie breathed a sigh of relief before following her into the house. If Estelle hadn't been here, she seriously didn't know what she would have done, besides put out a missing-persons report and possibly find another woman to dress up as Nana for the wedding. Maybe Logan would never have noticed.

'I was worried you were those terrible people that are

always trying to get me to join their cult,' Sylvia said with a cheerful smile as she led them through her house.

'Oh … yikes,' was all Annie could think to say. Mac chuckled from behind her.

'Estelle's lucky I let her stay the night,' Sylvia went on. Her pace was a slow shuffle, and they hadn't made it past the incredibly floral sitting room yet. 'You know her father and mine had a horrible falling out. Years ago, that was.'

'Probably sometime in the eighteen-hundreds,' Mac muttered, and Annie tried to jab him again, but he was ready for it and dodged her.

'But I couldn't very well put her out in the snow. Plus, she brought her lovely friend, Dot, so here we are.'

'That was very … charitable of you,' Annie said, and Sylvia beamed at her.

They found the missing women in a bright, sunroom in the back of the house. 'There they are,' Sylvia announced. 'You better not have taken anything while I was gone,' she said, shooting Estelle a glare.

'There's nothing here to steal,' Estelle said, glaring right back.

Dot at least had the courtesy to greet Annie and Mac.

'We are so sorry you had to come all this way to get us. It's my fault. I left the headlights on when we got here.'

She got up from her seat on the white wicker furniture where an ancient-looking dog was snoozing next to her. She gave Annie a big hug.

'It's no problem at all,' Annie chirped even though the whole thing had been a rather large problem. 'We were just worried about you.'

'I told Henry where we were going,' Estelle said. 'That man never listens.'

'Can I get you something to drink?' Sylvia asked, directing her question to Mac. She looked extra tiny standing beside him, her head barely coming up to his bicep.

'No, I'm all right. Thanks. We really need to get back on the road.'

'You sure? Such a tall drink of water like you must be thirsty or hungry. I could get you some cookies.'

Estelle scoffed from her perch on a rocking chair in the corner. 'Cookies? Is that what you're calling those dry bricks you tried serving us?'

'See, this is the sort of behavior her branch of the family is known for.' Sylvia wrapped a hand around Mac's arm. 'You remind me of my dead husband,' she added, gazing up at him.

He looked to Annie for help, but she was still too busy trying to figure out what the hell was going on and why they were all here.

'Well, if you've finished your business, Estelle, we really do need to get back so we're not late for the wedding.'

She wanted to scream, *You know, the wedding for your one and only grandson who you raised and who loves you more than anything?! That wedding?*

But she kept the smile pinned to her face and avoided Mac's panicked stare as Sylvia tucked herself closer into his side. Although she fully intended to tease him about his new girlfriend later.

'We'll be done with our business as soon as Sylvia forks over my rightful property.'

'Your property? How dare you!' Sylvia said, trembling with anger. She kept her grip on Mac's arm as she spoke. 'That heirloom has been in our family for generations and it's as much mine as it is yours.'

Estelle huffed, rising from her chair. 'Be that as it may, I have a grandson who needs it, and you don't.'

'Just because my grandkids didn't want it, doesn't mean I should pass it on to you after you come storming in here like you own the place.'

'They've been having this argument since we got here,' Dot whispered to Annie. 'I really didn't know what I was getting myself into when I agreed to drive her here. I thought it was a simple errand to pick up something for the wedding.'

'She duped you,' Annie whispered back.

'Totally.'

'I've been calling you for months,' Estelle went on. 'You could have given it to me weeks ago and we wouldn't be in this situation.'

Sylvia shrugged. 'I didn't get your messages.'

'Ha!' Estelle said, coming closer. 'Like my father always said, your family is full of liars.'

Sylvia gasped and Annie felt like she was a side character on a daytime soap opera. Mac shifted so he was in between the two cousins. If he had to break up a fight between these senior ladies, Annie would lose it. That definitely wasn't on her wedding bingo card.

'Ladies,' Mac said, flashing his most charming smile. 'I'm sure we can figure this out. We're all mature adults here, right?' He winked at Sylvia.

She giggled.

Okay, so maybe he *was* a really good groomsman. Annie had to give him that.

Sylvia blushed, patting a hand to her white curls. 'Well, maybe we could figure something out,' she said. 'You come with me.' She took Mac by the hand and led him out of the room. He glanced back once, his eyes wide, and Annie shrugged and wiggled her fingers in a wave goodbye. If he wanted to play the charmer, this was what he got.

'I really am sorry about all this,' Dot said again.

But Estelle was still fuming. 'It's not our fault the old wretch won't give me what's mine.'

Annie patted her shoulder. 'I'm sure we'll get it and we'll be back in plenty of time for the wedding, okay? Everything's going to be fine.'

The old dog let out a long sigh. Annie felt the same way.

'What is this heirloom, anyway, and why is it so important?' she asked while they waited for Mac and Sylvia to return.

'It's good luck,' Estelle said. 'It has been in my family for years and every bride that's worn it on her wedding night has had a long and happy marriage, so it's important. I had to come get it.'

'I'm sure Jeanie and Logan will have a long and happy marriage, no matter what,' Dot said.

'Well, I'd like to have a little extra insurance.'

'Did you wear it?' Annie asked, still wondering what the heck they were talking about. Jeanie already had her dress and shoes and jewelry for the day. What else was there?

'I didn't get to wear it,' Estelle said, 'because Sylvia claimed she lost it after her wedding. I didn't push it at the time, but Logan's too important to me for him to not have it for his bride.'

If Annie disregarded how this whole thing had upended her day and threatened the wedding, then she could almost see how it was a loving gesture from a grandmother to the grandson she'd raised. Almost.

'We're back,' Sylvia said, shuffling into the room. She had a wrapped parcel under one arm and Mac's hand in hers.

'I'm only giving this to you because Dot has been a lovely guest and Mac here really made my day. If it had been only you on my doorstep, I would have left you outside.'

Estelle huffed and held out her hand. 'Just give it to me already.'

'Estelle,' Annie hissed. 'Be nice.' Maybe if she had been nice from the start this whole thing wouldn't have happened, but Annie kept that part to herself. She didn't know what history these two old women had, but she was not about to get into it right now.

Estelle rolled her eyes like a teenager. But she cleared her throat and tried again. 'Please may we have the package so we can be on our way?'

Sylvia hesitated but then handed it over, and Annie breathed a sigh of relief.

'Thank you for your hospitality,' Dot said leaning down to give the woman a hug.

'You can come back anytime,' Sylvia said, patting her on the back. 'And that goes for you too,' she said, looking up at Mac. He leaned down and she gave him a little peck on the cheek.

'Thanks, Sylvia. We really appreciate your help,' he said, giving her hand one more squeeze.

'Okay, gang. We've got a wedding to get to,' Annie said, herding everyone out of the house. The dog finally woke up and barked as they closed the door behind them.

They all piled into Mac's enormous SUV truck-thing and, before they were even back on the highway, Annie had to know. 'So, what is it?' she asked.

Estelle unwrapped the package and held up some sort of fabric or garment. Annie still wasn't sure what she was looking at.

She turned around so she could get a better look at it. 'But what is it?'

'It's a nightgown,' the old woman replied, and Annie nearly choked on her spit.

It *was* a nightgown, a nightgown that was probably older than the country itself. The material was yellowed, and it had long sleeves and a high neck and would probably reach down to Jeanie's ankles. It was an actual nightmare. It was what an angry ghost would wear while haunting an old Victorian manor.

'Wow!' was all Annie could reply. She couldn't meet Dot's eye as she was currently very clearly trying not to laugh.

'You want Jeanie to wear that tonight?'

'Of course,' Estelle said. 'And if she does, she and Logan will have a long and happy marriage, guaranteed.' She beamed and Annie had to turn around before she started laughing. She could see Dot's shoulders beginning to shake. They had come all this way to retrieve an ancient nightie. Annie was pretty sure that if Jeanie did wear it, the thing would disintegrate as soon as Logan touched her. The thought had her snorting as she tried to stifle her laughter.

'Wait a minute,' Mac said, slowly piecing things together from his position in the driver's seat. 'Did we just drive to New Hampshire to pick up some magic, old-timey lingerie?'

That was when Annie and Dot completely lost it, descending into hysterical giggles. Even Estelle started to chuckle.

'I guess I forgot how old it was,' she said. 'I'm not sure it's going to hold up to another wedding night.'

The group laughed even harder at that. Annie was doubled over in the passenger seat, her sides aching.

'Can I please be there when you give it to them?' she asked between giggles. 'I can't wait to see the look on Logan's face when he sees it.'

'Jeanie's so sweet, she'll probably pretend she likes it,' Mac said, and the group broke down again.

'My God, this is insane,' Annie said, wiping the tears from her eyes.

'It really did seem like a good idea at the time,' Estelle said.

Dot patted her on her shoulder. 'It was a lovely idea. I'm sure Logan and Jeanie will appreciate the gesture.'

'Yeah, and silver lining: Mac almost got a girlfriend out of the deal,' Annie said.

'Sylvia was a very handsome woman,' he said straight-faced. 'Although I didn't love the part where she wanted to tell me how *loving* her dead husband used to be.'

Annie giggled. 'Big shoes to fill,' she said, nudging Mac's arm where it rested on the center console.

He shook his head and smiled at her. 'I'm not sure I could keep up with Sylvia, that's for sure.'

It was suddenly quiet in the backseat and Annie glanced back.

Dot smiled. 'What's going on between you two? Something's different.'

'Nothing's different,' Annie snapped.

'No.' Dot shook her head. 'Something's definitely different.' Her eyes lit up. 'You two finally had sex, didn't you?'

'Thank God,' Estelle said, rolling her eyes. 'Wait. What day is it? I might have won the pool.'

Annie's face flushed hot. She couldn't believe she had to have this conversation while trapped in a vehicle with Mac.

'We *didn't* have sex. Everything is the *same* between us. *Nothing* is going on, okay?'

Both women looked at her like they didn't believe a single word she was saying.

'Now, Annie, that's not entirely true.' Mac's voice was teasing and devious. *He wouldn't.*

'Don't you dare,' she said.

He held her gaze for a second before turning his eyes back to the road. 'Oh, that's right. I forgot I gave you one more day.'

'One more day for what?' Estelle piped up.

'One more day to keep pretending there's nothing going on between us,' he said, and Annie smacked him hard on the shoulder.

'Oops,' he said with a chuckle. 'Did I say too much?'

'I knew it,' Dot said triumphantly, sitting back in her seat. 'I can always sense these things.' Annie wanted to point out that the woman hadn't known when one of her employees had had a decades-long crush on her, but unfortunately, she'd been taught to respect her elders.

'Wait, did I win the bet or not?' Estelle asked.

'You didn't win,' Annie said, eyes straight ahead on the road. 'Nobody won.'

'Ain't that the truth,' Mac muttered from beside her.

And at this point Annie didn't know what winning looked like anymore.

Chapter Thirty-Five

Now

The Wedding

Mac had never been the kind of person to fantasize about his wedding day, but he'd be a liar if he said it didn't do something to him to see Annie walking down the aisle toward him. In a different world, a parallel universe, this could be *their* wedding. She could be walking to *him*.

Her gaze held his and everyone else in the room disappeared. Some part of his brain knew that he stood between Noah and Bennett, all in their dark-gray suits, a sprig of holly tucked in their lapels. He knew Logan waited at the altar for Jeanie. He knew the trees he'd helped Bennett string lights on were lit up and that the whole barn was twinkling with white Christmas lights and candles.

He knew that Estelle and Henry sat in the front row with Jeanie's parents as though Estelle hadn't been missing for the past twenty-four hours. He knew that Annie had played a big role in making this whole day perfect.

But as he watched Annie walk down the aisle, *she* was the only thing he knew, the only thing he saw, the only thing that mattered.

The bridesmaids wore deep-crimson dresses or, at least he assumed they all did. He hadn't taken his eyes off Annie long enough to confirm that, but he knew that her dress had long sleeves and a high neckline in the front, and it scooped low in the back. He imagined dancing with her later, pressing his hand to her bare skin. If she let him. Her blonde hair was in satiny curls over one shoulder and when he looked at her face she had tears in her eyes.

And it hit him again that she was so much better than the fantasy.

She reached the front and arranged herself next to Hazel and Kira. The music changed and the guests' attention turned to the bride. Annie's eyes stayed on him for a beat longer and he winked at her, expecting a scowl in return. Instead, he got a gentle smile before she turned her gaze to the bride.

Bennett nudged him from the side. 'Is that why we haven't seen you all day?' he whispered.

'What are you talking about?'

Noah blew out a disbelieving breath. 'You two were totally eye-fucking each other that whole walk down the aisle.'

'We were not.' *Had they been? Had he just eye-fucked Annie in front of the whole town?!*

One glance at Jacob's huge grin from the third row confirmed it. When the man started making kissy faces and drawing hearts in the air with his fingers, Mac had to look away.

Bennett chuckled. 'You absolutely were, but you can tell us all about it later.'

'I'm not telling you two anything.'

'She went from looking at you like she wanted to kill you to *that* over the course of a weekend. We definitely need to hear the story,' Noah whispered before turning back to Logan to hand him a handkerchief. The big guy had big tears rolling down his face at the sight of his soon-to-be wife.

It was sweet, really, and Mac tried to focus on the wedding ceremony instead of on Annie and what she might say after today was over. He hadn't meant to give her an ultimatum, and he didn't even expect her to have an answer for him. He only wanted her to *talk* to him. He was tired of the silence between them, the half-truths.

'We are gathered here today,' Mayor Kelly began, 'to marry two of our own, two people who this town holds very dear.' He smiled at both of them, and Jeanie reached forward to wipe a tear from Logan's cheek. She looked beautiful in sparkly white lace, like a fairy you would find in a frost-covered forest somewhere, and Mac knew if he were Logan he would be crying, too.

'Jeanie,' Mayor Kelly said, turning toward the bride, 'ever since you moved to town, we all knew you were special, and we knew that you were just the one to take care of our Logan.'

'And Logan,' he continued, turning toward the groom,

'this town, and your family and your friends have always wanted the best for you, and we know that the best is Jeanie.'

'Damn right she is,' Logan said, eliciting a laugh from the audience.

'Love is a funny thing,' the mayor went on. 'It's not always big or loud or over the top. Most of the time, it's quiet and unassuming. It's a shared cup of coffee on a rainy day or reading side by side together every night. It's finding the person who gets you. The person who will have your back through it all.

'*Your* person,' he added with a smile. 'And since we all know that you found that in each other, let's move on to the vows and get this party started.'

A few guests whooped at that suggestion.

Jeanie let out a teary laugh and reached behind her to grab the folded-up piece of paper Annie was handing her. She opened it and cleared her throat.

'Logan,' she started with a slight tremble in her voice. 'I never expected to find you. I never expected to find a home here, a *life* here, but I'm so glad I did. I promise to love you until we're both old and gray and I'll keep on loving you even after that. I promise to love your family like my own. I promise to never limit the number of chickens you can have.'

Logan laughed between his tears at that one and so did Mac. *That* was love. Unlimited chickens.

'I can't promise I'll keep our house tidy, but I will always help you make it a home. I love you and I promise to be your partner from now until forever.'

The entire bridal party was wiping their tears now and

Mac didn't know how poor Logan would make it through his own vows. Jeanie was a tough act to follow.

'Jeanie,' he started and then stopped to clear his throat. 'Jeanie…' Another pause. Mac knew speaking in front of the entire town was the last thing Logan wanted to do.

Jeanie leaned forward and whispered something in his ear and Logan laughed. 'You can do it,' she said, pecking him on the cheek.

'Jeanie,' he started again. 'I tried not to like you.'

Mac shook his head. *Dear God, that's a rough start.* But Jeanie was smiling. So maybe not too rough.

'I tried not to like you, but it was impossible because I actually like everything about you. I like how kind you are and how brave. I like how you move through the world looking for what brings you joy.

'I never lived my life like that. But you bring me joy every day and I promise to try to do the same for you. I promise to love you with my whole heart. Forever.'

Annie caught Mac's eye from the other side of the altar. What he wouldn't give to make the same sort of promises to her.

Mayor Kelly was wiping his eyes behind his glasses. 'That was beautiful, you two. Just beautiful. I'm so proud of you both,' he said as everyone composed themselves.

'Now down to the business of it. Jeanie, do you take this man to be your lawful wedded husband?'

Jeanie's smile was so big Mac could feel it in his own heart. 'I do,' she said, proudly.

'And Logan, do you take this woman—'

'I do,' he blurted before Pete could finish his line.

'Very good, very good,' the mayor said with a chuckle. 'The rings?'

Noah passed Logan the ring and he was quick to put it on Jeanie's finger, completely skipping the part where he was supposed to say something, but at this point the man was just ready to be married.

Jeanie beamed, tears sliding down on her face as she put Logan's ring on his finger. 'With this ring, I thee wed,' she said following the script and Logan turned even redder than he already was.

'Me too,' he said, and the audience laughed some more.

Mac thought there was so much love in this room he'd never felt anything like it, and it was all for them, all for these two people that they all loved so much.

And maybe for the first time since he'd been back, since the first time Annie told him how much she loved this town, he finally got it. He finally understood how special this place was and how lucky he was to be here.

He wiped his eyes. Christ, now he was crying, too.

'You may kiss the bride,' Mayor Kelly announced through his laughter.

Logan took Jeanie's face in his hands and kissed his wife.

The whole town cheered.

Annie stood from her seat at the table and waited for the room to quiet. When it finally did, she raised her glass of champagne.

'When you know someone for your entire life,' she

started, 'you can get protective of them, sometimes overly so.' She gave Jeanie a knowing look, remembering the day she and Hazel had warned her to be careful with Logan's heart. Jeanie smiled back.

'As Pete said, you want what's best for them, especially when you know that they are one of the best people in the world.'

She looked to where Logan sat with Jeanie at their sweetheart table in the center of the room. He looked absurdly handsome in his dark-gray suit and maroon tie. Handsome and happy. But for a moment she saw him as he was all those years ago. A sad, quiet little boy who she had immediately decided she needed to cheer up. And now Jeanie sat beside him, looking stunning in her wedding dress with her dark hair swept up off her neck. She sparkled in the muted lighting of the barn and Annie knew her relationship with Logan would be different now.

'Logan has been my best friend since we were five when I forced him to be.'

The room laughed at that.

'But now Logan has a new best friend,' she said, and saw the emotion flicker across his face. 'And he couldn't have found a better one. I will always be here for both of you but I'm so happy you have each other.'

She barely got the words out before the tears started, so she raised her glass and everyone followed suit.

'Cheers to the happy couple!'

She sat back down, using her napkin to dab at her eyes, hoping she hadn't destroyed her makeup again. That ceremony had already done a number on it.

Luckily it was Noah's turn next.

'Hey, everyone, I'm Noah. I *thought* I was the groom's best friend but I'm just now finding out I'm actually third in line.'

'Fourth,' Hazel said from her seat beside him, and everyone laughed, including Noah who shook his head.

'Fourth, I guess. But I'll take it, because for the first two years I knew him I was pretty sure the man hated me. As you all know, that's just part of Logan's charm.'

More laughs, even from Logan.

'Jeanie, on the other hand,' Noah went on, 'I liked right from the start, and I was pretty confident she liked me, too.' He winked and Jeanie shook her head, laughing.

'I couldn't think of a better couple,' Noah said. 'I mean except for maybe me and Hazel.' The crowd groaned and Hazel swatted him on the arm.

'What about us?' Kira shouted from her place beside Bennett.

Noah chuckled. 'We can all have different opinions about that, but since today is *their* day, let's raise our glasses to Jeanie and Logan.'

Again, the guests drank in the bride and groom's honor.

Noah sat back down, and Hazel leaned into his side. Her curls were tucked away from her face with a pretty silver comb and, while her dress matched Annie's in color, a gorgeous dark red, the cut was different. She'd chosen a lower neckline with spaghetti straps and Kira had gone with an off-the-shoulder choice. Annie's was modest in the front but dipped dangerously low in the back. She loved it and especially loved that Jeanie had let them choose what suited them best.

It was one more thing that made the wedding feel extra special.

Several rounds of champagne later and the speech portion of the evening had gotten completely out of control, which Annie probably should have seen coming. Somehow the microphone had started being passed around and everyone in town seemed to have something they wanted to say to the happy couple.

Annie thought maybe as co-maid of honor she should put a stop to it, but the bride and groom seemed to be enjoying themselves. So, she sat back, kicked off her shoes, and was enjoying the show.

'That don't-go-to-bed-angry advice is all wrong,' Isabel was saying, glass of champagne in hand. 'Sometimes you need to just sleep it off and wake up fresh.'

'Or even better go to bed and don't sleep!' Marissa suggested, eliciting hoots and hollers from her table of rowdy ladies.

Isabel raised her glass. 'Great. Even better, go to bed and don't sleep,' she said with a laugh. 'Cheers to the couple!'

'Cheers to Logan and Jeanie!'

The microphone was passed to Dot and she stood up. 'I wanted to say I'm so glad you two ended up here together. Deep down, I knew that giving Jeanie the café was a good idea. I just didn't realize how good it would be! It really worked out for all of us,' she said with a smile, looking down at Norm in the seat beside her. 'I'm so happy for you two.'

'And I'm forever grateful to you!' Jeanie called from the sweetheart table. Jeanie's face must hurt from smiling so much but Annie was thrilled to see the bride so happy and that they'd pulled this wedding off.

For the first time in weeks, she felt like she could finally breathe a sigh of relief. At least she did feel relieved until she looked across the room and caught Mac staring at her. What the hell was she going to do about that? It didn't help that he looked unfairly gorgeous in his suit or that he had watched her walk down the aisle like she was all he ever wanted.

She thought about what Pete had said during the ceremony. Was it remotely possible that the man who had broken her heart all those years ago actually might turn out to be *her person*?

'I just wanted to say a huge congratulations to my beautiful sister and her new husband,' Bennett said, taking the floor. 'And I also wanted to take a minute to say what an amazing job Kira did putting this wedding together.'

Kira smiled up at him as everyone applauded. 'I had plenty of help,' she said. 'Annie and Hazel, the best bridesmaids ever. Daisy, for the beautiful arrangements. And a huge shout out to Archer for this amazing food. I couldn't have done it by myself. So many people pitched in. I'm so happy to have had such an amazing couple be my first customers, but please do keep us in mind for future large events, hashtag kiranorthevents!'

Annie smiled. She couldn't help but remember last year at this time when Kira was doing everything in her power to not get sucked into the Dream Harbor vortex, and now here she was planning events for the town. This place had that effect on people. They came here sad or lost or alone until Dream Harbor worked its magic.

She looked over at Mac again. Had the town worked its magic on him? Of course, he'd live here for the first half of his life, but he'd been gone for so long. Was this place in his heart like it was in hers?

She watched him laughing with Noah and she thought about all the ways he had come back. For three years, she'd tried to pretend it wasn't true or it wasn't real or it wouldn't stick. But here he was, friends with her friends, renovating his parents' old house, running his dad's pub. Mac was here in Dream Harbor again. He had set up his life here and he wanted her. All she had to do was say yes.

She turned her attention back to the speeches in time to hear Cliff comparing marriage to fishing and making some sort of obscene, rod jokes. Maybe it was time for her to confiscate the microphone. She was about to when Mac took it.

He cleared his throat looking around the room. His gaze stuck on her only for a moment before flitting away.

'I wanted to say congratulations and to say thank you to Logan.'

Logan looked up, surprised, his eyebrows raised.

'Thanks for letting me have a clean slate with you, and for being one of the first people to welcome me back to town. It's funny how when we're young we feel like we need to get far away from where we grew up, or at least some of us do, in order to find ourselves. And I did learn a lot about myself while I was gone. I lived in a lot of amazing places, and I met a lot of interesting people but, in the end, I missed *home*. I missed the people here. I missed this.'

His gaze landed back on Annie. She felt her skin flush. Had he really missed her the whole time he was gone?

Mac cleared his throat.

'Anyway, I'm really happy for you, man, and thanks for letting me be a part of it. Cheers to the bride and groom and to Dream Harbor.'

'To Dream Harbor!' the crowd echoed, raising their glasses one more time.

Chapter Thirty-Six

Now

The Wedding (still)

'Daisy, that guy is totally checking you out,' Iris said, as she worked through her second plate of cookies. The gingerbread house had been a big hit, but Annie had also made several platters of cookies and pastries for the guests to eat. Iris seemed to be appreciating them very much.

'What guy? No, he isn't. What guy?' Daisy's head swiveled from side to side.

Iris laughed. 'That one over there with the glasses. He's been looking over here all night.'

Daisy glanced over to where Iris was pointing.

Annie, Daisy, and Iris were the only three left at their table. The chairs from the ceremony had been cleared and a dance floor was carved out between the tables. At the moment, Annie was watching Noah spin Hazel in circles while she giggled. Kira and Bennet had snuck off somewhere about an hour ago and Annie hadn't seen them since, but she had a pretty darn good idea of what they were doing. Weddings had that effect on people.

'Who even is that?' Daisy asked and Annie looked at the man in question.

'That's Elliot, the new architect. He's working on the inn,' she said.

'Wow, Jeanie really did invite every person in town to this wedding,' Iris said with a laugh.

'I know. Apparently, he was standing nearby when she went to the inn to work out the room availability for her visiting family. She felt bad and invited him, too.'

'Well, whoever he is, he's looking at Daisy like he wants to get to know her better,' Iris said, waggling her eyebrows. She had a hand over her growing belly and her bare feet propped up on the chair next to her. She looked tired but happy as she watched Archer slow-dance with Olive.

'That's adorable,' Daisy said, looking at them spinning in circles, Olive perched on Archer's feet.

Iris nodded. 'That's how they get you.'

'Well, if that didn't do it, the roast chicken definitely would have. It was so tender I wanted to cry,' Annie said, making the other women burst out laughing again.

'The man knows how to cook,' Iris said, 'that's for sure.'

Archer grinned at Iris from his spot on the dance floor and Olive waved. She looked adorable in her velvet Christmas dress, little patent leather Mary Janes on top of

Archer's dress shoes. Something across the room caught her eye and she came running over to Iris.

'Is that hot chocolate?' she asked, her face filled with the intensity of a girl who would go to the ends of the earth for chocolate. A girl after Annie's heart.

'It's actually a whole hot-chocolate bar,' Annie told her. 'With toppings.'

'Toppings?!' Olive squealed.

'Marshmallows, candy canes, little cookie bits, oh, and whipped cream.'

'Whipped cream!!'

Olive was practically vibrating now, and Annie ignored the look of horror on Iris's face. It was all part of the fun of being an honorary auntie.

'Yep. All the whipped cream you can eat.'

'Daddy!! Can I have some?' Olive turned around to where Archer was standing behind her, staring daggers at Annie. Annie smiled up at him.

'Sure, Liv, let's go.'

'Weddings are the best!' Olive was already halfway across the room before the sentence was fully out of her mouth.

'You're welcome,' Annie said, and Archer shook his head like he was resigned to the fact that Olive would never sleep again.

'You want anything?' he asked Iris, leaning down to kiss her.

'Well, all this talk about hot chocolate…'

Archer sighed but the little smile on his face betrayed him. He loved every minute of it.

'I'll get you one.'

'Extra marshmallows, please. It's for the baby.'

Archer laughed and pressed another kiss to her lips before straightening. 'Of course. For the baby.'

'Love you!' Iris called as he walked away.

'Wow.'

'I know,' Iris said with a smile.

Annie shook her head, debating if she also wanted hot chocolate, but instead turned her attention back to Daisy. 'So, are you going to go talk to him?'

'What? Talk to the architect guy? No, nope. No way. Not in the market for weirdos that stare at you from across the room. No, thank you.'

Annie laughed. 'Good call, although he is a pretty cute weirdo,' she said, remembering her short-lived plan to invite him to the wedding as her date.

Daisy peered over at him one more time. 'Cute, maybe, but I've sworn off men anyway.'

'Now hold on,' Iris said. 'You said you swore off love. That doesn't mean you have to swear off men altogether. You know they are good for other things,' she said with a wink.

Daisy laughed, tucking her dark hair behind her ear. She looked gorgeous in her slinky black dress. It really was no wonder the weird architect guy was staring at her.

'I forgot to mention,' Annie said. 'You don't need to worry about your curse ruining this marriage.'

'Really, and why's that? Because Logan and Jeanie love each other so much?'

'Nope,' Annie said with a grin. 'Because Estelle brought back a magic, olden-times nightie that will bring them good luck.'

'What the hell does that mean?' Iris asked.

'I tracked her to New Hampshire today where she was fighting with her ancient cousin over a nightgown that will now feature prominently in my nightmares. Oh, my God, see!'

Annie gestured over to where Estelle stood in front of Jeanie and Logan's table holding up the offensive garment.

Jeanie had a smile plastered on her face, but Logan looked like he wanted to crawl under the table and die.

Annie, Iris, and Daisy burst out laughing.

'Hey, Annie, looks like your sister is stealing your man,' Daisy said once they'd recovered from their fit of giggles.

Annie's head whipped to the dance floor where Mac was currently twirling her sister, Charlotte, in a slow circle.

Annie's brain short-circuited.

What the actual fuck.

'If you'll excuse me, ladies,' she said, getting up from her seat so fast their empty glasses rattled on the table. No time to track down her shoes; she marched across the room barefoot to where Elliot stood with wide eyes at her approach.

'I need you to dance with me,' she said, grabbing him by the hand.

'I actually … I just…'

'It really doesn't matter,' Annie cut him off. 'I need you to dance with me for one song. Okay? We're not getting married or anything. No need to worry.' She dragged him onto the dance floor.

Poor Elliot took one more glance at Daisy and followed Annie into the throng of dancers.

'Told you it would work,' Charlotte said, looking over his shoulder at where Annie had just charged onto the dance floor.

Mac could feel Annie's rage boring into the back of his head.

Of course it worked. How many times had they done this? He'd bring a date somewhere and then Annie did. Over and over again, they'd tormented each other.

He was tired of it but, if this was the only way to get Annie to pay attention, then he would do whatever it took. She'd been avoiding him all night, ever since they had walked back down the aisle together. Her arm had felt so right in his, he hadn't wanted to let go, but there were photos to be taken and toasts to be given. She'd even managed to scramble up the bridal party for the first dance and he'd ended up dancing with Hazel while Noah got to dance with Annie.

He told himself he was going to be patient. He was going to wait for the wedding to be over like he promised he would, but Annie, in that dress, was making it impossible. It hugged every delicious curve of her. Every dip, every delectable bit of her body was on display, and as the night wore on, Mac found himself with less and less patience.

So, when Annie's little sister, who insisted he call her 'Charlie' now, offered him a dance, it seemed like the perfect way to spur Annie into action.

Except there was a flaw in his plan because, as he slowly spun Charlie on the dance floor, he came face to face with

Annie in another man's arms. Who the hell was that guy with his hand on Annie's back, his fingertips grazing her bare skin in the exact place Mac had imagined touching all night? The guy from the inn? Whoever he was, Mac wanted him dead.

'You okay?' Charlie asked. 'You got all weirdly tense there for a minute.'

Mac cleared his throat, and Annie caught his eye over the shoulder of her dance partner. She gave him a satisfied little smirk.

'I think your sister might be the death of me,' he told her.

'She is the most stubborn person I know, so good luck with that.'

'Yeah, I know that. I've been trying to get her to forgive me for years now.'

'And how's that going?'

'She's dancing with another man, so not great.'

Charlie raised a brow. 'To be fair, you're dancing with another woman.'

'Good point,' he said as he watched Annie's hands wrap tighter around the man's neck until their bodies were nearly flush together. He practically growled with rage.

Or maybe he did growl, because Charlie pulled back, her eyebrows raised.

'Sorry.'

'Do you want to know what I think?' she said.

'Sure.' What did he have to lose? He was already failing at this and had been for years. Maybe one of the people who knew Annie best could finally help him figure it out.

'I know Annie thinks it's some big secret that you two

were together for a while there, but I knew, little sisters always know, and I know how upset she was when you left.'

'Shit, Charlie, I know. But how many times can I say I was a dumb kid and I'm sorry?'

She shook her head. 'That's not the main problem. Getting over heartbreak is easy but you bruised her *ego*. You know she loves to be perfect. But she was *wrong* about you. She fell for you and then you never came back. She hates to be wrong. You made her feel stupid and foolish and that is something she hates more than anything.'

'What do I do about it?'

'Well, that's the hard part. I'm not really sure. I guess she needs to know for certain that you're not going to do it again.'

Mac sighed. 'I'm trying.'

'Good. Keep trying. And when it works it will be so worth it. You know her, Mac. She might be stubborn, but that stubbornness translates to loyalty when she loves you. That girl will go to hell and back for the people she loves.'

'Yeah, I know.' Mac said, thinking about their road trip today. All to make sure Logan wasn't upset on his wedding day.

Annie and her dance partner turned, and Mac got to look at the man's face. He had dark-rimmed glasses and was blushing as if he was finding this whole scenario overwhelming. Mac almost felt bad for the guy. He knew he had nothing to do with this situation.

'Thanks, Charlie,' Mac said, giving her a peck on the cheek.

'Anytime,' she said, turning to find her date waiting for her.

Mac walked over to Annie and tapped her dance partner on the shoulder. 'Mind if I cut in?' he asked and the man looked instantly relieved, even as Annie looked like she might argue.

'Go right ahead,' he said quickly, releasing his grip on Annie. 'She's all yours.'

If only that were true.

Annie hesitated, like maybe she was going to leave him standing there like a fool but after an awkward silence she stepped into the circle of his arms.

'Dancing with my sister was a dirty move,' she said.

'You've been avoiding me, Annabelle. I had to do something.'

'Today is not about us.'

'Look around, Annie! *You did it.* The wedding was beautiful. People went wild for that gingerbread house. I'm pretty sure it was the most Logan cried today, which is saying a lot. The bride and the groom are happy.' He gestured to where Jeanie and Logan were slow-dancing, her head resting on his chest. They did look blissfully happy. 'Your job is done, so I would argue the rest of tonight *can* be about us.'

Surprisingly, she didn't argue but huffed an angry little sound that blew her warm breath over his neck. Her hands were on his shoulders, holding him at a distance like they were at some sort of middle-school dance and had been lectured by the chaperones to keep space between their bodies. His hands were on her hips and, every once in a while, his fingers grazed the bare skin of her back. He wanted to press his whole hand there and tug her closer. He wanted to feel the full length of her body, in that damn dress, pressed up against him.

'I think we regress when we're together,' he said, and Annie looked at him with a bemused expression.

'Oh, yeah?'

'Yeah, we act like we're teenagers again,' he said, taking her hand from his shoulder and twining it with his. He slid his other hand to the small of Annie's back and savored her small intake of breath as he pulled her closer. 'But I'm not a teenager anymore, Annie. I know what I want now.'

'And what's that?' Her voice was low and breathy and right beside his ear. She was close to him now, so close he could feel the rapid beat of her heart against his chest.

'You.' It was as simple as that. He'd been too scared to take what he wanted before. Too young, too unprepared. But not anymore.

'I want you, Annie, and I don't care if you need to fuck me like you hate me but you're leaving here with me tonight.'

'Is that so?' she said, like she was going to fight him on it, but there was no argument in her tone. Only curiosity, *interest*.

'Yes,' he said. 'As soon as we're done here, with whatever little tasks you come up with to stall for time and whatever bridesmaid duty you feel like you need to do, whenever that's done, I'm taking you back to my place to finish what we started.' *Or to start something brand new.*

It was a dangerous tactic, being that forceful with Annie. He was still half expecting to get a knee to the groin, but he was out of patience, out of time, out of sanity. Maybe Annie needed him to be stronger in his conviction that this could work, strong enough for the both of them. Strong enough to prove to her that this was right, that he wanted her and that he wasn't going anywhere. Maybe that's what he should have done from the start.

Judging by the way Annie hadn't kneed him in the balls, and instead had curled up even tighter against him, he might be on to something.

He didn't push his luck, but held her close, rocking her to the music, amazed that they had made it this far, that she was letting him hold her in public. That, in and of itself, was a miracle.

He trailed an index finger under the line of her dress and Annie shivered. A little further and his finger found the dimples above her ass. Torture.

'Are you not wearing underwear?' he whispered.

'Of course not, not with this dress,' she said, and he could feel her smile pressed against the side of his neck. Christ, if they weren't in a room full of people, he'd lift her dress right now and check for himself.

'Maybe we're not going to stay till the end after all,' he growled against her ear. 'I can't wait that long.'

Annie gasped at the feeling of his words on her skin.

'I can't just leave,' she said.

'For once, put yourself first, Annabelle. What do *you* want to do.'

She pulled back a little, finding his gaze. Her eyes were a bright, beautiful blue as she studied him. She wanted to say yes. He could tell. But she was holding back again, not wanting to make another mistake with him.

But this time wouldn't be a mistake. He was sure of that, too.

'What do you want?' he asked again, holding his breath. Praying for the answer that got them the hell out of here.

'You,' she said finally, the word barely more than a puff of air, but Mac heard it. It was all he needed. He took her by the hand leading her back to her now-empty table. 'Find your shoes,' he whispered a little too harshly in her ear, but he was a desperate man. 'I'm going to get our coats.'

He left her there in stunned silence and hoped she would still be there when he got back.

Chapter Thirty-Seven

Now

'Hey, there you are.' Logan came up behind her while she was grabbing her strappy heels from where she'd left them under the table.

'Hey. Everything okay?' Annie said, glancing around the room for Mac, afraid her plans were written all over her face.

'I wanted to thank you,' Logan said. 'For everything, but mostly for tracking down Nana today.'

'She told you, huh?'

Logan rolled his eyes. 'Yes, it came up while she was giving Jeanie that nightmare of a nightgown.'

Annie laughed. 'Be careful with that thing. I hear it's a family heirloom and it's lucky.'

'That thing isn't getting anywhere near Jeanie tonight,' he said. 'But thank you, really. That gingerbread house was amazing, and I know a lot of this day happened because of you.'

He wrapped her in his arms and gave her a big squeeze.

Annie squeezed back. 'I love you, you know,' she said.

'Yeah, I know. I love you, too.'

'My turn!' Jeanie said, coming up behind them and giving Annie her own big hug. 'Thank you for finding Nana,' she said, 'although I'm not super excited you brought her back with that nightgown.'

Annie winced. 'Yeah, sorry about that. I couldn't get her to part with it.'

Mac slid up to the table with both their coats over his arm and his face flushed, as though he'd been running around to find them and make it back in time before Annie changed her mind.

'Are you two leaving?' Jeanie asked.

'I... Well, I thought things seemed to be winding down...'

'Definitely! Thank you for everything!' Jeanie said. 'You should take off. You did an incredible job!' Her smirk made it clear she knew exactly what was going on here.

Logan, on the other hand, looked back and forth between Annie and Mac like he was confused about why they would be leaving together.

'Come on,' Jeanie said, tugging him by his arm. 'We've got more guests to thank.' She pulled him away and left Mac and Annie face to face. Annie was sure there were a million reasons she shouldn't go home with him, or at least there had been and now suddenly she couldn't remember any of them.

'Ready?' Mac asked.

Ready was not something Annie thought she'd ever be around Mac, but she grabbed her coat from his arm and started her way toward the door. His hand pressed to the small of her back and heat frizzed up her spine.

Outside the barn, groups of guests were huddled around several firepits, snuggled under cozy blankets with cups of hot drinks in their hands. Kira and Bennett were back from wherever they'd gone, looking happy and rosy-cheeked.

But Mac didn't let her get waylaid, his steady hand guiding her toward the cars.

'Are you two leaving?' Kira called from her spot by the fire.

'We have to check on the kittens!' Annie called back.

'Is that what we're calling it now?' Kira said with a laugh. 'Enjoy!'

'Worried about being the topic of town gossip tomorrow?' Mac asked, leading her toward his car.

'Not particularly,' Annie said, pulling her coat tighter around her. She had her strappy heels in her hand and a pair of boots on her feet to trudge through the snow. 'Just don't embarrass me.'

Last time at least no one knew what had happened between her and Mac. She didn't know if she could handle it if it was town news this time.

Mac turned to face her. 'I don't intend to,' he said.

'And what do you intend to do?'

Mac stepped closer until her back was pressed against the side of his car. His breath was hot on her neck, his hands tracing the curves of her hips.

'I thought we'd start with a kiss,' he said, and Annie realized that even with all their fooling around the past two days they hadn't kissed. It had been over a decade since they had, and suddenly, she wanted that more than anything. She stared at Mac in the moonlight, caught in his gaze, *waiting*.

But he didn't make her wait long. His mouth was on hers before she could second-guess it. And once it was there it was like it had never left. Kissing Mac was the most natural thing she'd ever done.

His lips were insistent and hot, pressed to hers in the cold night. Years of heartbreak melted away. She let her hands slip into his hair and his grip tightened on her hips. Soon his tongue was sliding against hers, urgent and wanting. He pressed her harder against the car, his hands roving over the dips and curves of her body, like he couldn't wait to get her inside before he touched every part of her, like he had to do it now.

'This damn dress,' he growled into her mouth, lifting one of her legs and pushing the dress up over her thigh, wedging himself there. Annie clung to him, her hands fisted in his suit jacket, years of tension and hurt and longing finally surging to the surface.

'Mac,' she gasped as he pushed against her, sending sparks of pleasure through her body.

'I've wanted you for so long. I've wanted you forever,' he said, sucking the delicate skin of her neck, her ear.

It wasn't until they heard boots crunching in the snow toward them that Annie paused, pressing her hands against Mac's chest.

'We can't do this here,' she hissed. 'We have to go.'

Mac blinked like he was returning to reality, only now realizing they were in a snowy field between parked cars.

The night sky was cold and dark behind his head.

'We have to go,' Annie said again.

He kissed her again one more time, quickly, and when he pulled back his face was lit up like the stars.

'Yeah, okay, let's go.' He went around to the driver side while Annie got in. Luckily, they weren't blocked in by anyone and were able to maneuver out of the field pretty easily. Annie snuck a peek at him in the driver seat, and he glanced back with a smile.

'Don't chicken out now, Annabelle,' he said, putting a hand on her thigh. He left it there, tracing little circles with his fingers.

'I'm not chickening out,' she said as his fingers inched higher.

'Are you really not wearing panties?'

Annie swallowed hard. 'I told you I can't with this dress.'

'Show me.'

Annie's heart rate ratcheted up, her pulse quickening, her blood turning molten hot.

'I can't. You'll drive off the road and kill us both.'

Mac let out a low chuckle and Annie wasn't sure how she had resisted him for this long, because right now she felt like she couldn't wait another second.

'Okay, then I won't look.'

Annie made no such promise and watched as Mac pulled up her dress little by little, his fingers tugging up the fabric while his eyes stayed on the road. When the hem was high enough, he slipped his hand under her dress, and she gasped at the sensation of his skin on hers.

That hand traveled up her thigh until it met the crease

between her leg and her hip. The place where Mac discovered she was not lying.

'Jesus, Annie,' he rumbled 'Completely bare.'

Annie's whimper echoed through the car. She didn't look at Mac's face, couldn't meet his eye, but she kept her focus on his hand. His hand that had now found the apex of her thighs, one finger dipping down to where she was wet and aching. She squirmed in her seat.

'Spread your legs for me,' Mac rasped.

And she did. Didn't even fight about it. Didn't even *want* to fight about it. It was nice to not have to think about it, to not worry about what the next step should be. She just did it.

And was rewarded with Mac's fingers on her clit. She grabbed onto his forearm. He pressed harder, his fingers making tight circles, winding her up.

'I've dreamed about this,' he groaned.

'You dreamed this exact thing?' she asked, incredulous even in her pleasure.

'Annie, I've dreamed about having you in every possible way,' he said, quickening his pace.

Annie's head dropped back on the seat, her legs beginning to tremble as they made their way down dark back roads to Mac's house.

She was close. Pleasure building as Mac increased his speed and pressure. Close, so close. Her back arched against the seat, feet scrambling for purchase.

'Mac...'

'We're here,' he said, pulling his hand from her dress.

Annie spun to face him, eyes wide. 'What are you

doing?' she asked, shock and frustration spiraling through her.

'We're here,' he repeated, flashing that obnoxious smirk.

'I was almost there! You need to keep going.'

He chuckled. 'Now, Annie, if you're going to fuck me like you hate me, I had to give you a little more ammunition,' he said before stepping out of the car.

What the hell just happened?

She sat there in disbelief staring at him walking to the house. She almost considered calling an Uber and getting the hell out of here. Then she looked down, saw her dress hiked halfway up her thighs, thought about how Mac's hand had felt there, and she really only had one choice.

Follow him in and fuck his brains out.

Chapter Thirty-Eight

Now

Annie walked into his house looking murderous. Gorgeous and murderous. Her cheeks were still flushed pink from what they'd just done on the drive here, her hair in golden curls over her shoulder, her body like a walking fantasy in that red dress. She looked like some kind of goddess sent here to personally kick his ass.

It had been an act of cowardice to provoke her like that, but Mac was afraid that this was the only way he could have her, that if he showed her any more of the truth she would just run. So instead, he'd fallen into old habits and pissed her off and prayed she wouldn't leave.

She had ditched her boots and coat by the door and stood seething in the middle of his kitchen; seething because she wanted *more*.

And that's exactly what Mac wanted, too.

'Hey, Annabelle,' he said with a slow grin, the one she hated.

'Don't *hey Annabelle* me!' she hissed. 'What the hell was that?'

'A preview,' Mac said, trying to keep up his confident smile even as he was doubting the wisdom of this plan.

Annie's eyes narrowed at him in a familiar glare, but there was something different about it. This time there was heat behind it, *desire*. Maybe there had been all along.

She huffed with impatience. 'And is that *all* I get? A preview?'

Mac grinned. 'Hell no, you get the whole damn show.'

He strode across the kitchen and took her face in his hands, dropping his mouth to hers before she could say another word, diving between her lips with his tongue, devouring her. Every little moan and whimper was his. *Finally*.

Her hands were greedy in his hair, pushing the jacket from his shoulders until he tossed it aside. They somehow made it upstairs like that, grappling with each other, grabbing and pulling and kissing. He pushed Annie against the wall when they made it to the top, pressing against her. She pulled his hair, bit his bottom lip. And he wanted all of it, all the punishment she could give him and more until finally she could forgive him.

He steered them into his bedroom as Annie tore at the buttons on the front of his shirt, clawing at him to get it off. He pushed her hands away, undoing the buttons himself, popping a few off in the process. Annie's laugh was slightly unhinged.

He pulled back long enough to take his shirt off before

Annie was on him again, kissing and tugging at his clothes, nipping at the skin on his throat.

'Take your dress off, Annie,' he rumbled. 'Please,' he added between wild, sloppy kisses. He felt like he was coming apart at the seams, completely undone, but he needed to see her, all of her.

She let go of him, breathing hard. Their gazes locked as she slipped the dress down off one shoulder and then the other. Down her arms, over her chest, her waist, her hips until she had shimmied out of the entire thing and stood in front of him completely naked.

An injured, desperate sound escaped his lips. *'Fuck.'* The word was more sound than coherent thought, but it was all he could manage to say.

Underneath all her hard scowls and sharp remarks, Annie was actually all soft, golden curves. And he wanted to lick every single one.

'Now you,' she said, and Mac was happy to oblige, quickly pulling off his undershirt and kicking off his dress pants.

'Keep going,' Annie said with a smirk, waiting for him to shuck his boxer briefs. He tucked his thumbs in the elastic waistband and held Annie's gaze as he pulled them down, letting his cock spring free. Annie tipped her head to the side like she was assessing the situation. Like she hadn't seen it up close and personal this morning.

Mac couldn't help but laugh. 'Jesus Christ, Annie, did you scare the absolute shit out of every other guy you slept with?'

Annie shrugged. 'Probably.'

He stepped toward her. 'Lucky for you, you don't scare me.'

She wrapped her arms around his neck, pressing her body against his and Mac nearly blacked out.

'You're absolutely fucking gorgeous. You know that, right?' he whispered against her ear.

'Thanks for noticing.'

'I've always noticed.'

His cock pressed against the delicate skin of her stomach and, if she kept kissing his neck like that, he was afraid that little preview might be all she got tonight after all.

'Get on the bed.' He didn't recognize his own voice. Who was this man who made demands like that? But he wanted Annie like nothing he'd ever wanted, and this felt like his last chance. Like if he didn't convince her tonight, he'd have to give her up forever.

By whatever miracle was working in his favor this weekend, she did get on the bed and the sight of her there nearly killed him. She practically shimmered in the moonlight coming in through his window. She was like a dream.

He crawled on top of her, needing to feel her skin on his, needing to know she wasn't a dream. Not anymore. This time she was real.

He kissed her. Every inch, every gorgeous expanse of skin. He kissed and licked and bit until Annie was squirming underneath him, writhing in his bed sheets.

She kissed him back, her nails scratching tracks on his back, her legs wrapping around his waist, pulling him closer.

He looked down at her and every memory, every

moment, every regret tumbled together. He had loved this woman for most of his life. He'd known her for nearly all of it. And he knew he wanted to be with her for the rest of it.

'Annie, I…'

'Don't,' she said, like she knew a confession, one last declaration, was coming. 'We still have half an hour,' she said, glancing at the clock. It was eleven-thirty. Another half hour and it would be tomorrow, the day she'd promised they would finally talk.

'I still have thirty minutes,' she said, giving his shoulder a shove. He laid back on the mattress and let her climb on top of him straddling his waist. She was watching him like she was expecting him to stop her, but nothing could stop this.

'Condoms are in the bedside table drawer,' he said, and Annie smiled. She reached over and grabbed one out of the top drawer, tearing the little packet open with her teeth. He hissed as she slid it over his length, her fingers on him an exquisite torture.

She notched his cock at her entrance pausing to look at him with those blue eyes one more time and then she took him one inch at a time. So slowly time stood still until she was fully seated, and Mac's breath was caught in his throat.

'Holy shit,' Annie gasped, leaning forward, her hands braced on his shoulders. He held tight to her hips, fingers digging into her flesh as they both adjusted to the intensity of the moment.

'Look at me, Annie,' he said, and she opened her eyes.

They were flipped from the last time they did this. It felt like the entire world had flipped since then, but this thing between them still felt more right than anything Mac had ever felt. And, by the way Annie was looking at him, she felt it too.

Tears had gathered in her eyes, and he reached up to brush them away.

'Go ahead, darling,' he said. 'Fuck me like you hate me.'

Annie shook her head and whispered, 'But I don't hate you.'

She leaned down and kissed him slow and deep, her hips mimicking the motion and Mac was lost. Lost to the world. Lost to everything except *this*. Annie had found him again.

They stayed like that for a long time, kissing and rocking with him inside her and her little moans filling the room, fucking like they didn't hate each other at all. When it all became too much, she picked up the pace, grinding against him, chasing her pleasure.

Her blue-eyed gaze held his as she came, the cries racking her body and his name like a chant from her lips.

Annie collapsed onto Mac's chest, her breath sawing in and out of her. She could feel his racing heart beneath her cheek.

He was running his hands up and down her sides and murmuring sweet words against the top of her head. If this was supposed to have been hate-sex, they had done something very wrong. But who was she kidding? Of course she didn't hate him. That had been the problem all along, hadn't it?

Mac rolled them so he was on top of her, and she

realized he was still hard inside of her. He kissed her gently on her lips and cheeks, down the side of her neck.

'You okay?' he murmured.

The best Annie could do was a contented little humming sound. She could feel Mac's grin on her neck.

He thrust his hips, and a spark of pleasure shot through her, aftershocks from that earthquake of an orgasm.

'You know that shady little motel the kids used to party at outside of town?' he asked, still kissing her, her collar bones, her shoulders.

'Yeah?' Why on earth would he be bringing that place up now?

'That's where I spent most of that year away.'

'Mac, what are you talking about?'

He looked up, meeting her eyes. 'I only traveled for the first couple of months, and then I got overwhelmed and sort of freaked out and I spent the rest of the time in that motel. Too afraid to come home and too afraid to go anywhere else.'

Annie stared at him speechless, her legs still wrapped around his waist, her fingers still trailing along the muscles of his back.

'You weren't wrong about me, Annie. I *was* in love with you. I wanted to come home to you, but I felt like too big of a loser to do it.'

'Mac.' She breathed his name, feelings she'd kept at bay for years threatening to tumble out of her.

'After that, I did travel for real, and it was amazing, and *good* for me. I wasn't lying about that. But three years ago, I was in town visiting my parents and I saw you through the window of the café and that's when I decided to move home for good.'

Annie shook her head, her hair brushing along the pillow. What was he telling her? 'No, no, you moved home so your parents could retire.'

'No, I convinced my parents to retire once I did move home, but I came back for *you*. I saw you through that window and I knew I would never find everything I was looking for out there. Annie, I came back on the off chance that I could convince you to give us another try. I never stopped loving you. I still haven't.'

He came back for *her*. He *loved* her. He still did. Hearing those words did exactly what she was afraid they would. They cracked Annie wide open. She took his face in her hands and kissed him with everything she had until he was moving again, thrusting into her. She clung to him as another orgasm tore through her. Crying, she whispered that she loved him too, that she always had.

Mac's movements became faster, more erratic until he came, groaning her name. He pressed his forehead against her shoulder, his breath cooling the sweat on her chest.

She ran her hands over his shoulders.

'I love you, Mac Sullivan,' she said and when he looked at her his smile lit up the room.

Chapter Thirty-Nine

Now

'So, this is it now?' Annie asked. 'We're together or something?'

They were still in bed, and it was well past midnight, but Annie was starving, so they'd raided his fridge for leftovers from the pub. She was wearing another one of his old T-shirts and a pair of sweats, wrapped up in one of his blankets with a plate of cold fried chicken in front of her. She'd never looked more beautiful.

Mac smiled at her question. 'I could formally ask you, if you think that would help.'

Annie tipped her head, considering it.

'It might,' she said with a teasing grin. 'It just seems like an abrupt change, like I'm supposed to be nice to you now? It's weird.'

Mac laughed. 'You don't have to be nice to me all of the time, but I'll take *some* of the time.'

'I'll see what I can do,' she said with a shrug, taking a bite of chicken and then licking her fingers clean.

'Don't you think we deserve to be together after all this time?'

'Well, you still haven't formally asked me, so I'm not sure if we *are* together.' There was that teasing smile again. He wanted to kiss it from her lips. He liked that he was allowed to now.

'Annabelle Andrews, will you be my girlfriend?'

She tipped her head like she was thinking about it. Mac growled her name again and she threw her head back and laughed.

'Okay, yes, I will be your girlfriend.'

He liked the sound of that a little too much for a grown man, but he'd waited for a really long time to hear it.

The kittens had apparently smelled the chicken and were mewing from beside the bed. He leaned over and scooped them up by the scruff and deposited them in the blankets. Annie picked off little bits of chicken to feed to them and they tripped over each other to get to them.

'I think maybe it's better it worked out this way,' Mac said, stealing a piece of chicken for himself.

Annie raised an eyebrow. 'Really? You think it's better that we wasted all this time hating each other?'

'I never hated you, Annie.'

She rolled her eyes again, but a blush worked its way up her cheeks.

'Whatever,' she said.

'I think it's better,' Mac went on, 'because what was going to happen between us when we were nineteen?

I mean, what are the odds we would have lived happily ever after when we were so young?'

'It does happen sometimes.'

'Yeah, but now we have our own shit sorted out.'

Annie gave him a bemused smile. 'You have all your shit sorted out?'

'I like to think so,' he said. 'Took me a while, but I finally figured out that living here is actually really lucky, that plenty of people would jump at the chance to have my life, that my dad built a great business with loyal customers and I'm happy to have taken it over. It's a *good* life. And you have your baking empire. You don't need to worry about me getting in your way while you build it.'

'I was never worried about that.'

Maybe she hadn't been, but he had. He'd never wanted to hold her back.

She shrugged again. 'But maybe you're right. Maybe it is better this way, although it does still feel like we wasted a lot of time. I know a lot of that was my fault. I know you tried to apologize.'

'The way I remember it, I *did* apologize, and you told me to get the fuck out of your store.'

'Oh, right. That's what happened. Sorry about that.'

Mac crawled across the bed toward her. And kissed her lips. Because he could. 'You're forgiven.'

She smiled. 'So are you.'

He lay back in the pillows and Annie put the plate aside and joined him. The kittens promptly crawled on top of his chest, curling up together in a fuzzy heap.

'Okay,' he said. 'Current biggest fear?'

Annie rolled to face him. 'Probably the way the town is going to react to this little development.'

'Yikes.' Mac cringed at the thought. He had no desire to be the topic of town gossip, but it was a small price to pay.

'What about you?'

Mac turned his head to look at her, keeping a hand over the kittens, not wanting to disturb them. 'That if you're in my bed, I'll never want to get out of it again.'

Annie smiled. 'Good one. We will have to get up eventually but I'm free tomorrow.'

'You're free? To stay in bed all day with me tomorrow?'

'Why is that such a surprise?'

'You're *never* free. I don't believe that you don't have a to-do list a mile long for tomorrow.'

Annie shrugged, looking relaxed and happy. 'Maybe I got rid of it.'

'That's the sexiest thing you've ever said.'

She laughed, her nose crinkling, and he thought he was the luckiest person in the world to get to see that every day. He would never take it for granted.

'So, what do you think of me now?' he asked.

Annie was looking at him again, her expression tender. 'I think you're my person. I think you're someone I can trust and love. And I think you look really freaking cute with kittens piled on top of you.'

Mac grinned and one of the kittens clamped their little claws into his still bare chest.

'Oh God! I think this one just cut off a nipple.'

Annie cackled so hard tears ran down her cheeks. Mac removed the cats and deposited them back into the box beside the bed, rubbing his chest as he settled next to Annie. She was still laughing at him.

'That one really got me.'

'Poor baby,' she said, between giggles, kissing the tip of his nose.

He wrapped an arm around her and tugged her close, right where he planned to keep her from now on.

'So,' she said, snuggling in tight, her hands over his heart. 'What do you think of me now?'

That was an easy one.

'I think you're the love of my life.'

Epilogue

A New Favorite Christmas

Annie had spent the last week in Mac's bed. Well, they'd gotten out of it to do their jobs and all that. Annie had had plenty of Christmas orders to fill and nieces and nephews to babysit, and Mac was slammed at the pub with everyone wanting to have their end of year office parties there, but every night they'd fallen into bed together and it had been lovely. They were back in their own little bubble. Conveniently, their new relationship simply hadn't come up in the outside world. But all that ended today. It was Christmas morning, and they were headed to Logan's farm for Estelle's annual Christmas open house this afternoon. And then everyone would finally know Annie's deep dark secret. She was in love with Mac Sullivan. She was only a little nervous.

She reached out an arm to Mac's side of the bed but found it empty. A kitten was draped across her neck and another over her eyes like a little furry blindfold. She gently lifted him up and moved him to the side, blinking in the early morning light.

Where did Mac go? She was always the first one up, having to get to the bakery early, but of course everything was closed today so she'd taken the opportunity to sleep in. She was sure Mac's warm body had been beside her not that long ago.

That was when she smelled smoke.

What the hell?

She tossed off the blankets and scooped up the kittens, hurrying down the stairs. She skidded into the kitchen in nothing but her cozy socks and another one of Mac's old T-shirts as plumes of smoke escaped the oven.

'Mac, what are you doing?!'

He yanked a cookie sheet from the smoking oven and dumped it into the sink, turning on the water. Steam hissed up from the mess. He took a dish towel and was waving the smoke out the window when he finally looked up at her.

'Uh … Merry Christmas?'

'Merry Christmas?! Is setting the house on fire your big surprise?'

He took her in, barely dressed and with the cats in her arms and let out a laugh.

'What? I was ready to evacuate,' she said, putting the cats down. They quickly scampered over to their food dish which luckily was not on fire.

'What were you doing down here?' she asked, coming further into the kitchen now that she was reasonably sure it was safe. Laid out on the counter were what looked to be several batches of burnt, deformed, or undercooked Christmas cookies.

Mac sighed. 'I was trying to make you a Christmas present.'

'You were making me a Christmas present?' she said, her voice getting all high-pitched and sappy like when she talked to the kittens.

'Don't look at me like that.' Mac narrowed his eyes at her in mock anger.

'Like what?' Annie teased.

'Like I'm some sort of injured puppy.'

Annie laughed. 'Sorry, it's nice of you to try but this is clearly a disaster.' She gestured to the dozens of inedible cookies. Maybe the birds would eat them?

Mac hung his head in shame, even as his shoulders shook with laughter.

'It seemed like a good idea at the time,' he said. 'I thought about how you're always making cookies for everyone else, so maybe I should make some for you. But it turns out cooking and baking are two very different skills. One I can do, and one I definitely can't.'

Annie walked across the kitchen and wrapped her arms around his neck. 'This was a very sweet effort,' she said, reaching up to kiss him. He tasted like coffee and sugar-cookie dough. 'But there's no way I'm eating these cookies.'

Mac laughed, kissing her back. 'Oh God, no.'

Annie glanced over his shoulder and caught sight of Mr. Prescott through the kitchen window. 'The mailman still lives next door?!' she gasped, scooting out of his line of sight.

'Yep,' said Mac, amusement written across his face at her

attempts at hiding. 'You know everyone is finding out today.'

'I know.'

'And then there's no turning back. You're stuck with me,' he said, standing in front of her, crowding her against the counter.

'And you're stuck with me.' Her arms were around his neck, playing with the short hair at the back of his head. She couldn't seem to get enough of touching him. For years, she'd resisted it and now she wanted to have her hands on him all the time. Luckily, Mac seemed to feel the same way.

Mac kissed her slow and deep and not at all appropriately for the mailman to witness. He put his hands on her waist and lifted her up onto the counter, keeping his body between her legs.

'Stuck with you is exactly where I want to be,' he said with a grin.

'I got you a present, too,' she said, and Mac's eyebrows rose.

'Really?'

'Of course. You thought I wasn't going to get you a Christmas present?' she teased.

'I honestly wasn't sure.' And it hit her again how new this all still was. Sometimes it felt like they were rushing into everything and then other times it felt like they had been slowly inching toward this for so long that she was more than happy to jump right into the middle of a serious relationship. But they clearly hadn't worked out all the details yet.

She hopped down from the counter and went to get the

gift she'd been hiding upstairs. She brought it into the kitchen hidden behind her back, suddenly nervous to give it to him.

'It's not much,' she said.

'I got you a bunch of burnt cookies, so I think you're going to come out ahead on this one,' Mac said with a laugh.

Annie quickly handed him the gift before she chickened out.

'A postcard?'

'I said it wasn't much. I always felt bad that I didn't write back to you that time. You reached out and I ignored it. I regret it.'

Mac's expression was tender as he turned over the postcard and read, 'Dear Mac, *sorry it took so long to write back. I hope you had an amazing journey but I'm so glad it brought you back to me. Love, Annie.'*

He was smiling when he looked up from the postcard, and Annie stepped toward him, needing to be in his arms again, which he quickly wrapped around her. He pressed a kiss to the top of her head.

'So did I win first Christmas gift-giving?' she asked.

'Absolutely,' he said with a laugh. 'You win, Annie.'

She held him a minute longer, enjoying the feel of him before pulling back.

'I think I have time to help you make a fresh batch,' she said with a smile that Mac promptly kissed.

'No way, you have today off. You sit over there with your feet up. I can at least make you breakfast.'

'Sounds good to me. '

She scooped up a kitten and made herself comfortable at the table, while Mac got breakfast ready and she tried to enjoy their last morning as a secret.

'How do you think everyone's going to react?' Annie asked as they walked up the path to Logan's big front porch. There were dozens of cars out front. Clearly the party was in full swing. They would have been here sooner, but Mac's biggest fear was coming true. With Annie in his bed, he couldn't seem to get out of it. And she'd been more than happy to stay there with him. It wasn't a bad problem to have.

But now, thanks to that, they were late, and it looked like half the town was in there. Mac could hear the Christmas music and laughter spilling out into the cold afternoon.

'I really don't think people are going to be as surprised as you think they are,' he said.

'Why would they not be surprised? We've been horrible to each other over the past few years.'

'Annie, please…'

'Please what?'

'Everyone saw us leave the wedding together.'

'Yeah, but before that we hated each other. I still think people will be shocked.'

Mac scoffed. 'There's *always* been something between us and I'm pretty sure it's been obvious.'

'Obvious? No way. Maybe you've been obvious but not me.' She stomped up the stairs to the porch, her ponytail swinging angrily. She still hated to be wrong.

There was no point in knocking today. Everyone just came and went as they pleased. So, Annie opened the door, and Mac grabbed her hand as they walked into the farmhouse.

The place was bursting at the seams. They barely made it through the door before three little girls raced past them followed by a flustered Archer and a laughing Noah.

'You need your coat if you're going to go outside,' Archer called out as he attempted to wrestle one of the little girls, Olive, into her winter coat.

'Cece's not wearing a coat,' she accused, pointing to one of the other girls.

'She will be,' Noah said, tossing his niece Cece a winter coat. The third seemed to be already in hers and barreling out the door.

'Wait for us, Ivy!' Cece shouted at her cousin.

'Me too!' Olive yelled as they all ran out into the yard.

'Do not leave that front yard!' Archer called after them.

'Merry Christmas to you, too,' Annie yelled as the girls blew past.

'Hey! Merry Christmas!' Noah said, noticing them now that his uncle duties were complete.

'Yeah, Merry Christmas, guys,' Archer said, straightening from his crouch on the floor where he'd been waging the winter coat battle. Neither man mentioned the fact that Mac was clinging tight to Annie's hand, but Noah's smile grew.

'Come on in,' he said. 'I'm sure everyone will be *so excited* to see you.'

They didn't make it any farther into the house before they were accosted by Jeanie and Hazel.

'Merry Christmas!' Jeanie said. 'So happy you guys made it!'

'Thanks for having us,' Mac said, mimicking the way Jeanie had addressed them as a couple. 'Shouldn't you be on a honeymoon or something?'

Jeanie waved a hand. 'No, we put it off till after the holidays. We didn't want to miss out on all of this.' She gestured to the absolute chaos around her, smiling like it was the best thing in the world. She took their coats and Mac grabbed Annie's hand again. She shot him a little glare but didn't pull away.

Hazel stood quietly, her gaze flicking between the two of them and a Cheshire-cat grin on her face.

'So' she said. 'Did you get what you wanted for Christmas, Mac?'

'Definitely,' he said.

'That's nice.'

'It's really nice, thank you.'

Annie growled another angry little sound.

'Seriously?!' she said. 'None of you are going to comment on this?' She lifted their linked hands between them.

'Comment on what?' Logan said, emerging from the kitchen.

'On this,' Annie said, still waving their hands around. 'On me and Mac and … and *us* and we're a thing now and everyone's acting like it's *normal*.'

'You're a thing now?' Logan said, narrowing his eyes, and for a second Mac thought he might actually be about to give some sort of *if you ever hurt her* best-friend lecture, but instead, he blew out a long sigh and said, 'Oh, thank God.'

Hazel burst out laughing and Noah could barely hide his mirth behind his hand.

'Whatever,' Annie said. 'You guys are all jerks.' She led Mac into the living room wishing various townsfolk a Merry Christmas as they went. Not a single one acted surprised to see them together.

'Well, aren't you two cozy?' Kira said when she found them together next to the Christmas tree. Bennett had his arm wrapped around her like he was some sort of human blanket.

'We're very cozy,' Annie said, 'but not a damn person seems surprised about it.'

Kira laughed. 'Well, I'm happy for you, even though no one is surprised.'

'Me too!' Iris chimed in from her seat on the sofa. She was wedged in between Isabel and Kaori and they both grinned up at Annie.

'We've been waiting for this for so long,' Isabel said. 'What a lovely Christmas present you've given us all!'

'Oh, shut up,' Annie said with a laugh and Mac tugged her in closer, planting a kiss on her head.

The whole room broke out into oohs and aahs and Annie turned bright red even as her smile grew. It was just as embarrassing as he knew it would be. But after all this time he would take whatever crap Dream Harbor wanted to give him as long as it meant he got to have Annie.

'Mac!' Jacob gasped, coming into the room. 'Did you finally get your happily ever after?!'

A guy goes to one romantic fiction book-club meeting, and he never hears the end of it! But he wasn't even mad about it. Jacob was right: second-chance romances just hit different.

Mac grinned. 'I sure did.'

And after eleven years he finally had a new favorite Christmas.

Acknowledgments

We're five books into Dream Harbor now and what a wild ride it has been! This series has changed my life in so many ways and I have you all to thank. I have had a lot of readers tell me that these books have brought them comfort in tough times, that they feel like a hug in book, that they read these books for an escape—for a *break*—for a little shot of happiness. All I can say to that is that I am so honored and proud to be able to do this job for you.

I didn't do it alone, of course. A huge thank you to Charlotte Ledger and the entire One More Chapter team and everyone at HarperCollins US and UK that make these books possible. Thank you to Jennie Rothwell for continuing to make working on this series such a joy. Our brainstorming sessions are one of my favorite parts of this gig!

Thank you to Amy Tannenbaum for jumping into the middle of this Dream Harbor craziness and becoming an integral part of the team. And thank you for all your expertise and advice (and for always asking how my wrist is feeling!).

And as always, thank you to my family for cheering me on every step of the way. Thank you for reading, coming to book signings, and for telling literally everyone you know about my books. It is both terribly embarrassing and wonderfully supportive at the same time.

With the success of this series I've had the amazing opportunity to go on several book tours, and while it has been so exciting for me to meet readers, it has also meant leaving home for stretches at a time. So, thank you to my kids for excusing my absence and for sharing me with the world every once in a while. And thanks for being so well behaved while I'm gone.

And lastly, thank you to my husband. There is no one I'd rather be on this ride with than you. (And I'm really happy we got together in high school and just stayed that way instead of breaking up like these two dummies.) Love you xo

Dream Harbor's not done yet, so I hope you'll come back for more!

DO YOU LOVE LAURIE GILMORE?

Why not become a Dreamer
and be the first to hear
from Laurie Gilmore about:

New books
Special and exclusive editions
Additional content
Events and signings

Sign up to the newsletter or follow her at:
thelauriegilmore.com

Pre-order the new spring romance in Dream Harbor now!
Coming May 2026

Daisy is fed up with being unlucky in love, and after several weddings she has done the flowers for end in divorce, her beloved flower shop has gained a reputation of being cursed, thanks to Mayor Kelly's infamous visions.

Dream Harbor newcomer **Elliot** has been adjusting to town life following his own relationship turmoil. And until now he's avoided the flower shop at all costs. If the mayor is correct, he doesn't need any more bad luck in his life.

But with his family coming to visit, Elliot finds himself reluctantly in front of Daisy's store in need of some flowers. As the petals blossom in the sunlight, Daisy and Elliot might find that love comes when you're least expecting it…

Available in paperback, ebook and audio!

When **Jeanie's** aunt gifts her the beloved Pumpkin Spice Café in the small town of Dream Harbor, Jeanie jumps at the chance for a fresh start away from her very dull desk job.

Logan is a local farmer who avoids Dream Harbor's gossip at all costs. But Jeanie's arrival disrupts Logan's routine and he wants nothing to do with the irritatingly upbeat new girl, except that he finds himself inexplicably drawn to her.

Will Jeanie's happy-go-lucky attitude win over the grumpy-but-gorgeous Logan, or has this city girl found the one person in town who won't fall for her charm, or her pumpkin spice lattes…

Available in paperback, ebook and audio!

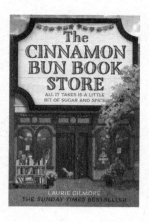

The CINNAMON BUN BOOK STORE

ALL IT TAKES IS A LITTLE BIT OF SUGAR AND SPICE

LAURIE GILMORE

THE SUNDAY TIMES BESTSELLER

When a secret message turns up hidden in a book in the Cinnamon Bun Bookstore, **Hazel** can't understand it. As more secret codes appear between the pages, she decides to follow the trail of clues... she just needs someone to help her out.

Gorgeous and outgoing fisherman, **Noah**, is always up for an adventure. And a scavenger hunt sounds like a lot of fun. Even better that the cute bookseller he's been crushing on for months is the one who wants his help!

Hazel didn't go looking for romance, but as the treasure hunt leads her and Noah around Dream Harbor, their undeniable chemistry might be just as hot as the fresh-out-of-the-oven cinnamon buns the bookstore sells...

Available in paperback, ebook and audio!

Kira North hates Christmas. Which is unfortunate since she just bought a Christmas tree farm in a town that's too cute for its own good.

Bennett Ellis is on vacation in Dream Harbor trying to take a break from both his life and his constant desire to always fix things.

But somehow fate finds Ben trapped by a blanket of snow at Kira's farm, and, despite her Grinchiest first impressions, with the the promise of a warming hot chocolate, maybe, just maybe, these they will have a Christmas they'll remember forever…

Available in paperback, ebook and audio!

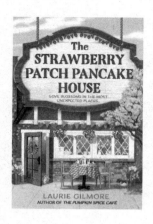

As a world-renowned chef, single dad **Archer** never planned on moving to a small town, let alone running a pancake house. But Dream Harbor needs a new chef, and Archer needs a community to help raise his daughter.

Iris has never managed to hold down a job. So when it's suggested that Archer is looking for a live-in nanny, she almost runs in the opposite direction.

Now, Iris finds herself in a whole new world. One where her gorgeous new boss lives right across the hall and likes to cook topless... Keeping everything strictly professional should be easy, right?

Available in paperback, ebook and audio!

ONE MORE CHAPTER

YOUR NUMBER ONE STOP

FOR PAGETURNING BOOKS

The author and One More Chapter would like to thank everyone who contributed to the publication of this story...

Analytics
Abigail Fryer

Audio
Fionnuala Barrett
Ciara Briggs

Contracts
Laura Amos
Inigo Vyvyan

Design
Lucy Bennett
Fiona Greenway
Liane Payne
Dean Russell

Digital Sales
Laura Daley
Lydia Grainge
Hannah Lismore

eCommerce
Laura Carpenter
Madeline ODonovan
Charlotte Stevens
Christina Storey
Jo Surman
Rachel Ward

Editorial
Kara Daniel
CJ Harter
Charlotte Ledger
Jennie Rothwell
Sofia Salazar Studer
Emily Thomas
Helen Williams

Harper360
Emily Gerbner
Ariana Juarez
Jean Marie Kelly
emma sullivan
Sophia Wilhelm

International Sales
Peter Borcsok
Ruth Burrow
Colleen Simpson
Ben Wright

Inventory
Sarah Callaghan
Kirsty Norman

Marketing & Publicity
Chloe Cummings
Grace Edwards
Roisin O'Shea

Operations
Melissa Okusanya
Hannah Stamp

Production
Denis Manson
Simon Moore
Francesca Tuzzeo

Rights
Ashton Mucha
Alisah Saghir
Zoe Shine
Aisling Smyth
Lucy Vanderbilt

Trade Marketing
Ben Hurd
Eleanor Slater

The HarperCollins Distribution Team

The HarperCollins Finance & Royalties Team

The HarperCollins Legal Team

The HarperCollins Technology Team

UK Sales
Isabel Coburn
Jay Cochrane
Sabina Lewis
Holly Martin
Harriet Williams
Leah Woods

And every other essential link in the chain from delivery drivers to booksellers to librarians and beyond!